CONCRETE FAERY

Book I of the Troutespond Series

Elizabeth Priest

Luna Press PUBLISHING

Text Copyright © 2018 Elizabeth Priest
Cover Design 2018 Bede Rogerson

First published by Luna Press Publishing, Edinburgh, 2018

www.lunapresspublishing.com

ISBN-13: 978-1-911143-41-3

Contents

For Catwin, who's read every word.

White Lights

They'd replaced the streetlights out the front of my house with new power-saving ones that cast a sickly grey, giving the street the atmosphere of a zombie film. It wasn't the cheeriest night I'd spent wide awake staring mindlessly out of the window.

My story began, as many do, at stupid o'clock in the morning. The witching hour: a time known only to unnatural creatures, or drunken partygoers staggering home like the cast of said zombie film.

And me, though I was definitely neither of those. I was sitting at my window. There was a lot of stuff I could have been doing instead. Reading, perhaps. Writing my university application. Finishing coursework due in in the next few weeks. But I had gone to bed, and that meant drawing a line under regular activities. I had chosen watching the new streetlights and I was going to see it through, because some decisions you just have to live with. It was late: this was what passed for logic.

It wasn't like the lights even did very much—they just glowed dimly. Perhaps, I thought, it was some sort of diabolical plan. These lights weren't even bright enough to drive safely by. I could imagine a squad of hippies infiltrating local governments across the country, cackling to themselves as they advised the use of the bulbs, knowing they were reducing power consumption and taking thousands of cars off the roads in one fell swoop.

Not that I was likely to see a car plough across the road and flip over the low brick wall that edged our garden any time soon. I lived in on a back street in Troutespond, Middle of Nowhere, and the amount of stuff that happened here was zero. There were weird out-of-the-way-small-town things—fairs and the occasional town meeting—but those didn't get everyone talking for weeks to come. A missing cat made the front page of the Troutespond Chronicle.

As if the universe had read my mind, a cat streaked into view. I mean it was moving very fast, rather than completely naked. This is rural England, not some fairytale land where animals habitually wear top hats and dinner jackets (though for some reason almost never trousers). This cat was a long-haired thing, huge and pampered-looking. It must have been from one of the bigger detached houses down the road, where they had proper lawns in their front gardens. Soon another cat came along, thin and furious, haring after the first in full kamikaze attack mode, ready to claw off huge chunks of fuzzy hair. The first cat fled. The second followed, yowling all the way.

Stillness sunk back in, like the world was snuggling under a big duvet of quiet, much like the quilt I should have been under. The world remained grey and grew more boring by the minute, not a fox or badger wandering by, not a single car grumbling down the main road that lay beyond our street. I wondered if it might not be better just to lie down and stare at the ceiling instead. But to my amazement more than one distraction came along in a single night. And what an improvement on a catfight it was… A young man (not a pimply teenager like all the boys we knew, the ones at college who would talk to us) came around the corner. He was tall, scruffy, and had white guy dreadlocks—long, tangled, and hanging loose to his shoulder blades. He blended in well with the background; his hair was black, his T-shirt dark grey, jeans a lighter grey to match the pale paving slabs.

I shrank back behind my curtains, immediately terrified that he'd see me. But he didn't look up, and I got bolder with my peeking. I didn't have any lights on, but the streetlights were probably at least strong enough to outline my pasty, freckled face for anyone to see if they scanned the row of houses. On the other hand, he seemed completely uninterested in the houses around him, mooching along with his hands in his pockets and minding his own business.

He cut across the street and glanced around as if checking the ground, then sat down right on the pavement opposite my neighbour's house. With his head tipped back to face the stars, I could just make out that his eyes were closed like he was meditating. I couldn't understand it. Why would anyone want to sit on the chilly pavement, wearing just a T-shirt and jeans, in the middle of a night in March? I knew every face in the town, if not their names. And yet I had never seen this man before. Had I missed the buzz of someone new? Someone with dreadlocks and the gleam of metal piercings on his face should have caused such loud tutting in the post office it could have been heard off in the hills. The old women of this town had more than enough snottiness just for my mum's hippie style, and she was fairly normal aside from the tie-dye.

I had to find out what this was all about, sniff around and see what he was doing on our territory. I could see a relaxed smile, a calmness to the way he sat. More likely than not he was drunk or on drugs. He'd probably sold his coat for more drugs, which was a pity. In my limited experience of gawking at them in bigger towns, guys who wore ripped jeans and T-shirts with some sort of grubby band artwork on had the most amazing long coats, usually studded, hanging with belts and at the very least riddled with safety pins. It was an admiration of these coats more than anything that made me stare. People with their act together about personal style like that freaked me out, sporting jeans and T-shirts all year round.

But something about this man wasn't giving me the usual warning signals after my panicked first glance.

I slipped on the flip-flops that always sat beside my bed instead of slippers or house shoes, already beginning to wonder if this was entirely sane. I'd diagnosed him as being a druggie, but I found myself sneaking over to the door and peering out into the hall. From my parents' room I could hear gentle snores from my mum. My spongy flip-flops cushioned my steps as I made my way down the stairs, avoiding the creaky patches. I grabbed the spare keys from the shelf in the hall and pushed the door open. The air was icy after the centrally-heated warmth of our house, but I went out without grabbing a coat. It felt sort of rude to my guest. He probably wasn't going to care that all I was wearing was a T-shirt and some bright yellow pantaloons that I had stolen from my mum to stop her ever daring wear them in public. It still sort of felt more polite not to bundle myself up to gawp at him like he was an exhibit in a zoo, putting us on the same footing as strange, nocturnal outside people without proper winter clothes. Late-night logic at work again.

My flip-flops scuffed along the path. I stopped at the tall hedge that grows by our gatepost and makes it impossible to get out the drive without nearly causing major traffic incidents (if there ever was major traffic on our road in the first place). I snapped a twig off the hedge for self-defence.

But when I stepped out onto the street and into plain view I froze, the twig hanging uselessly at my side. This close to the strange dreadlocked man I lost all my will to bother him. He was so serene, and I could tell he meant no harm, although I didn't know how I knew that: it was just that he radiated this sense of peace. All I could say for sure was that I felt completely relaxed about him being there, all the niggling doubts that he might suddenly leap up and come at me with a knife vanishing away. He may as well have been another lamppost. I just stood there, watching him.

He had enough metal shoved through his face to not be safe near a magnet shop: eyebrow piercing, a stud in his nose, two glinting points beneath his lower lip. This failed to disguise his plain, heavy features. He was probably unattractive to many people, and would be even if you cut his hair and put him in an inoffensive polo shirt. He was a dorky friend if we go by film casting stereotypes—maybe the clutzy sidekick or secondary villain. Not the face of a major player. Not like I was one to talk. I fell so hard into the clutzy sidekick box I was amazed I hadn't broken both legs.

After a few seconds, as I was beginning to wonder if this was an awkward moment or if he genuinely hadn't noticed me, he took a small tin whistle from his pocket, put it to his lips and blew such a gentle tune that I couldn't believe it came from a whistle. I had fond memories of music lessons when we were younger, where Tanya and I would try to deafen each other with the various instruments, and we always held onto a tin whistle as a weapon of mutually assured destruction. And the key to being thrown out to sit in the office for the rest of the hour. From his lips, though, it sounded as sweet as the classiest flute—yet as mysterious as the wind in the hills. I sat down abruptly before I could ask myself why I wanted to do it, and listened.

His music danced through the still night air, leaping about through pitches, occasionally catching on a note like the sound had startled him so much with the intensity that he had to try it again and again. The warbling sounds should have sent curtains flying back, windows being levered open to shout insults down at the street, but the stillness of the houses around us remained intact, like I was the only one who could hear the high-pitched trilling.

As suddenly as he had started, he stopped. Maybe I'd sat there ten seconds, maybe it had been five minutes. I couldn't tell you. He lowered the whistle and looked over at me with his pale grey eyes catching the white streetlight above him. He smiled mysteriously. What other smile could someone produce at that point?

I was about to ask him who he was, but he raised his hand. I shut my mouth, much more interested in what he'd open the conversation with. I didn't feel I could contribute more than confused noises after the scene he'd made.

"Well met," he said. "You can't talk to me yet. I will explain later. Goodnight." He unfolded his long legs, trousers flapping around the large rips at the knee, exposing the bony leg behind the fabric. He stood up, turned, and walked off, all while I sat there, my mouth hanging wide open again like the holes in his trousers, incapable of asking any of the questions I wanted.

With a huge shiver running through me, it finally occurred to me that I was sitting on the freezing pavement with bare legs. My arms had huge goosepimples, and I was shaking like crazy, so much it was hard to struggle up again. The backs of my legs groaned in complaint, throbbing from the cold as I straightened them and stamped on the ground, accompanied by loud flaps from my sandals.

I glanced over my shoulder as I hurried back to the house. The dreadlocked man was disappearing around the corner.

I reckoned the experience had been in the top ten of strangest things that had ever happened to me. I went inside to make myself a cup of tea.

"It Was Only a Lollipop, Sir…"

I'd love to say that I had portentous dreams, the whispering of the universe sneaking in to tempt me with suggestions of what was to come, but when I finally blacked out from exhaustion I slept through the night, and most of my morning routine. The ringing of my alarm clock failed to rouse me. The sound of it was so offensive that the neighbours two houses down complained during the time I was making five am starts for my paper round when I was ten, but I slept on. It wasn't until my mum shook me awake an hour or so after the blaring bell that I knew it was a new day.

"Come on, Ally, there's ten minutes until you have to be at school!" Her cheerful morning voice echoed through my head better than any alarm. The added incentive that she would start tidying my tiny nook of a bedroom if I lay inert for too long usually inspired me to sit up. That morning, though, I had to commune with the gods of pillows and duvets a little more.

"College," I mumbled to my pillow. "I stopped going to school two years ago."

There was a scraping of china on wood in my peripheral hearing. I opened an eye a crack to see the tasselled edge of her hand-knitted poncho disappear from view as she picked up my mug. "Tut tut, were you drinking tea late at night? You know it'll keep you up. No wonder it's so difficult to wake you in the mornings…."

"Ten… minutes?" I groaned, more annoyed at her using the same tone of voice on me as she had when I was seven and refusing to wake up for school than actually paying attention to the words she said. Why was I so tired? More than any normal morning, that is, as I never did go to bed at the time I was supposed to. The words that I had just repeated sank in at last, before the rather strangely passive magical experience of last night ever came to my thoughts.

"Ten minutes!" I leapt out of bed and began grabbing the first clothes I could see. I realised I'd picked up my bright yellow shirt with the leering banana on the front, but momentum carried me out of the room before I reconsidered and found something more fitting my dreamy mood. I could hear Mum laughing all the way down the stairs as I dived into the bathroom to repair as much of the damage of sleep as I could.

Mum had toast waiting for me when I got downstairs; I grabbed it and ran upstairs, but I gave up on it due to lack of time and fear of choking as I searched for my backpack under furniture: I crammed the hot buttery bread through the bars of Jimmy-Three-Paws's cage. Hamsters can eat toast, right? Jimmy had survived a freakishly long time under my care so I was assuming that nothing could kill him now. Through carelessness I had apparently created an immortal monster… I would have to watch out for him gnawing through the bars and coming for me as I slept.

Nine and a half minutes after waking I thundered down the stairs, backpack in hand. I grabbed one of Mum's lumpy cardigans off a peg in the hall. Dad was waiting at the door, arms folded, glancing down at his watch. He had the door open as I skidded up to it and almost knocked over his briefcase. His look of horror as he grabbed it out of my path was plain: I swear he loved that case more than me. It was the son he'd never had. He should be grateful—there was no chance Mum would try to hippie up his briefcase with more than a heart-shaped sticker on the inside lining.

"Sorry-I'm-late-will-you-give-me-a-lift-to-college?" I asked in a rush, trying to shove my arm into a sleeve while still wearing a backpack on it. I looked around but couldn't see any shoes in the downstairs hall: Mum must have tidied them away to the cupboard under the stairs. All that remained was a 'pair' of mismatched flip-flops, discarded at the foot of the stairs at four a.m. because I wasn't confident in my ability to carry a full mug of tea upstairs while sneaking around in flapping shoes.

"Of course," he sighed, well used to ferrying me the five minute walk to college whenever I slept too late. I really only asked any more because it was polite. I knew he had been waiting for me.

So I hopped into the car for the agonising minute or so of being late I regularly endured of a morning.

As we pulled out of the drive my eyes fell on the spot where Dreadlocks Guy had sat. In broad daylight there was nothing witching about it at all. The street was direly suburban, all clean curbs and low brick walls. The murderous scrawny cat was sleeping on a fence, its tail flicking lazily, foe vanquished.

It was as if I was seeing my town for the first time, but instead of the veil lifting to reveal all the wonder and magic of the world, something struck home: Troutespond made a huge deal about its 'interesting' history. Growing up here, every corner had seemed full of mystery and surprise when I played games on its quiet streets with Teb and Tanya, turning it into a wonderland of imagination, full of spies and elves and pirates. But how much of that was just me being easily amused? Maybe it didn't just *look* normal. What if it was the same as every other town in the country? The fact I had never dared entertain that thought before probably said a lot about me; more so the gutting disappointment that came with it.

"Say, Dad? Has anything weird *ever* happened here?"

"I wouldn't know. You'd have to ask your mum," he said. He turned and gave me that hopeful smile which always means a dad joke is on the way. My heart sank. "After all, I just use this place as a pit stop on my commute."

I almost wept as I slumped down in my seat until the belt cut into my neck. Sadly not enough to kill me. "Nuh," I said, trying to be the good supportive daughter when he told jokes that didn't even have punchlines. Or anything else that could inherently be considered a joke despite what he was suggesting with his elevated tone of voice.

Fortunately we pulled up outside the school before he could say anything else embarrassing. Something so bad it would follow me into school in a cloud of boring and everyone would know he'd said it, somehow. I did say the town was a small place; the school was reasonably far outside the town limits, on the other side from our house. Yet we'd only got one Dad 'joke' before the drive was over.

I flung open my car door long before I'd managed to struggle free of the seatbelt and almost whacked a lady dressed in white who was walking past. "Sorry!" I yelled, tugging wildly on the belt. She didn't look around, but swung her long red hair in a way I thought was expressive enough.

"Good luck, kiddo," Dad called as I hopped out of the car.

"Bye-Dad-thanks-love-you," I replied, most of those words spilling over my shoulder long after I'd shut the door, as I dashed through the gates. He was probably too busy putting his briefcase into the front seat and buckling it in to care.

There were two schools connected to the town. St Troute's, the posh Catholic school in an old medieval nunnery up north of the town, in the hills, and Troutespond Comprehensive, a pebble-dashed monster from the seventies. The old Catholic school had an elite sixth form of about thirty students who all went on to Oxford or Cambridge. The Comprehensive sucked up students from all around the local area. Guess which one I have to go to? The Comprehensive was the only new thing that had come to the town after the motorway had cut alarmingly close to us in the seventies, and depressingly the only part of the town apart from the wonky steeple of the church that could be seen from the motorway. It made a great symbol of the coming oppression when seen on return from a holiday. Just a few more months before I'd be laughing at it on my trips home from university... Until then, the big green-cement and dull-windowed box glowered down at me as I crossed the playground, reverting back to being eleven years old in my heart thanks to the endless repetition of this ritual.

I almost tripped into the building and staggered along the obnoxiously quiet corridors, flip-flops slapping on the lino. How dare everyone already be settled down into their lessons? I was barely five minutes out of sync with the rest of them. Yet here they all were pretending like they'd been here an hour already. I was fairly certain the clocks only went back on a Sunday; I couldn't have fallen out of one hour and into the next without noticing.

"Late again, Miss Guardian?"

I squealed and spun around; I'd missed seeing our rotund headmaster, Mr Plebsy, lurking in a doorway. He stepped out, stomach bulging towards me, smug grin stretching out like the gaps between the buttons on his shirt.

"Sorry sir! Some dreadlocked hooligan was playing music outside my window at three in the morning, and made me sleep clean through my alarm." I hoped playing the 'can complain like an old lady' card would win some points, but he must have hated his mother, because it just made his smile more malicious.

"Keep your love life and school separate, Miss Guardian," he growled, fierce and threatening to laugh.

"Technically since it happened at home, I did," I replied, annoyed not to be taken seriously, though really I ought to have seen that coming.

"What class are you meant to be in?" As sixth formers we were supposed to have human rights, but they assumed that since we hadn't gone to the marginally worse sixth form college twelve miles away in Bilsworth, we were technically their prisoners for another two years. I was amazed they'd even relaxed uniform rules for us.

"Maths with Miss Lemon, sir."

"I'll be having a word." He turned and stalked off. Then, as I began haring away off to my class, he called without even looking around, "And no running in the corridors!"

Ugly flip-flops slapping on the lino at a more reasonable pace, I went off to my history class with Mr Brooke.

*

My palms were still sweating from my encounter with the headmaster when I received my second horrible shock of the day. As I rounded the corner I saw Mr Brooke stomping towards me on one of his rainforest-decimating trips to the photocopier. I flattened myself into a gap in the lockers and waited for him to pass, my heart pounding. And, let me stress, because I was late and in deep trouble, and not because he was the teacher that all the girls fancied.

Unlike most other A Level classes there were over two dozen students in the classroom, and only six of them were male. If we're casting from the movies then Mr Brooke would be the implausibly young pretty-boy, hair spiked up and the finest layer of stubble on his chin, who's taking his first grown-up role and isn't quite pulling it off. The audience would be smirking as they remember his ridiculous teen actor roles and cooing over how adorable he was trying to act like a big grown-up man now. He'd been here three years, and I couldn't believe all the hormonal squealing from his students hadn't broken him within a week.

He didn't notice me and carried on his way. Even his charm wasn't enough to trump the queue for the photocopier in the morning, when all the burly coffee-breath'd teachers of yore had their long-held printer dibs to call on. The first five minutes of his class were usually bitching about said teachers, so I knew I hadn't missed much except some gossip Teb would relay to me in good time if I needed to know it. I waited until he was gone around the corner, and unstuck myself from the nook I'd shoved myself into. Several pink blobs of gum came away with me, glued to Mum's cardigan. I groaned. I would be even more hideously late if I popped to the toilets to go through the trouble of cleaning it; I'd feel vaguely disgusting and sticky all day in any case because toilet tissue, little slivers of pink soap and lukewarm water aren't ideal gum-removal agents. I stripped the cardigan off and abandoned it to the top of the lockers, where all sorts of wrecked PE shoes and damaged textbooks lurked, unclaimed for generations of students.

Bare arms beginning to goosepimple in the tepid hallway, I hurried to the classroom. With any luck Mr Brooke hadn't taken the register yet and I could slide in and pretend like I'd been there all along. While he was pretty cool, I did have this habit of being consistently late since History always seemed to be the first lesson of the day, and winding up the guy who marks your coursework is never a good idea.

People hardly even glanced up as I walked into the room. The only ones who paid any attention, in this blissful remaining ten minutes of my life in obscurity and normality, were Tanya and Teb, sitting either side of my empty seat.

"Ally! Hey! Ally!" Tanya called, waving from the side of the room and nearly taking Teb's eye out since she hadn't put her pen down first. Teb caught hold of the waving appendage and gently pushed it down to the table.

I crossed the room as stealthily as I could, stealing a handful of lollipops from the jar Mr Brooke kept on his desk as bribes to the evil year nines just for sitting still and turning up to his class. He never offered them to his sixth formers but I'd say we'd eaten more than half of the jar anyway. I could count ten students with little white sticks hanging out of their mouth right that moment (and I was pretty sure only one of those was an unlit cigarette).

As I walked up to the table I threw Teb and Tanya a lollipop each. I might not have been that great at throwing, but Teb snatched hers right out of the air. Tanya missed by a mile because she had still been waving and she dived to get the errant sweet from under the table in a puff of rigid green lace.

"Nice skirt," I said as I dropped down into the seat between them, working on unwrapping my own lollipop. I took in her completely green, sparkling attire and revised my opinion. "Er. I think."

"It's less than a week until the fair," she said. "I'm getting into the mood."

"Oh no," I said, recognising her manic grin that meant trouble was afoot and it was much better not to ask questions in case I ended up being the foot. I tipped my seat back, shoving the lollipop into my mouth at the same time with no regard to health and safety. "Did he take the register?" I asked around the sweet.

"Aren't you going to ask Tanya how she plans to celebrate the coming of spring this year?" Teb asked, faking disappointment over a mirthful gleam in her dark eyes. If anyone loves crazy things more than Tanya, it was Teb's love of *watching* Tanya enjoy mad stuff.

"No, I still have the scars from last time. Am I in trouble?"

"Answered for you," Teb said calmly. "One day you're going to just not come in, and I will be in *so much* trouble for covering for you all the time. Tanya wants us to dance in the fair."

"Can't. Helping Mum," I said at once, purely in self-defence, catching the table as my chair wobbled and almost tipped back.

"Of course she can spare you for half an hour!" Tanya said, tossing her long blonde pigtails back over her shoulders with an irritated flick. Between her dress sense and hairstyle of choice it was easy to forget she was the eldest. When she turned her big baby-blue eyes on you it was easy to forget she was a *teenager*. "She's a fellow earth-child. She understands!"

"It's *important*," Teb giggled. "A luck or fertility ritual; seven years good luck or—"

"Your money back?"

"Or you get pregnant within the year," Tanya said. Unlike Teb, her blue eyes were shining entirely with fascination and I knew her too well to doubt she believed it completely.

Teb snorted with laughter, unable to hold back her contempt at the weird pagan practices of the town. Her parents were firm atheists and had done their best to bring her up right, much to the disappointment of a vast family back in India. Also much to the disappointment of her best friend Tanya here and now. "Yeah, *like* that is going to happen."

"We're nearly eighteen, Teb. In ye olde times we'd have all popped out a dozen by now," I pointed out, waving my hands vaguely in the direction of the infamous Miner's Lung display. The noticeboard was supposed to be about family life in Victorian Times, my reason for gesturing at it, but Tanya had gone overboard with her disgusting project, a mass of diseased-looking cotton balls expertly painted and modelled to cause maximum nausea, and Mr Brooke had stuck it up as a warning to the year nines.

"Now, making up fake historical facts within the walls of the classroom is definitely seven years bad luck," Teb declared.

"So you'll do the dance?" Tanya pressed.

"You're both nuts," I said.

"Come on," Teb complained. "With a mum like yours, how can you *not* believe this sort of nonsense?"

I shook my head, trying to find a way to explain it. It was this kind of wacky local folklore, and my mum's rampant enjoyment of it, which was what constantly fooled me into thinking that Troutespond was something special. She had dragged me around fairs and bonfires all my life. The town was out of the way and had a negligible amount of interest even to people within the county, for most of the year. I remained dubious that our medieval history, pagan holidays and a three year rotation between Bilsworth and Ransley for hosting a mead and cider festival went any further back than an emergency meeting of the town's tourism board after the motorway removed significant footfall in lost motorists looking for public toilets and somewhere to get a sandwich and cup of tea. I even doubted how long the stone circle had stood on the hill overlooking the town. Just how many winters did it take for some rocks to lichen up and start looking ancient? Being old was the first line on their CV.

But Tanya ate all of it up. Her main pastime in the summer seemed to be long walks, often on her own, to "commune" with the woodlands. The pathways were dotted with notices containing snippets of history and information—put up by the town council and most likely made up. But she had them all memorised. Her end-of-college-forever project was a massive local history survey, and for the last few months her favourite teacher had been the geriatric head of Geography, a man now entirely ruled by the moustache he played host to. His shrivelled stature had not diminished his memory of Troutespond back to Napoleonic times, confirming our youthful theory that he was at least two hundred years old.

Learning history was fine, but getting caught up in the mythos of this town? It was a step too far into gullibility. Maybe it made me as dull as my dad, but that was how I felt.

I forced a sarcastic sort of look to my face, giving up on saying all that, and looked at Teb. "And what religion did your parents attempt to raise you in?"

She coughed.

"I rest my case. Just because it's an alternate religion doesn't mean I'm indoctrinated into it like a cult. You should be *glad* I'm on your side—one of the sensible ones."

Teb coughed again, this time to cover up laughter. "You should know there's absolutely no fun in that. I only hang around with you and Tanya to see what weird things you'll do next..."

"You mean what weird stuff she'll make me scapegoat for." If I'd been a little off-hand with Mr Plebsy, it was because he'd been blaming me for Tanya-caused problems since our first week in year seven when she hacked the school computers in an IT lesson and changed everyone's names to ones from a certain series about a teenage wizard. There's still some stationery in the office which was printed during that brief time we were Hogwarts School of Witchcraft and

Wizardry. Tanya had tricked me into showing up wearing my Hufflepuff scarf that day, so *of course* I was under suspicion.

Mr Brooke finally returned, cutting short our conversation. I cowered down in my seat, folding up my gangly stature so I was the same height as my friends, but he didn't pay me any attention. He wasn't paying anyone attention; his arms were empty of the papers he'd gone out to copy, and he walked right in without looking around. He sat stiffly, his eyes pointed down at his desk. For a moment I worried that he was going to start counting lollipops, but he didn't move.

"Got a crush?" Teb asked, nudging me.

"N-no!" I protested, caught out by her tone when I was genuinely worried. "Look at him, though… Is he okay?"

He carried on doing nothing, his eyes wide like he was trying to memorise the pattern on his desk surface.

"He was fine this morning," Tanya said, sucking on the lollipop I'd given her in an extremely blatant way. I frowned harder. Teachers have bat-like hearing for picking out the crinkling of sweet wrappers in a noisy classroom. A couple of people looked like they'd tried to swallow their lollipops, stick and all, when he walked in and were making muffled choking noises. But he hadn't flinched.

By then the rest of the class were shooting him worried glances, their own conversations interrupted by his return. We were all unsure if we were allowed to keep chatting, I guess.

"Maybe he got some bad news while he was out of the room?" Teb suggested anxiously.

"Maybe *you* are the one who cares about him?" I said. She pinched me on the arm. Of course she was the one with the crush on him, but didn't want to admit it, so she always joked I did if I so much as raised my hand to ask him not to rub some notes off the board because I'd been messing around and not copied them properly. Teb hated being reminded that she suffered an occasional weakness for tall boys, a problem which had become more pronounced since the morons around us had hit puberty and shot up like beanstalks. She insisted that she would rather study than be dragged on what passed for a "date" in this area, but I still caught her sighing sometimes when Mr Brooke handed her a photocopied sheet about Russian prisoners of war or anything else suspiciously un-sighworthy. Or being far too eager to raise her hand in a class she was only taking because we both were.

Students were looking up like meerkats now, faces popping up and pointing front, paying more attention than they ever did in the lessons. A bit of drama always livened up a dull Thursday morning.

A blonde girl sitting with her pretty friends within cleavage range at the front of the class adjusted her shirt and then stuck up her hand. "Um, sir?"

Mr Brooke didn't look up.

"Wow," I said. "He's broken." I stood up and, flip-flops making sticky noises against my sweaty feet, approached his desk. I could feel absolutely every eye on me in the still room. I think they knew what I was about to do, but I didn't. Wish one of them had thought to warn me.

"Ally!" Teb hissed. "Sit back down!"

"Sir, are you okay?" I asked. I bent down a little to peer at his blank face. His eyes were practically bugging, almost with fear if I had to put an emotion on it. The rest of his pretty features were rigid. I snapped my fingers under his nose. Nothing happened. I poked him on the forehead. No reaction.

I leaned back and dipped my hand into the lollipop jar.

"Ally—no!" Teb cried.

I guiltily drew my hand back with several lollies clasped in my fist. The jar wobbled, and crashed to the classroom floor as I tried to step back stealthily. Mr Brooke's head shot up and his blank eyes stared right through me. With a squeal I fell back, bumping into the front row of desks occupied by Mr Brooke's fan club, causing more little shrieks. But they were all drowned out as his mouth fell open and he began to scream and scream and scream, unintelligible babbling noises mixed with stretches of yelling as loud and long as his throat could manage.

I stumbled around, almost losing a flip-flop as I dashed back to my seat, bruised and dazed with horror.

"Back! Back!" Teb cried, making a cross with her fingers. "We don't know you! We didn't tell you to do that! Tanya will back me up." Behind me I heard, over the screaming, the classroom door slam open against the wall, shaking all the posters—someone running to get help.

I looked at Tanya. She was watching Mr Brooke, and for a moment her face looked gleeful before she turned to look up at me, mastering her love of chaos as she pretended to be as serene as ever. "You poked him in front of the whole class. Can't help you there."

Teb had pulled a long ruler out of her bag and she jabbed at my hand where I clutched the table, trying to pry me off it as if she was scared of coming into contact with the deep crap I was in.

So that was probably up into the top five weirdest things that had ever happened to me, and it definitely bumped events from the night before right out of the top ten.

Alana Larbie

I wound up sitting outside Mr Plebsy's office, wondering how on earth to defend myself. "Yes, I got three hours sleep, and I'm in a curious mood where I poke things for no reason. He was like that when I got there." I was used to being branded as trouble through no fault of my own, but I'd never felt quite so sure I had only been in the wrong place at the wrong time as I did then. Tanya almost certainly hadn't been involved…

There was another girl sitting outside the office, three seats down. We were sharing the experience of not enjoying the row of hard, brown-on-brown chairs made of recycled bathtubs and shaved hedgehogs that were lined up against the wall. The legs were too short to comfortably seat my lanky frame, so I stretched out, flip-flops proudly displayed in front of me. We were in a tiny waiting alcove decorated like a fifties living room. We had a view of the car park through the window opposite, I think so the worst offenders could watch and wait for their parents to come collect them, an additional bit of psychological torture. Or a reminder of the outside world and freedom to leave for the rest of us.

I guess something in the beige of the wallpaper inspired me to be sociable where I would normally be mopy. Anything to take my mind off the trouble I was in. I turned to the other girl.

"Hey there, I'm the victim of random demonic activity. How are you?"

"Well, happy not to be the only one," the other girl said. "I'm new here."

"Ah, nice to meet you, Newbie. I'm Ally G." She stared at me and my utter failure to be cool. I really couldn't pull that joke off, and if my dad hadn't jumped on it, it would never have occurred to me. Look what you'd done, father; your terrible attempts to be hip a century late have rubbed off on your previously far hipper and less dorky daughter, and doomed her for all eternity! One day I will have nothing left but a businessman's sense of humour and will cry myself to sleep between terrible puns and non-jokes.

I cleared my throat. A lasting silence yawned between us. I considered beating myself to death with my sparkly blue flip-flop. This girl was pretty in a way that wasn't anywhere near as slutty as the girls from the front row of the history class. She would have been quite cool wherever she'd come from, her short dyed-black hair styled in the typical fake-messy wavy way that was popular at the moment, and she wore a frilly patterned shirt, black with little red roses all over. She had the required pumps (bright red) and skinny jeans, chunky, vividly coloured plastic beads around her wrist, and just a bit too much eyeliner to finish it off. She had the usual scowl of someone who expected to fit in with a certain crowd, met me and found someone to assure them of their position in society.

"Man, how long does it take to load a screaming guy into an ambulance?" I said, after a bit. Might as well let her in on the day's gossip, even if it did revolve around me. When she went out to start bonding with all the girls with hair parted at the exact same point as her she could smugly assure them she had all the details already. "Everyone in this school wants to sleep with Mr Brooke, or I suppose they did until he became damaged goods today," I added helpfully, trying to sound like the kind of girls who sat in the front row. "I think Mr Plebsy does as well. He seemed awfully mad at me for breaking the history teacher. Or maybe he just sees Mr Brooke as school property? I'm not entirely sure, but I break enough of that already. Butterfingers." I laughed weakly.

More cold stares. Jeez, how lame had I managed to make myself look? Good going, Ally.

"So where are you from?" I asked, to fill the yawning chasm of social ineptitude.

"St Fish's," she drawled, amazing me by bothering to reply at all. The response made it doubly surprising. St Troute's sucked up all the well-to-do kids, regardless of their religion, with its excellent results and gold star reports from inspectors. I could tell she was one of them since she'd called it St Fish's, something those weirdos liked to do. We had St Fish everything here in common slang. Even the church released its newsletter as "St Fish's On The Hill."

"So why transfer here?" I said, "You *must* be in Sixth Form, right?" She might have been short but there was something outwardly mature about her.

She nodded. "Like I said, I'm also a victim of random demonic activity."

"You weren't kidding?" I sat up straighter in my chair.

She shook her head. Her reddish-brown eyes seemed suddenly too wide and staring and, despite the utterly bizarre mental breakdown of Mr Brooke, she was what creeped me out the most at that moment. "All the school cafeteria custard turned to brimstone. They blamed it on me... I was in the wrong place in the wrong time, talking about cranking the school. I didn't even know it had happened until later. What happened here? To this Mr Brooke character?" There was the faintest hint of an accent to her words, the slightest softness, a turn up at the end of her sentences, which made me wonder if she wasn't British. Canadian, maybe. She had been here a long time whatever the case; her accent was nearly grammar-school flawless.

"He went to get photocopies and came back all stare-y and silent, so I poked him a bit, and he started screaming his lungs out." I shrugged, "No official word on what happened yet, but the whole class saw me stick a lollipop in his face. Kind of by accident."

"You're *crazy*," she said, eyebrows shooting up.

"Says Miss Brimstone Delight."

"That wasn't me!"

"You're still sitting in *our* Head Teacher's office begging to join our crappy, second-rate college," I pointed out.

The chasm of social ineptitude shook under the earthquake of 'your foot in it', and split into the newly-named 'pits of utter despair in you, Alexandria Thebes Guardian'. No wonder I'd had the same two friends since primary school and no one else, *ever*. Even Tanya managed to have an occasional back-up friend of the month for when we fell out, and boys talked to Teb—as much as she wanted to ignore them.

The new girl and I went back to staring angrily at each other, me only because she was looking at *me* all squint-eyed. And glaring at her saved me from getting down to that flip-flop beating I owed myself. Better to direct my embarrassment at her in anger than starting to sob quietly in public.

Finally Mr Plebsy returned, his white hair standing on end from repeatedly running his hand through it. "Come," he snapped at me, shaking a sausage finger my way.

I stood up with a long-suffering sigh. I rolled my eyes at the girl, but she just shook her head a little and looked away, no sympathy. It wasn't like I'd done anything to deserve it from her. I dragged myself into Mr Plebsy's office.

"Now. Sit down. What happened?"

I flopped into one of the padded chairs in front of his desk, feeling that I knew the scene depressingly well. Mr Plebsy lowered himself into his own chair with a grunt from him and a groan from the poor thing he sat on. He leaned back with another long creak and folded his hands together, resting them on the shelf his stomach made. "Do you have anything to say?"

I shook my head.

"Last I saw of Ian, they had him restrained and were tranquillising him as they took him away. Now, I've only worked with Ian three years, but he was a calm man—'cool' as you kids might say. He got on with his students, aside from the year nines, anyway, and everyone loved him… Perhaps a bit too much. Would you care to explain what you did to make such a man snap? I spoke to him personally this morning and he was fine."

"A-actually, I was going to see if he was okay. See, he came back from the photocopier a little strange—" (How many more times was I going to explain this today?) "——and I asked him if he was okay. And, er, that was when he started screaming his head off. I was so startled I knocked over his lollipop jar, but that's about it. Yep. Maybe one of the evil year nines put a hex on him," I suggested, since dark magic was the flavour of the day.

He scowled at me. "You still lied to me this morning."

"I was confused—I got three hours sleep, sir. I went to the wrong room!"

"You don't *take* maths. I got my secretary to check the registers."

I sat there in silence, picking at a hole in my jeans.

He gave up first. "Do me a favour; look after that new girl today? Lovely girl, Alana, right up your street, and we need more St. Fish defectors to boost our A Level scores. Try and keep her out of trouble."

"I can promise nothing."

"Remember I personally oversee *all* the sixth-formers' university references."

"We'll be good as gold, sir." I stood up and, in a moment of panic, gave him a swift bow because I'd been watching too many films set in the Middle Ages with my mum recently. I hurried from the office.

"Wait outside until I'm done talking to Alana!" he called after me.

I sighed and slouched against the wall by his door. I jerked my thumb back behind me. "You're up next, Alana."

They talked for what felt like an awful lot longer than the time it took to hand over a map and timetable and tell her that she wasn't allowed off school property during breaks and free periods. I wondered what she had really done to get kicked out of school with two months left before the exams. She was joining us to take the exams, if she was in the same year as me. It was bizarre. If he'd booted me out for this incident I would have stayed home and done whatever home-schoolers do to get their qualifications, because the effort of re-enrolling somewhere else for what was probably six more classes in each subject was probably way too much.

When Alana came out of Plebsy's office he reminded her, "No funny stuff while you're here!"

She waited until he'd closed the door behind him, then stuck her middle finger up at it.

"We call him 'The Pleb'," I said helpfully, wondering if we could bond over mutual dislike of the portly head teacher.

She scowled at me, her fluffy hair puffing out more than ever. Though she was only about five foot two, she managed to seem a little menacing to me from down there, like a hissing cat. "I don't need looking after!"

"Well, I'm tailing you wherever you go for the rest of the day then, because Mr Pleb has it in for me, and I don't trust him not to ask all the teachers if we were hanging out."

She shook her head with a darkly amused and rather private smile: she was laughing at me, not with me. Without wasting more time on this conversation, she set off out of the offices. "Just show me where the common room is."

"Hey, I could tell you *all* the cool places to hang out around here," I said, trailing after her as threatened. She turned and looked over her shoulder, giving me a once-over from the mismatched blue and purple flip-flops, the ripped jeans (and not stylishly so) and the shabby T-shirt.

"I doubt it," she said. She set off again.

"Ally!" Tanya came skipping out from around a corner, stepping right into my path. "Teb wants to know, have you been expelled or is it safe to be seen with you?"

"Yeah—the only punishment I got was looking after this new kid…" I turned to gesture to Alana, but she'd vanished, taking advantage of my abrupt stop. "Oh. Great. We've got to find her before Mr Plebsy sees her running around unaccompanied."

"She's gone to the common room," Tanya said, pointing to a sign on the wall advertising the library and common room.

I sighed. "We were going there anyway."

*

We found Alana standing at the side of the common room, arms folded, glaring at the small groups of people gathered there.

Most of our history class were in the battered room since the only other option was the library; they were lounging about on worn sofas with their feet on cluttered coffee tables, sitting in circles on the balding brown carpet that looked much like the deputy head's head, or fiddling with the exposed innards of the TV in an attempt to change the channel. The aforementioned school administrator, as the only person with a remote control, persisted in changing it to BBC News since some wankers had broken the front off in a fight over channels.

Incidentally, when I mentioned my obscurity coming to an end, it wasn't with these guys. Yes, the class looked up, and there was rippled laughter and murmuring, and one of the boys initiated a slow, sarcastic clap for me that quite a number of people in the room, including Tanya, took up, but then they pretty much instantly lost attention and went back to texting and gossiping about more interesting people. For my part, I had never been bullied because A: I had an attack Tanya at my disposal if anyone actually upset me, and B: they just… didn't. The most I could muster to insults was a confused, "Er, okay?" and my refusal to break down in front of bullies generally meant they left me alone, except that to a small population of the school I had been known as "Beanstalk" instead of any name I'd picked for myself. By sixth form, most of those people had dropped out to have children or start the sort of work one gets having spent one's education drawing pictures of me being as tall as Godzilla instead of paying attention in lessons. I wasn't above feeling like I'd won.

Alana was looking pretty dubious about the ability of a group of nearly-adult-people to make a new friend (with cool clothes and good hair) without mockery. She was loitering at the edge of the room with the sort of expression I knew best from Indiana Jones' face when he uncovered various things full of snakes. No one had instantly adopted her yet; no one seemed to know her from around the town or through mutual friends, which surprised me: even a loner like me knew everyone around my age in the town's back stories and faces from my earliest years. Alana had to commute from Bilsworth or further afield: it was the only logical explanation.

Alana spotted us and frowned. She was about to make a run for one of the private study rooms to hide but Tanya pushed me aside and rushed over to her. "Ooh, new kid!" she said, eyes shining. "I wouldn't have expected one so late in our school career. You have an incredible aura."

"Thanks," Alana said, before my face and palm could meet each other. What had started as an average slap to the forehead over Tanya and her idea of what a first impression should be took on double intensity thanks to Alana's response. No one should *encourage* Tanya, especially if they're only trying to be friendly out of fear, as I hoped would be the logical reason for Alana's response. The other option was that she meant it, and I felt that meant I should intervene.

"Okay, Tanya, you can stop..." I started to say, but Teb stepped forward from wherever she'd been hiding from the shame of being associated with me.

"Okay, you *look* normal, but you're talking to us. We have to keep her; I need a friend that I can be seen in public with."

"I'm not abnormal," I grumbled, but Tanya and I had taken a back-seat role to her new bonding experience.

"Hello to you too," Alana said, giving Teb a rather more approving look, relieved to find someone who knew what modern hairstyles were.

Teb stuck out her hand, a wicked smirk on her face at a chance to use her full name, long as I was tall. "Teb Nandi. And you are?"

"Just call her 'Teb'," I mouthed over Teb's shoulder as Alana blinked in surprise. I had a little hope left that I could bond with Alana before my friends snatched her away.

"Alana Larbie."

"I bet you get tired of saying that too many times."

"You can talk!"

"Come on," Teb said, a genuine smile appearing. "Let's ditch these losers and have an honest-to-God conversation about shoes and celebrities and other crap that's on TV in the evenings."

"Okay!" Alana said brightly. Teb linked arms with her, and they turned their backs on us and walked into the small computer room to the side of the common room.

I exchanged looks with Tanya. Teb had always been the 'normal' one in our group, but it had never occurred to me that she might actually like that instead of suffering through her affliction as we teased her for not being weird.

"Looks like we're going to have to start buying fashion magazines again," I sighed.

Tanya put a comforting hand on my shoulder. "I hate it as much as you."

Fun and Games

Once we were sitting in the computer room, having a vicious tournament of a silly repetitive online game to pass the three-hour gap in our timetable, we actually turned the conversation to the reason we had no history class. We filled Alana in on the events properly; she asked a lot of questions. Teb did her best to make it sound completely my fault that everything had happened. After that we moved to theories of why it had happened.

"Definitely demonic possession," Tanya observed, opening up a bag of Wotsits.

"I heard he was having an affair," Teb said.

"He's not married," I pointed out, clicking madly.

"Ooh, how would you know?" Teb jeered, prying open the Tupperware box her sandwiches lived in (ham and cheese with the crusts cut off, every day).

Tanya clung to her argument, though it was getting pretty shaky: "He still lives with his mother. Same difference."

"What, so his mysterious girlfriend breaks up with him, or his mum finds out, and suddenly he goes into meltdown?" I asked, trying to work out what she was saying since it was better than dignifying Teb's comment with an answer. The way she went on it felt like having a crush was nothing more than emotional weakness.

"Do you have a better idea?"

My screen flashed red as I crashed and burned. I sat back and tried to think. Alana was watching me. She was clicking without really looking at the screen, but I didn't think she'd died once. She gave me an "Ew, your face," look and turned back to her screen, nose still crinkled.

I had looked right into Mr Brooke's eyes and seen the fear in them. It wasn't manic screaming. It was panicked. Animalistic screaming, like all his humanity was stripped away and he was screaming because that was the only option left to him. I distractedly pressed "New Game", since I wasn't going to be able to calm myself down with tea until I got home. I had a single Rice Krispies bar in my bag from yesterday and I was going to have to make that last. Fortunately the horrible guff of Tanya's crisps was enough to put anyone off food.

"His girlfriend broke up with him, and he was so cut up about it he got possessed by demons," Alana said.

"Don't try and make them both happy," I said over the chill that ran down my back at the calm, assured way she said that. "It doesn't work."

"We should go look in his room for clues," Alana said, ignoring my advice.

"It'll be like trying to get into a crime scene—and twice as dangerous," I said. I had a few hundred more points to beat Tanya's best score... Just needed to drag the conversation out a little longer...

"Worth a try," Teb said. "I'm bored and the alternative to this is doing research for our coursework or revising for our exams."

"Those are months away," I complained.

"Still, we should make a start... Never know what might happen!"

Alana jammed her finger against the off button without bothering to save her progress, even though she had about a million points, more than Tanya would get in three games, and jumped up. "Come on. What are you losers waiting for?"

"Three more apples!" I said.

She leaned over and gave my computer a hard shutdown as well.

*

We crept down the corridors, past room after room of years seven to eleven hard at work terrorising their teachers and even some sixth formers lazily writing notes to each other.

"Why *are* we sneaking?" Teb said, strolling along behind us. "It looks suspicious, and all the teachers know who we are if they catch us anyway." She plucked the thick lilac sweater she wore, a bright contrast to the grey and green uniforms we'd suffered since before we were teenagers, "And it's obvious we're sixth formers and don't have to be in a lesson—and Ally is notorious for the whole Mr Brooke thing already, so they should know we're skipping history once they spot her skulking about."

"It *looks* dramatic," Tanya said, flat against the wall. Her wide blue eyes darted about, then she dashed across a space between some lockers.

"Watch out," I said, tapping a locker door, "there's a lot of gum stuck down the sides of them." Ah, to sound wise for five seconds. Teb's look told me she *knew*. I stopped attempting to be worldly before I accidentally revealed any other sources of deep shame.

Mr Brooke's classroom was understandably empty, but Tanya cautiously jiggled the handle and the door opened at once. There was an utter lack of crime scene tape on the other side.

"Top security," Alana agreed. She gave me a lingering eye-roll, and pushed past me into the room, flicking on the lights.

I glanced up and down the bland green-painted corridor to check no one was watching, and darted after the others.

"Is it really safe for me to be seen here so soon after I was accused of assaulting him?" I asked. "Someone might think I've come to hex him one more time and finish him off…" Since we'd all been at school with each other since we were toddlers, it was really hard to shake a rumour even at seventeen or eighteen. After Mum once did Tarot cards at a school fête (making a killing from adults bored of tombola and watching children catch rubber ducks with magnets) everyone had started saying that she was a witch and so was I, because that's what nine year olds assume logic is.

"I think we'll be okay," Teb said, sliding open the top drawer of Mr Brooke's desk while I stood hopping from foot to foot and glancing over my shoulder. Alana stooped and picked up a handful of lollipops from the floor. She pocketed most of them but opened up a lime-flavoured one and stuck it right into her mouth without stopping to consider that maybe they were evidence, cursed or those really horrible sour ones.

"Who takes a TV guide to school?" Teb complained, rummaging through the drawers of what was apparently a serial pack-rat.

"Someone who cares more about going home and watching crap than the lessons he teaches," Alana said, the lollipop's white stick bobbing about as she talked.

We instantly launched into defence of Mr Brooke—"He's one of the best teachers in this school!" Teb cried.

"He does the best projects!" Tanya pointed out, voice muffled from within the cupboard.

"Free lollipops!" I added; pretty much the greatest reason to like him.

Alana shook her head, as if she couldn't believe us. She busied herself examining the desk: she lifted the now mostly empty jar of lollies and sniffed inside it. She ran a finger across the top of the desk and riffled through the piles of homework sitting on the corner of the table. She frowned, looking serious as she held up his coffee mug and peered into it. I had no idea if she had the best deadpan humour I'd ever seen out of the TV, or if she really believed she was looking for something and would know it when she saw it. I remembered that she was the one agreeing with the "demons" explanation, and shivered a little despite myself. And despite the fact I had yet to find replacement sleeves.

"Okay, there is nothing sinister here," Teb said, pushing his drawers closed, having missed Alana's whole show while she searched for incriminating evidence.

"Or here," Tanya said from inside his cupboard. She emerged shoving a ream of coloured paper into her backpack.

"That's theft," I said around the lollipop that Alana had handed me (so far the day really wasn't too much of a loss… A little psychological trauma was eased nicely by the extra round of free sweets).

"Anything to report?" Teb asked.

I looked around. "Er… Nothing demonic on the walls."

"God, you're an idiot sometimes," Teb said, moderately affectionately. "Whatever happened here, I don't think we're going to find out about it. Let's go play Tetris until lunch."

It turned out that Alana had some sort of unholy skill with tetrominos as well.

The Dancing Girl

Two hours of Literature later I emerged into the sun, blinking. It was a still day, the air mild, so that if I stood in the sun it didn't feel like a punishment.

"Ally, you're freezing," Teb said, giving my arm a rub that left it feeling burnt. "Let's stop by Tanya's and grab you a jacket."

I looked at Tanya's odd get-up: she was wearing a chunky lime green bomber jacket over her frilly springtime clothes.

"I think I'll pass."

"You are in no position to complain about fashion."

The day had passed without any noticeable changes in any of our other teachers' behaviours. Of course, they were acting neurotic, paranoid, jumpy, mean-bordering-on-sadistic, and, conversely, having nervous breakdowns in the loos between lessons. But that was all par for the course with most of our teachers. None of them had had a proper freak out that warranted any special attention—considering we'd had teachers running about on the roof before, they *really* had to go out of their way now. Mr Brooke had been surprising mostly because he seemed more well-balanced than most. I suppose the school had to get to him eventually.

We'd met, as always, outside the school gates. History was the only class all of us took together. I was pretty sure Teb took it because Tanya and I had and she wanted to have a lesson with both of us. Not that you would ever get her to admit to a single insecure thought. Alana turned up a few moments after Teb, so I had assumed they'd come out of their class together. Not that Alana had waited around and stalked one of us out of college. As we walked down the narrow pavement that lined the twisty road between town and school, I spotted Teb giving Alana some pretty suspicious looks, along the lines of "who invited her anyway?"

Tanya happened to be walking just in front of me. "Did you tell Alana to meet us?" I whispered in her ear.

"No," she replied in a slightly more obvious stage whisper. Alana didn't look around. Tanya didn't offer a justification or mad theory for why we had this clinger-on. It left me wondering if I had been the one to ask Alana to join us, and then somehow forgotten it. I was *fairly* sure most of my day was accounted for, but that Tetris marathon had gotten pretty mind-numbing, so who knows what I might have said to cheer things up a bit?

I walked along thinking of how no one could remember the fourth musketeer (poor d'Artagnan didn't even make it into the title). I'd always felt sympathy for him, but suddenly I was looking at this from a completely different perspective, and not the most popular one: everyone loves a new girl story from the point of view of the scared arrival on the scene. It led me to musing on how easily Alana could be completely wiped from my memory to be a stranger all over again if I had a slight bump to the head at some point; just looking up and finding a weird person sitting in the middle of our insular little trio, acting like one of us, apparently convinced she was one of the team. I almost wished I could go back and flub the introduction even more badly to drive her away before this started.

*

"I said, cheer up Ally!" I looked up to see Tanya grinning at me, and realised I'd zoned out. We'd walked all the way into the heart of town while I'd been thinking, and were surrounded by tall timber-framed houses and the ancient church. Tanya turned and skipped over to greet the war memorial statue that she was infatuated with and cared for much more consistently than any of her fleeting attempts to maintain a boyfriend. Legend goes that in both World Wars, ten men from the village (when Troutespond was still a tiny village of ten houses and a post office) went out to fight, and in both nine returned. Where it gets weird is that it was the same man who didn't make it back both times. Teb thought it was an administrative error. Tanya believed he was like our own personal King Arthur, rising to defend the village, returning to Avalon with a glorious heroic death when it was all over. I thought someone had paid for a really nice statue of the bloke in 1920, and in 1946 no one had felt like paying for a new one so fudged some new dates onto the bronze plaque.

Tanya climbed up on the bench beside his plinth and leaned over to wrap her green fuzzy scarf around his neck.

As Alana sighed and rolled her eyes yet again, my gaze wandered over the town square. Charity shops, tea rooms, antiques, second-hand books… with no nod to actual needs for everyday conveniences. We still had our post office, if only because we were so small and isolated the government probably forgot us entirely when they nerfed the service. The road down to the green was lined with local greengrocers and butchers, and some arty little shops that

26

sold sparkly things and statues made from coat hangers. Away from the scenic historic centre—a tourist trap for old ladies and hipsters—there was a single One Stop Shop hiding under a Tudor façade, and a supermarket in the suburbs of Bilsworth several miles down the road where we got everything else.

St Troute's Church looked down on the town centre from its slight hill. It was a small, crumbling thing of mostly flint and worn stone, and in constant need of fundraisers and jumble sales to keep its roof and tower intact. Only its intentionally leaning design had stopped it collapsing sooner. It was perched atop what Tanya said was an old barrow with a Bronze Age king in it and I assumed was actually just a big mound of earth to make the church taller than all the other buildings on the street, since it was so stumpy. With slopes sharply down on both sides of it, there was no room for buttresses or anything to keep it upright in a strong breeze. One wing of it was always in scaffolding, propping it up on all sides, but work had stalled because of endangered bats. You haven't lived until you've attended a town meeting and listened to pro-bats versus pro-church. The pond that our town took part of its name from was somewhere on the other side of the grounds, historic monument to a *really* lame miracle.

While I moped and shivered, Tanya had a real agenda. Hopping down from the statue's plinth, she dramatically slammed a foot down on the bench next to Alana, and leaned over her knee to inspect the new girl.

Alana stared back unflinchingly. But she was fiddling almost obsessively with the zip on her bag, hugged to her side under one arm.

"So… Marmite. Love it or hate it?"

Alana stole a glance at me and Teb. We shrugged in accidental unison.

"It's… Okay. I prefer Twiglets to eating it on toast."

Tanya nodded thoughtfully, rubbing an imaginary beard on her chin. "They're taking the hobbits to…"

"Isengard." Alana sounded more confident: whether she had watched the films as many times as Tanya, our resident fantasy nerd, or she had just learnt the game Tanya was playing, she had warmed up to it.

"When you grow up, you want to be?"

"Would you call me unoriginal for saying investigative journalist?"

"Depends if you say it just to make yourself sound interesting, or if you actively pursue that dream. Don't worry, we have time to wait on that one." Tanya seemed a little less intense, perhaps realising that none of us could have told Alana our real life goal if asked on the spur of the moment. Teb flitted between high-flying careers, and was smart and driven enough to succeed if she ever landed on one. There was always the chance she wouldn't. Tanya was guarded about her future, I think because she had no idea. She was good at computers in a way Teb and I weren't, but she wasn't a programmer *or* creative: just good at using software and the internet. Since super hackers were an imaginary Hollywood career, she would probably become an average office worker and get done for embezzling after a few decades exploiting the big companies she worked for with her creative account books. As for me… I heard a three-year Literature degree was a great way to procrastinate over actually deciding what you wanted to do with your life.

"Well, I was going to ask you what do I have in my pocket but I wasted my Lord of the Rings reference already…"Tanya removed her foot from the bench and rocked back on her heels.

"That's from the Hobbit," Alana said helpfully.

Tanya smiled. "Yes, of course it is. Look, the point is, we're totally cool with you following us around, as long as you're only surly because that's your personality, not because you resent being stuck with us. Do you have other friends from St Fish's?"

Alana wordlessly shook her head, her eyes downcast.

"I won't ask what made you leave in your final year of college, in the final term as well. Do you have anything you want to ask us? I mean, we've hung out a fair bit today already, but do you know for certain we're all compatible friends?"

Alana looked right at me. "We are," she said. "I know it."

I looked away, a little scared of why she would be so intense and focussed on me. Tanya had it right to question what Alana was doing. When we'd first met she had hated me, so I thought. By the time we were done 'investigating' Mr Brooke's nervous breakdown, she just seemed to assume she was one of us, and had even stopped giving me the stink eye. By now she was, by her standards, fawning over us.

I pretended to be checking out a group of boys who were waiting at the bus stop until Tanya suddenly found a second wind for ridiculous questions and bombarded Alana again, treating it as a game for fun instead of learning.

"Answer me these questions three, and my Kit-Kat I shall give to thee…"

My eyes stopped on a figure sitting cross-legged on the pavement outside the florists. I would have recognised those dreadlocks anywhere (if only because of their rarity on a high street such as ours). He was still in his tatty, torn clothes from last night, still missing a coat. His tin whistle was raised to his lips yet again. I couldn't hear any music; the dozen people wandering about the little triangle space between church and shops weren't making enough noise to drown out anything.

I nudged Teb. "Hey, look." I pointed, then went through a long charade of trying to explain what I wanted her to see, who he was and where he was sitting. Finally she saw him and whistled.

"Look at those piercings… It's amazing he hasn't been stoned to death by the old ladies for dressing like that." He was definitely getting some evil looks as they hobbled past. "Why are you pointing him out? Do you think he's cute?" she asked in an odd way that seemed hopeful as much as mocking.

"Are you kidding me? He's just *strange*."

"Well thank goodness for that. I was getting worried about your choice in men,"Teb said, leaning back, losing interest again already.

"I'm going to go over and ask him what he meant last night," I decided out loud, standing up and heaving my backpack onto my shoulder.

A hand caught my arm. Tanya had broken off from her guessing game with Alana, and looked up at me with that weird earnest face I sort of dreaded seeing. In all my years of knowing her, that face had always been the harbinger of trouble. "Don't, Ally... You can't talk to him yet."

Tanya and I stared each other out for a moment before I pulled my arm free. "What is *with* everyone today?" I demanded, rightly freaked out at that point to hear his words from the night before echoed back at me.

"Ahem," Teb said, making a chopping gesture to exclude herself from 'everyone'. "As far as I can see, *you* are the one who is acting odder than normal."

"Okay, fine," I said, and sat down again, leaning my head on Teb's shoulder because she was warm, and I could see that my fingers had gone an unnatural white. She was my last little rock of normality, and it had struck me just how odd my day had been so far. Did I really want to go tempt it again? Things in my life had been reasonably sane for a long time up until last night... I wasn't even sure I'd woken up properly today. Maybe I was still dreaming, time stretching out into eternity while I waited for the death knell of my alarm clock to go off. I was determined to make it through the day with nothing else weird happening—though it was my mum's turn to cook tonight. My current plan of action may not have stood up against that. She's melted bread before. And claimed she meant to do it.

Before I could really argue my "everyone is crazy today!" point any more, Dreadlocks Guy began to play the tin whistle he was holding. I think most of the town centre stopped in its tracks. Those of us within a few dozen feet instantly gravitated over, the four of us looking at each other, not saying a word before we hurried to get to the front of the quickly-drawn crowd. I hadn't known this many people could even *be* in the town centre all at once, but there were about fifty people peering out of doors and windows, or heading over to join us. I hadn't known there were that many people in the *town*. Tanya grabbed my hand as a reminder of her warning, pulling me to stand at her side before I could get any funny ideas. She needn't have worried—it was far from my mind. I wasn't going to stop him playing for anything.

He didn't look up. His eyes were closed, the same peaceful look on his face as the night before. The notes sounded so clear and sharp in the cool afternoon air that I could almost feel them as a physical, icy line that ran in zigzags from the end of his whistle. The sound was harrowing, the tune wonderfully controlled and complex. I wasn't sure, as good as it was, how it had drawn such a crowd so quickly, but then I wasn't really sure of anything while the notes danced around us, jabbing every so often at nerve endings and painful spots on my soul until I was shivering and tearful.

A woman wrapped up in a long fuzzy white winter coat stepped from the crowd, a cream scarf over the lower half of her face. She took a couple of dainty steps into the clear space around the man. He didn't look up at all. She unknotted the scarf with delicate tugs, pulled it free with a rippling of silky material and dropped it at her side. Then she slid the coat off her shoulders, letting it collapse in a heavy pile of cloth behind her. She wore white denim shorts that stopped just above her knees, and a white tank top with silver sparkly bits. I felt warm in comparison. And ugly—she was model-beautiful, in the kind of airbrushed way you never expect to see in real life. Long auburn hair fell to her waist, layered and feathered up to chin-length at the front so it ended in wisps. Her eyes were closed, and she was apparently more caught up in the music than anyone else. Perhaps that was why the cold didn't seem to affect her. I remembered how I'd sat on the cold ground in the middle of the night. The song he'd played me then had been *nothing* compared to this. He could have had me sunbathing in the Arctic with that sort of playing.

The lady stepped delicately out of her tall-heeled white shoes and took another small step forwards, resting on her toes. Then she started to dance to the music of the tin whistle, twisting and swirling, her feet barely seeming to touch the ground, never coming close to accidentally punching an audience member in the face, though she never once opened her eyes. *It had to be a show*, I thought. He'd had some plants in the crowd who'd rushed over, drawing everyone like us who didn't know what was going on, and she was some hired dancer…

I couldn't figure out why I was having such a hard time convincing myself of that.

I felt Tanya clinging harder and harder to me as the music continued, but I was so enraptured by the dance I couldn't look away, so controlled by the music I didn't think to look over my shoulder and ask if she was okay.

The music built up to a manic pace, and then… I wasn't sure what happened, but there was silence. The dancer was gone, shed clothes and all. The crowd was drifting away. I stayed, staring, as Dreadlocks Guy calmly stood up, pocketing the tin whistle. He walked off, ignoring the many coins that had been dropped on the ground in front of him. Several people seemed to jump and reach for their phones, realising too late they missed the recording of a lifetime, like they'd been about to reach before the moment hit them all at once and the message arrived at their hand five minutes late.

Just as the strange man reached the corner, he looked over his shoulder at me as I stood there shivering and gnawing my lip. A smile flickered over his face, maybe even a wink aimed my way. He stepped into an alleyway between two shops and he was gone.

"What was *that* about?" Teb asked me. I looked over and shrugged, finally realising I was just staring at the glittering empty pavement. Alana, next to Teb, looked more disgruntled than anything, but then she hadn't displayed a wide range of happy faces in the brief time that I had known her. I wanted to catch her eye, ask her what she thought, to see if she felt as strange about it. Teb's reaction was more… unperturbed. Uncertain what she'd seen, I thought: the way her eyebrow quirked up was a sign that she was actually puzzled. Even that was only fleeting: the moment seemed to be slipping away from her entirely, until I wondered if she really did think she had seen nothing out of the ordinary, that our frantic reaction as the music started was nothing more than a quick conversation topic, a new thing to be sarcastic about.

Something told me Alana would be better suited for the conversation I wanted to have. She was at least a bit more credible, open to other suggestions. She believed in demons, after all. But Alana wasn't looking at anyone. I turned, following her vacant gaze past my shoulder as I realised that this silence was because we were waiting for Tanya to fill it with a mystic wise saying. She was no longer at my side.

"Did you see where Tanya went?" I asked, looking around with misplaced panic, not wanting to try and think too hard over what we'd just seen. Had something gone wrong in my brain and I'd misplaced a few seconds where the girl danced off?

"No," Teb said, by now looking totally recovered, like we had walked over here for completely sane reasons and she could give evidence to back that up if you asked her. "She must have got bored and wandered off to look at shops." It was about the least likely thing that Tanya would have done when something odd had been happening right in front of her (I remembered her grin when Mr Brooke had his attack), but on the other hand Tanya may have done it because it was so unlikely she would have done it. I think. To be honest, you stop using logic when considering that girl.

Teb pulled out her phone, and soon had it pressed to her ear, listening with a frown, "It's off," she said. "Or she hung up on me."

"Is that usual?" Alana asked. We shrugged. It was hit and miss with Tanya. She hadn't seemed in a particularly antisocial mood that day. But then she didn't often care about phone technology on a good day either—it was more a matter of feeling courteous to Teb, who of course was normal about having a phone. I was a sporadic replier to our group chat unless I was having a mad panic over stuff, demanding to know when was the last time they'd seen x bit of my property or when y homework was due or…

"Well, it's not like this town is unsafe—why don't we go look at a few shops, assume she went home and call her house after waiting for an hour so we don't look like crazy people?" Teb suggested. "Calm down, Ally, she's not going to die because we took our eyes off of her for five minutes…"

I tried not to hop about in an agitated way.

"Is she always like this?" Alana asked, apparently amused. She had to have seen the odd way the dancer disappeared! Why was she taking Teb's side? She had been the one talking about demons all morning!

Teb shook her head, putting a motherly arm around my shoulders. "There was some business with her hamster a few years ago… Now she thinks it's okay to freak out about everything." With her spare hand she had gotten her purse out, and she steered me over to the ice cream van parked on the side of the road by the green, eternally optimistic in weather like this. Still, it paid to get a good spot before the fair in the coming weekend. "Generally her weirdness can be cured with Mr Whippy, for future reference."

I felt demeaned being talked about like that, happy I was getting ice cream, and still confused and worried, most of my brain functions diverted to conflicting puzzling over the disappearances of the dancer and Tanya, and plans of action to find my friend, and playing out horrible scenarios for where she might have gone and what had happened to her there… Kidnapped by the circus and made to scrub down zombie freaks while sewing footballs in a sweatshop run by notable serial killers… That sort of thing.

Alana hung back with me while Teb bought everyone an ice cream. "Tanya will be fine," she said, in the same smug know-all way she said everything to me. It wasn't a friendly reassurance. More like a "Shut up and stop whimpering."

"Yeah, how do you know?" I asked, hoping perhaps that line ended with Tanya grabbing me from behind and shouting "BOO!" because Alana could see what was going on over my shoulder. I glanced around but there was no one there.

Alana shrugged, "She's being looked after, nothing bad can happen to her."

I stared at her. "What is *that* supposed to mean?"

"I dunno. Take your reassurance and shut up."

I knew she'd been thinking that at me. I regretted bugging her until she actually said it, no matter how stupid I thought she sounded. *How* could she know something like that? She didn't. Something in the air today was making me think that she could have known. I was the one who sounded stupid for asking for evidence.

Teb called my name and waved from the ice cream truck, and I hurried over to get my 99 before it became a splat on the pavement. Of all the odd things that had happened today, I could probably have least expected being grateful for ice cream until now. Alana and I retreated to the benches to lick our cones, glaring at each other over the cones, too riddled with brain freeze and placated with sugar to continue our half-hearted argument.

St Troute

We began methodically searching through the shops that circled the high street once we were done crunching up the ends of our cones. Teb was in favour of splitting up to get my panic attack over and done with, still so certain that Tanya had slipped away she seemed this close to telling me she'd *seen* her walk into a tea shop, though I knew she had been right at my side until she wasn't. Alana was being clingy. Neither response surprised me. I ended up dragging Alana through the row of charity shops while Teb went to look into the cafés.

The charity shops were the hottest shops on the block—Oxfam, British Heart Foundation, Relief Fund Romania… They were the great exchange between everyone in the town, the background noise behind the loud jumble sales every few Sundays. No one threw anything away if it could be helped. They donated it where it would be purchased for a short time by the next lucky owner, until it did the rounds like that unfortunate bottle of tombola wine that someone picked up in Corfu, never dared open, and has now been won about three hundred times in the monthly church raffle. Four times by the original owner.

Occasionally the shops would be inundated with new goodies after the death of an old lady, until their shelves bulged with odd-smelling stock, mostly in the cardigan and cushion variety. I think that these shops were how Tanya got her hands on most of her odder items of clothing.

St. Troute's local charity (an outpost of the church, run by the same few evangelical old ladies) funded town projects, and served, like the post office, as main gossip post and socialising hub. It sold less clothes than the others, having only a few clattering rails of limp garments from the twenties. It was mostly an antique shop, of the "I'm sure everything in here is haunted or cursed!" variety.

Furniture, teapots, garden gnomes, and grinning monkey ornaments all needed somewhere to go when they were no longer wanted (if they had ever been), and that was the boxes outside this shop, with "20p" stickers plastered haphazardly over them, discounted for the high chance that taking them home would fill your house with poltergeists. I'd saved this shop for last—handy, as it was on the end of the row—as I intended to have a good nosey round to see what else had turned up there in the last few weeks, to calm my nerves maybe by buying a few dusty old books I had no space for in my titchy room… I had heard horror stories about university housing's proportions, but after a few tours I was excited for the upgrade.

When we went into the shop I was assaulted by the oppressively dusty, mildewy smell of the old books and furniture, the undertones of polish and brass giving it a peculiar flavour. I had a mental image of myself working there in ten years, another weird lady in a long cardigan and too-big glasses peering accusingly at anyone who touched the china or crystal. I *really* needed to get out of this town and stay out when I went to university. If I ever made it out of here, I'd never be homesick with this smell coming from half my possessions.

Alana looked around with a rather bored expression, taking in the shelves of brass and china with a weary air, as if she'd seen it all before. Perhaps she had—it wasn't like she'd dropped into this town from another planet. I hoped.

I peered around a corner, hoping Tanya might just be sitting on one of her favourite horrible old armchairs, a girls' almanac from the 1900s spread on her lap, but the furniture corner was empty. Alana tapped my arm; "Hey, let's go down here." She gestured the fenced-off hole in the floor, the spiral staircase in it the only way down to a basement level of yet more junk.

I looked at the rickety, creaky stairs and swallowed hard. "Hold on a minute," I said and turned to the dear old lady who sat behind the counter at the front of the shop. She was watching us warily, as if we were likely to start pocketing miniature teapots by the dozen if unobserved. "Hey, Mrs Potts. Have you seen Tanya around?"

"Not lately, dear. Sorry. Is your mother coming to the meeting tomorrow? Tell her I'll drop the agenda by on my way home, and she should bring some of those delicious—"

"Sorry, no time for gossip." I backed off, bumped into Alana, and grabbed her sleeve to start dragging her to the door. "Come on," I said.

"We should go down there," Alana repeated, refusing to budge. I hastily let go of her sleeve because I had a feeling she'd know how to kill me if I ripped it.

"What?" What was with everyone seeming to know these utterly bizarre absolutes about the world today? No you can't talk to me, yes we absolutely have to go down there… If the world wanted me to know something, surely it could just come out and say it?

"Down here," she repeated, already setting foot on the wonky spiral stairs.

"Why? Now is really not the time to be exploring…"

She turned, grabbed my arm, and somehow managed to keep on walking down the spiral stairs, dragging me after her. I yanked my arm free and followed reluctantly, clinging to the rail with a shaking hand. She made no further attempts to drag me to my doom.

Downstairs the shop was darker, lit only by a few unsheltered bulbs hanging at irregular intervals along the ceiling. The air tasted cool and a little damp. There were brown water stains on the walls, but the goods down here were clean and smelled only as bad as old ladies and dust. It was all lamps, ornaments, plates, dolls, teddy bears, and straining boxes of old comic books that probably contained some thousand pound gems if you knew anything about collecting them. The basement was split up into lots of little rooms, white-painted cinderblocks creating rather arbitrary barriers, as if the builder had known that junk shops need lots of nooks and corners but no rhyme or reason and had just gone crazy with the theme. Maybe the patches of black mould had been sprayed on for authenticity.

It was in a narrow alcove that we found Tanya. A bench took up a lot of the few square feet of the space, and that was covered with figurines. There were little china people and twee ceramic animals that looked like they should be standing on a Victorian mantelpiece—though not in such great numbers: they seemed more like the massed ranks of an army. Among the human figures were a selection of gaudily dressed sailors, girls in fluttering dresses and prominent public figures with disproportionately huge heads. Tanya was sitting on a ratty vinyl barstool, one of a set of six, her back to a vast dollhouse with peeling wallpaper and broken stairs to make any full-scale haunted house proud.

She was playing with a few of the figurines. I moved closer to see what she was doing, curious despite my confusion and annoyance. She'd lined some of them up—dancing girls wearing many different bright colours, all following an incredibly battered old Pied Piper in enamel yellow and red. The dancing girl right behind him was dressed all in white, her hair a luminous red. I felt a little chill run through me. Knowing Tanya as I did, this could only end with a pile of broken china on the floor.

"Tanya?" I asked. I wasn't sure what the question was.

She started, turning to look at me with those wide, staring eyes, and a smile jumped onto her face. With her stupid bunches, hair hanging into her eyes, the puffy skirt and her skinny frame, she looked like she could have been ten years old.

"Hi Ally! How come you had ice cream without me?" She had the same priorities as a child as well.

I didn't even ask how she knew, although I did run the back of my hand over my face just in case she wasn't psychic and I was merely displaying the evidence. "Let's go."

"Okay, but you should buy this." She picked up the only non-china thing on the table: a polished recorder of dark brown wood, the head in a paler cream.

"What would I want with that? You know I'm completely musically inept…"

"It's meant to be yours." She stated it so simply I didn't think before I reached out and took it. Like how she'd possibly known about the ice cream, this was just another Tanya moment: she had them often. It *would* have been her to repeat the catchphrase of the day back to me. I turned it in my hands, looking at the light-touch carving that ran around the length of it, a swirling abstract pattern that looked a bit like leaves or flowers. There might once have been gold paint on the design but it was rubbed almost completely away. The design itself was worn smooth in many places where the instrument had been held by long-passed hands. A little sticky price tag on it said "£0.75p". This shop had ordered some extremely optimistic price stickers, considering most things came out under a fiver.

"Alright, whatever. If it gets you out of here…" On a whim, I grabbed the red-haired dancing figurine as well, in case it was a clue. I'd been trained well by Enid Blyton to look for clues all the time, and damned if I wasn't going to acquire them the one time it seemed actually relevant to be looking.

Tanya seemed perfectly happy with my decision. She hopped down from the stool and gestured at us to make a move. I turned to see the tail end of Alana's expression after she'd watched this whole exchange—her face just lightening up from a frown, her forehead uncreasing. She needed a poke to start moving, as if she were still lost in thought.

"My mum knows a spell that will make your face freeze like that," I said as we wove our way back to the stairs.

Alana seemed surprised. "She's a witch?"

"Yeah, but not a bad one!" Tanya said, relentlessly jumping in wherever valiant jumping was not needed.

"Also, you know, magic and spells aren't real," I said, scowling at her, realising Ally's mum jokes were not going to work in front of Alana.

"Chill out," Alana said. "I'm the last person who'd judge a witch." She clattered on up the stairs without stopping to explain that statement.

*

We met up with Teb again, and I got thoroughly mocked for my panic. "Hey, look, it's Tanya," she said as the three of us walked up to her, sitting on one of the benches again, clearly having been less than bothered about making a thorough search. "And she even has the same number of limbs she did when we last saw her! My god! Can it be…? She only has one head too! Who would have thought it?"

"It's not a bad thing that I worry about my friends," I grumbled.

"Calling us at three a.m. because you had a scary dream about the Queen turning cannibal and eating us on the school trip isn't exactly normal."

"I don't even remember making that call. I must have done it in my sleep!"

"Which just goes to show you're all the more abnormal."

"You've already had this argument," Tanya pointed out helpfully. "It's not so exciting the second time. Let's skip the part where Teb calls Ally crazy and you both sulk, and…"

"And go home," I said. "I'm fed up with today—you can be sure I'm not going to call *either* of you, asleep or not, for at least a few hours."

"She says that," Teb said. Alana nodded wisely, like she could already know me so well, and gave me a rather mocking smile. At least I knew now that the corners of her mouth could theoretically be set to an "Up" position.

After that we went our separate ways, Teb still rolling her eyes at me for making such a panic over Tanya's disappearance.

"It must be something in the water here," I said to Alana as I waved goodbye to the others. She was still standing next to me, head tipped a little to the side, watching me with a half-smile that deeply unnerved me. I wanted to start the hike back to my house, music on my phone turned up loud to keep the real world at bay behind a wall of prog-rock ambient new age chanting that was my mum's current big thing at home. But Alana was in the way of my sojourn with a few minutes of much-needed sparkly guitar solos, and my in-built British politeness stopped me walking off and leaving her despite having not said goodbye. Also, I was more than a little worried that if I took a step she would come too, until she'd followed me back to my house and officially ruined what little there was left to enjoy of today.

"Do you not have a home to go to?" I asked her, genuinely concerned. Dad had a very firm line about homeless puppies. He'd probably say the same about homeless hipsters.

"Sure I do," she said. "I want to show you something first."

"What? You could have just said."

"Follow me." She beckoned, and turned towards the church.

"You aren't going to try and convert me, are you?" I asked, suddenly remembering that she had come from the Catholic school. "Because that witchcraft thing—it's just my mum and I'm not even sure tea leaves and tarot cards count as *proper* witchery: I was only joking about her knowing spells…"

Alana laughed, cutting into any more babbling I might have done on the subject.

I decided that I hated today as I grudgingly followed her across the town square and up the path to the church. This time next year I was going to stay in bed *all* day and not come out even for a mug of tea. March is rubbish anyway. And I don't think I'm going to find many ardent defenders to tell me otherwise. I'd just point out the window at the gathering rain clouds and my point would make itself.

I breathed in musty church smell at the arched doorway—old building and old person smells. I knew the church well from school plays, occasional forced Christmas carol services, and jumble sales.

Contrary to the ravings of the women who claim it's the cornerstone of the community and all that stuff, the church was utterly empty inside. Colder days reminded the devout they could just tune into *Songs of Praise* and have a cup of tea. Alana waited for the heavy wooden door to close behind us, sealing us into the religious atmosphere. She took a few steps, her shoes ringing in the stone ambience of the place. The church was small but still suitably dramatic, with its narrow windows and ancient round arches lining the aisles. The stained glass was shiny clean, and blue and red light fell in spots across the floor and wooden pews, filtered through a badly-proportioned depiction of St Troute being drowned. The air was cool and dusty, but at least my breath was not coming in puffs.

I thought she would follow the dramatic precedent TV had instilled in my imagination and walk straight up the centre of the church, but she cut sideways to a private altar in the south aisle. There was a low, coffin-shaped stone ledge protruding from the wall, a paler crack in the dark-with-time limestone, like it had been broken into at some point. There were a few carvings of angels and oak leaves on the arch around it. The centre of the arch contained a face with leaves spewing out of its mouth. They twisted away around the rest of the pillars either side. I recognised the motif as the Green Man, and this one carving more than anything formed the town's firm and demented belief that the fair was all about him. I had never understood how they could take something from a Christian location and insist it backed up their pagan practices—or indeed why something leafy and odd would show up in a Christian church—but I wasn't slightly insane with religious or festival excitement, so what did I know? Tanya was the one to ask for an explanation.

Over the simple tomb there was nothing but a small alcove containing a statue of a man with his hands held out oddly, one a few inches above the other, curved like gripping something large and invisible. Time had left most of the icons in the building similarly confused about their purpose or intended number of limbs. The statue itself was almost all worn away, the face a blur with a nose, the hair marked in ridges like ropes along his misshapen, vaguely triangular head.

"What's this, then?" None of the many school visits had included a proper tour.

"The tomb of St Troute." She said it matter-of-factly, but I backed off right away, convinced he might sense my heathen blood and rise to start smiting. Odder things had already happened today. This could have made it into the top three of all time if it had happened.

"Don't worry," Alana said, rolling her eyes. I was feeling extremely muddled, so I couldn't say what I had actually expected to happen.

"So why are we here to pay our respects to someone who died a thousand years ago?"

"It's not the tomb that interests me. Look at the statue."

I glanced down several times at the big block of stone that came up to my knee as I leaned over it to inspect the statue. The rock failed to crack open further and fiery wrath did not emerge. "Is he one of those saints they stole all the bits from and sold them as relics?" I asked, swallowing hard.

"Nah, he's just your average backwoods local saint—I doubt Rome even knows who he is. 'Saint' was a term they just liked throwing around back in the day. You do something nice, someone says you're probably a saint."

I wouldn't have known—we learned about him in classes back in primary school about little local history things. I knew he'd been a wandering traveller who saved a girl from drowning in the pond, died himself but sort of didn't, in a rather fuzzily recorded way (I was thinking CPR was invented at that point in history), and gone on to stay here performing regular miracles for the rest of his life. The church was a rather solid testament to his life, if he had actually built it, but I couldn't help listing the levitating ducks miracle as my favourite act of his, because it was so utterly pointless and extremely fun to draw as a kid when we'd all had to produce a pamphlet on his life as a classroom task.

I stuck my finger down between the statue's hands. "Huh, looks like he could be holding something…"

"Something thin and about ten inches long?" Alana prompted. I turned and gave her a look I'd learned well from Teb—one eye screwed up, the other under a massively raised eyebrow, my top lip curling back. Though I think I usually raised both eyebrows at once when I tried it.

Alana rolled her eyes. "What did you just *buy*?"

My expression cleared. "Oh… really?" I dug around in my backpack, dropped it on the stone tomb, now totally over my fear of saints, and I held up the little recorder. "It does look like it fits…"

"Sure wouldn't hurt to try it."

I glanced around in case there was a priest nearby, but our voices were the only sounds disturbing the still air. I shoved it up into the statue's hands with little ceremony, wiggling it and easing it a little more gently once I had to line it up with the second hand, not wanting to snap a piece off the statue nor damage my new recorder. The instrument came to a stop against his stone lips, and I leaned back, leaving it held perfectly.

"Okay… One question: What the *hell*?" I made another paranoid check of the surroundings. "I do history. I know what a thousand year old statue looks like compared to a recorder that's probably barely a hundred years old. Why is there a connection? How do you even know about it?"

"Someone local clearly likes the size and shape," Alana said. "Perhaps it is an older design, used right since whenever. Maybe there's some deeper meaning behind it, I don't—"

"Oh, don't you dare go Da Vinci Code on me. I only just got over the last few horrible plot twists today. Either tell me some fact or don't tell me some theory." Tanya used to play a fun game that there were conspiracy theories everywhere (I imagined them as sort of horrible monsters before I worked out that it was a concept). In the game there were government agents in the town. Every time we saw someone wearing a business suit we had to follow them in case they led us to a secret base, then we filed reports in one of my dad's old briefcases. Growing up and finding out what conspiracies actually were didn't make me feel any better about having one pointed out under my nose.

"You are a strange creature," Alana informed me. "All I wanted was to see if it fit, because seventy-five pence is extremely cheap for the antique value of one of the matching set of whistles. Here is the reason for Tanya's odd behaviour: she knew this and wanted you to benefit from it. Give it to me and I'll see what I can get for it on eBay for you when I get home. I'll take ten percent of the profits. Easy." She shrugged like everyone knew about antiques. Perhaps if I watched more *Antiques Roadshow* I would have been less surprised by all this.

"It's okay," I said, pulling the recorder loose and putting it back into my rucksack. "I'm not starving on the streets yet or anything. I'll keep it for now."

"Are you sure?"

"Yes. Even if I paid for it, it's still sort of a present from Tanya if it's worth something significant... I'd feel guilty about pawning it right away." And I felt worried about why Alana knew about these things in the first place: maybe I would get Tanya alone some time soon and ask her the *real* reason she'd made me buy it. If there was a conspiracy afoot, Alana had just dodged telling me about it: I had a feeling she wouldn't explain further if I tried asking, and I didn't particularly want to stand around talking in the freezing church all afternoon either. Mad as I sometimes found Tanya, I could trust her to tell me something I ought to know.

Alana rolled her eyes. I wondered if she'd tie knots in her optic nerves from doing that too often.

"If you're just going to be sarcastic can I go home now?" I asked.

"Sure—I just brought you here to see if this recorder was as special as I thought it might be."

I gave her one more suspicious look and left. She didn't follow me out of the church and home like a lost puppy, to my relief.

Three of Cups

I was cold and miserable as I flip-flopped slowly home. My feet were chafing, and I'd stumbled over a twig and maimed my toes in my hurry to get away from Alana before she had second thoughts about stalking me. It wasn't until I was around the corner and past the One Stop Shop that I slowed down at all.

A wind had got up, and the dark, raggedy clouds that I had seen earlier were blowing in heavy clumps over the hills towards the town. They didn't mean our town well at all, I could tell—they were coming to flood the pond and make the streets slippery, to force the sickly streetlights on a few hours early, and to do their best to make me run home. I shook a fist at them, not caring if anyone saw me communing with nature this way, and hoisted my bag up further on my shoulder, trying to increase my walking pace as fast as I could without tearing up my feet.

As if to mock me, a group of boys in hoodies on skateboards came zooming past, wolf-whistling and jeering as they grew level. I flicked a middle finger at them when their backs were safely turned, and sighed. Damn them and their light-hearted attitudes and cheap and easy transportation. If only I had anything remotely approaching a sense of balance...

The first drops of rain came hurtling down when I was walking up my drive, as if they personally hated the ground. The house was a generic blocky modern thing, small and detached. Its one redeeming factor that stopped it being a cube with a pointy roof was a tiny awning over the door, barely wide enough for someone to hide under as they looked for their keys. I dashed for its safety as the rain got acquainted with the ground.

By that point the fact I had a key was the least of my concerns: my fingers were useless white sticks on the end of my hands, and with icy rain pelting down on them as I tried to open my backpack to get to the keys I only fumbled helplessly with the zip. I was going to drown before I managed to get to them. I gave up and hammered on the door, yelling "Lemme in!" until it swung open, letting out a waft of central heating and cinnamon incense, a few chords of traditional Indio-African-influenced heavy metal doing their best to struggle over the loud rain.

"Aw, honey!" my mum cried as I tripped, dripping and shivering, into the hall, dropping my bag just past the threshold, leaving flip-flops behind as I threw myself prostrate before the radiator. "You should have taken one of my cardigans!"

I stopped myself from rubbing my face on the brown-painted iron bars, realising I didn't want first-degree burns on top of everything else, and smiled pathetically at her—grateful she hadn't noticed my cardigan-snatching antics that morning. Okay, so maybe I could blame a little of my misery on myself. And Bob McChewy who put the gum down the sides of the lockers, of course. Whoever he was.

"I have just had a day full of the weirdest crap you can imagine," I said, "Please, please, let's have a normal evening and not mention it, okay?"

"Sure, I have about a million turtles to braid for the fair—you can sit and help me if you like," she said, her fuzzy slippers slapping on her heels as she headed over to the kitchen, turning down the tortured sitar noises on the way.

Mum's long turquoise skirt was making a kind of papery, rustling noise from the lining under the satin that puffed it out about a meter in diameter. It was a noise I appreciated from my childhood, where I'd spent a lot of time lying on the floor in the warmest spots I could find during cold winters

"You used to dance all over the house," I said dreamily, lulled to sleepiness by the radiator, as my red hands throbbed with recovering heat.

"And nearly broke my leg falling down the stairs when I misjudged a pirouette," she reminded me, as the kettle clicked and started a familiar hissing bubble right away—someone had been having tea already. "As you grow up you find you can't do the crazy things you used to…"

"… so you find new things," I finished for her, well-used to her set of favourite sayings.

"Indeed," she said, now rustling back over and dropping a wicker turtle on me. I sat up and tucked it under one arm as I went into the cluttered lounge. I moved a pile of the dinner-plate sized turtles that had invaded our living room, taking over the sofa and chairs and coffee table, odd corners, lampshades, bookcases, and television. They were cute, often wonky, woven from dark wicker, sometimes painted with gaudy poster-paint spots and smiles. They were expertly crafted by a woman with *far* too much time on her hands. I decided I'd better start leaving the family computer pointedly resting on Open University degree courses on Herbalism or Astronomy, or some such thing which shared a book-list with Hogwarts.

I pulled a big hairy fake-fur throw around my shoulders, huddling close to the end of the room with the genuine working fireplace (an amusing month had passed watching my poor father try to install it to prove he could do it better than the big burly builder Mum kept sparkling at, who did it in a day. Dad always claimed he'd set all the groundwork, and it was just the unimpressive finishing touches the builder had done. Dad had pretty much un-boarded the fireplace and bought a stove over the time he'd 'worked' on it, if you didn't count all the time he spent standing around with his hands on his hips saying "Hmmm" occasionally when he thought we were laughing at him).

"So tell me about your day," Mum offered, coming back into the living room with two steaming hot mugs of tea as I got to work braiding the easy bit—the shells—and she picked up a half-finished one, doing the fiddly head and neck. In the background the music changed to folk music played with a tractor engine providing the percussion, something she'd screamed with laughter about when she found a video of online, and tracked down all their recordings.

She gave me a comforting smile, but being in the same room with her was enough. Hunched over some work, she formed the same image of my mum I'd held all through my life—and it was unbelievably comforting to have that continuity, considering how unpredictable she was otherwise. She had the same sort of nose as I did, long and curved and splattered with freckles, but she had grown into it and I thought she was beautiful in her own way... Well, I would say that: I was hoping against hope I aged like her and not into some twisted, wicked witch-looking woman. With a leaf-patterned shawl draped over her shoulders and her homemade feather earrings hanging down past her shoulders she looked like an otherworldly creature, the mad storyteller, dancer and artist of my childhood, much better than any imaginary friend.

"Oh gods, it was bad," I sighed, "Mr Brooke—" I let her get over her giggling, since she'd rather taken to him on Parents' Evenings "—totally went mad... In a bad way!" I quickly summarised those events, and moved onto things that bothered me more, almost surprised to find how by the by the weird fit had become to me. "I got lumbered with this new girl from St Fish's who's a *nightmare*, and she hates me... When we went into town after college..." I hesitated—don't tell parents how late you were up the last night, no matter how cool they are—"there was this guy with a whistle who drew a huge crowd, and this lady danced for him, and then everything went all like... I don't know... And then she was gone. It wasn't like how I *normally* zone out, and anyway it didn't feel like any time had passed, and my head felt weird afterwards... But Teb and even Alana wouldn't say they saw anything strange. And that was when Tanya vanished and..."

"Breathe, darling," Mum said, without looking up from twisting strands of straw around each other.

I did so before continuing, a little less frantically, "I think there's something strange going on..." I trailed off with a plaintive look. Mum smiled at me. If there was ever someone to turn to with a zany theory... I braced myself for a

Tanya-esque reply, something along the lines of, "Well, now you know—here's your funny hat, welcome the Secret Council of St Troute," or maybe, "The girl knows too much—she must be destroyed!" (Cue Robo-Mum transformation sequence, *et voila*—giant robot anime.)

"Huh, I knew this place had an odd history… It's half the reason I got your father to move here," she bit her lip, "I don't know what this would all be, though. I've never heard of any *modern* St Troute legends…"

"Did I say that I was looking for modern legends? Actually…" I gave her a sad look, conveying my *not you too*, "did I even mention St. Troute?"

"Well, no, but you were thinking it, weren't you? You said it was a man playing a whistle, and that's a huge motif of St Troute's later life. I just assumed…"

"Assumed?"

"Okay, so me and some of the others from the coven have discussed this in the past and we *think* there's a connection…"

"So you know who the man is? That I saw playing? I mean, people have seen him before?"

Mum shrugged a little. "It's said that St Troute's blessing of luck continued on the village. What's to say he didn't stick around as well? They don't believe it but I wouldn't put it past him."

I felt a little ill now: my mind strayed to the antique instrument buried in my backpack, which had been left to steam beside the radiator. "And why is there any lore about him playing a recorder—a whistle? Why is that his thing?" Why did one have to come to me?

"All I've really heard apart from the dull, Christian stuff is something about pagan representations, and stuff like that. Like maybe he was some indigenous belief, same as the Green Man iconography in the church… A piper is a strong image, used lots of places. Pied Piper and all…"

The home phone rang, making mum and me jump. She hopped up to answer it while I hastily set down my tea and dabbed at hot tea splashes on my leg with the throw from the back of the sofa.

"Aloha?" Mum sang. She looked over at me. "Is your phone out of battery, Ally?"

I shrugged. "It might be. It doesn't last very long these days. Why?"

"Tanya on line one!"

"We don't have a line two," I reminded her. I got up reluctantly, my legs throbbing as a reminder that I wasn't quite done recuperating from my busy day. I padded over to the phone.

"Hey?"

"Hi Ally!" Tanya's voice was so bright that it would have hurt my eyes had we been in the same room.

"What now?"

"So cynical!" she chuckled. "Ally, amazing stuff happens all the time, all around us, and you have the cheek to sound bored when I try to tell you about it.”

“You’re not ‘telling’ me anything right now. You’re lecturing me.”

“Well maybe you need a lecture after how grumpy you were all day. This is about him, isn’t it? The man in the black and white and a bit of grey as camouflage.”

“How would you know…? Why would this be important?”

“Oh Ally… Ally, Ally, Ally. I’ll show you exactly how important this is. If you give me the time and belief to prove it.”

“I’m not giving you anything,” I said, by this point deeply uncomfortable with the way this conversation had turned.

“You need to live a little,” Tanya warned me, all the sunniness gone from her voice. “You’ll see.”

“Tanya, what are you…” I was talking to a buzzing hum on the other end of the line.

I shrugged and looked over at Mum, who was busy weaving her turtle and pretending that she didn’t listen in to all the phone calls I was forced to have in her presence. “Well, she’ll probably bring some mad book into college tomorrow and spout off about how it means that there are fairies at the end of our garden. She should really know better. In just a few months she’ll be living on her own a hundred miles from here. I dread to think what sort of trouble she will get into.” I flopped back onto the sofa and grabbed the shell that I had abandoned.

“Ally, honey, you’re not much better at coping on your own,” Mum reminded me, a soft voice but a harsh truth. “Look at you. We send you out into the world, just for a couple of lessons, and even though you’re almost eighteen you still come back chilled to the bone, bleeding and bedraggled.”

“Today was not a normal day!” I complained.

“You never have a normal day, sweetie.”

“Oh!” I said, something about all our talk of normal days reminding me of who I really blamed for the oddness of the day. I started back to my feet and sent my turtle flying, nearly knocking over our tea. “Tanya was playing with a model Pied Piper in the junk shop.”

“The St Fish one?”

“Yeah,” I nodded, a twinge going off in my guts. “The St Troute one.” Funny that *his* shop would have all this stuff related to my mad theories in it… Or were they Alana or Tanya’s mad theories? Without communicating with each other as far as I knew, both had been prodding me towards strange ideas ever since Alana arrived in our lives.

Mum put down her turtle and took a sip of tea, watching me with glittering green eyes over the rim of the cup. When she put the mug down on a failed, flat turtle which had joined the legions of homemade coasters, she spoke carefully: “I think I may know a spell that might be useful here.”

“Since when do your spells actually do anything?” Considering we still lived here in this house with the three foot wide kitchen, broom-cupboard second bedroom and clanking radiators, I couldn't imagine any beneficial magic had ever been turned our way. The leaking roof last winter had to be just about the biggest sign that my mum had zero control over the elements.

"Sweetie, you didn't really think my 'book group' was a book group, did you? You've sat in this very room when my coven met before!"

I mumbled something about the internet being deeply engrossing, not wanting to admit I'd willingly blocked out my mum playing pretend because I was still too close to my own memories of doing it as a child to let her do it as an adult.

"Aww, Ally…"

"Well has a spell you've done *ever* worked?"

"They certainly don't have *any* effect on you… Gods know I've tried to will a boyfriend on you every time I go near my ritual table."

"You *what?!*"

She grinned at me, looking like a teenager again, giggling with a long, wicker-scratched hand held over her mouth, in the universal "Oopsie!" gesture.

I rolled my eyes. "You'd better make this good."

*

We went into Mum and Dad's bedroom, both of us holding our cups of tea, shuffling along in slippers, wrapped in cardigans. I felt like we were an uprooted group of gossiping ladies, not hip and happening practitioners of an ancient religion.

Their room was the usual explosion of conflicting interests you found when Mum and Dad were compared side by side—very Spartan, IKEA furniture, attacked with glitter glue, spangly shawls hung from every surface, handmade pretty things my mum had created sitting on various surfaces or hanging from the lampshade. An industrial grade dreamcatcher hung from the wall over their bed, made from a hula-hoop, a whole reel of fat rainbow-coloured yarn, and ostrich feathers Mum had obtained from a classy craft shop and left around the house everywhere until she'd found uses for them all. When I slept under it, it was like being knocked out from the moment my eyes closed until they opened again… Though maybe the extremely comfortable bed also helped with that, with the dozen handmade blankets and throws.

A wall of mirrored closets faced us as we went into the room, and I flinched and looked away with an "Urgh…" as I realised just how badly I needed a long hot bath and a few days' sleep. I'd have settled for a comb: I was probably one more day of failed upkeep from having dreadlocks of my own. I washed regularly but my hair had abandonment issues, the strands desperately knotting themselves together even in the time it took to brush from one side to the other.

Mum tutted at me as she slid back one of the closet doors to allow out a

46

waft of more spicy incense. Inside was what had once been a wardrobe space—the hanger rail had been taken out, but the waist-high drawers at the bottom remained, a black and gold cloth thrown over them, splattered with dribbly wax. Several twisted and deformed homemade candles dotted across the surface were to blame. Apart from them the cabinet was covered in sparkly things, lucky things, and magical bits and bobs like stones and feathers and seasonal leaves, pots of powdered substances, and a few hair ties I *think* were just accidentally left there, unless they were some of mine that Mum had been using to put spells on me. The drawers were neatly labelled, contrary to the mess on top—"Oils", "Cards", "Clay", "Spell Books", and so on.

She opened the cards drawer and took out a set of Tarot cards, big fat ones with glossy backs, that she shuffled with an expert move that would have had most people backing nervously away if they found themselves in a game of poker with her. Then she tapped them on the surface to square them, and put them back in the drawer.

"Wait, you're not going to do Tarot cards?" I said, feeling rather cheated. If she turned out to be a practising Wiccan in a universe where spells did something after all, validating all those jokes from my friends and the school as a whole, then she might as well be doing it *right*. Maybe there was a reason I'd never realised she was serious about it before.

"Oh, nervous tic," she said, "Do you *want* me to do it?"

I shrugged. She pulled them out again and did another quick hand movement that had them utterly reshuffled before I could follow what she'd done. She fanned them out a bit—"Pick a card, any card."

"Um." I took one.

"'Kay, don't show me, don't show me, remember what it is."

I looked down at the three of cups—a jolly old time being had by the little drunken people painted on this card—and nodded.

"Right, stick it back in the pack," she said, holding them out again. I looked at her curiously, but complied.

There was another rapid flicking noise as she shuffled them, then she shook them, listened thoughtfully to the pack, cried, "Aha!" and produced the three of cups from her voluminous sleeve.

"And?" I asked, unimpressed.

"Is this your card?"

I nodded. "What does it *mean*, though?"

She looked down at it, thoughtful. "That I still haven't lost my flair… Was almost a magician's assistant once, you know…" She got that faraway reminiscing look. "But your father didn't approve of the outfit. I still have it …"

"*Mum.*"

"Oh! Right! Well, there's a book somewhere in one of these drawers…You can look it up while I set up the spell." While I'd been distracted and annoyed she'd finally started doing something that looked like real magic, setting a couple of candles up and dripping oils around them. She took a pinch of something from one of the pots and sprinkled it in a neat circle—sand, I thought. Or salt. She lit a couple of the candles with a lighter with a pentagram drawn on it in marker, then sat back for a moment, watching it critically. Then she shrugged.

"Once been seen, Twice be heard, Thrice be what the hell are you doing in our town, Piper?"

I sighed, slumping down on the bed to look up at the light fixtures. I didn't think Mum was mad in the typical sense, but she was officially unemployable, and from time to time I could see why. She'd had a nervous breakdown at a very young age—I'd had to get the story from Dad, so it had been unembellished, and as dull as a story about your slightly-dotty mother could be. Since then she had spells of chatting to the fairies or wandering off following ley lines late at night when everyone was sleeping. I'd always thought she'd known perfectly well what she was doing, because she usually expressed it pretty well as she chatted about the books she'd read on the subject over dinner, or tried to explain it to Teb, who sat interested and cynical through most of it. I mean, people wrote books *agreeing* with her style of crazy. It wasn't like she thought the wallpaper was going to eat her. I'd always accepted it, and found it sort of odd that everyone else didn't think about natural energies all the time or whatever when I was growing up. It wasn't until I realised Teb found the whole thing hilarious that I understood this wasn't normal.

But whatever strangeness was in the air today, it had missed Mum by about a hundred miles, and her personal mythology had reached a whole new level of harmless wacky. Honestly—I'd have felt rather better if she'd gone rigid, started twitching, then reeled off a ton of prophetic crap about the end times. This was just making me feel anxious for *her*.

The faint strains of a tin whistle floated up in the silence that followed Mum's question. I tumbled over the edge of the bed, sending comforters and cushions flying as I ran to the window.

He was back, sitting in the same place as last night, playing his whistle for all he was worth despite the soaking the clouds were giving him. His shirt looked black, plastered flat to a thin frame. The dreadlocks hung limply. I looked back at Mum, and she grinned at me. "I knew it would work."

"Is this an answer?" I asked, watching the rain streaming down his face.

She nodded.

"What does it mean?"

She shrugged, "He's the Piper."

"Well what does *that* mean?"

"Three of cups—frivolity and fun," she said. "I think he'll finally speak to you at the fair."

Okay, never mind, everyone in the whole freakin' town had caught it.

Don't Follow The Pied Piper

I ran to my room, my mum's call of "I said he'll talk to you at the fair!" echoing after me completely unheeded. I was listening hard for the sound of that whistle as I pulled on socks, sought out my rarely-remembered trainers, and grabbed my coat. Thus properly equipped for the day's weather, I hurtled through the house.

As I opened the door the whistling stopped short. I tripped down the drive and broke into a sprint when I saw the Piper heading for the corner of the road, ambling along in his usual unconcerned way. Even in the pouring icy rain he was still only wearing a T-shirt and jeans. It was this odd little fact that made him seem strange to me, more than anything else about him. He wasn't blinking as the rain splashed against his face. He didn't even seem properly wet… The rain was hitting him, but I looked considerably more like a drowned rat and I had only been outside for twenty seconds.

"Get back here!" I gasped, putting on a new burst of speed as he vanished around the corner. "I'm not waiting another two days to talk to you!" If everyone was so insistent I had to talk to him in the first place, then why couldn't I do it now? He'd proven it wasn't like he didn't know how to talk, and I had plenty of questions all stored up already thanks to Alana and Tanya trying to out-weird each other all day long.

He led me down onto the little road that linked my street with the high street, where the houses were tall and clumped together. He stuck out easily against this classy scenery, but was already at the corner onto the high street, though by all rights I should have caught him up seeing as I was running and he was strolling along. I was soaked through and having to push my hair out of my face just to avoid tripping over my own feet, let alone to keep tabs on my quarry.

I knew the town perfectly after eighteen years wandering around the tiny place, but he was still managing to throw me using the alleys that zig-zagged between the houses, old joining with new paths. He doubled back again and again, taking me back and forth between the two parallel roads, and he was always just a bit too far ahead of me, only there to signpost where I should turn next. I lost sight of him for good as the lights beaming out of the One Stop Shop blinded me. Blinking as I stumbled past the shop, I couldn't see a single inch of dreadlock flicking around a corner to tell me where to go next. Darkness had hit quickly in the lousy weather and the wretchedness of the day sunk in as I stopped to breathe in their doorway. I had a stitch, and I was gasping air that was made of knives.

After a while I carried on walking, heading out of town, because I had too much momentum to stop for long. I concentrated on doubling up and making asthmatic noises.

I didn't want to give up. When I'd caught a little breath I turned up my speed to half power walk, half jog, and continued on after where I assumed he'd gone. I made it all the way out onto the recently-straightened road that led down to the motorway. Looking down it, I could see the rise of the hills, covered with woods, to my left, where I had no hope of following him, and down to the skate park and motorway to my right, the land clear aside from a small copse of trees beside the huge road. It was impossible he could be there unless he'd teleported into the trees. I wouldn't have put it past him.

Dejected, I turned to sulk home, water running down my face and dripping from the ratty strands of my hair. My trainers squelched around my feet, filling up with soggy pavement grit. I remembered how he had stopped to wink at me after playing for the dancing girl. He hadn't given me the slightest look this time... I felt as hurt from being ignored as I did from being annoyed at losing him and this great opportunity Mum had got for me.

I made it a few hundred yards into town before I saw him through the rain, leaning against the florists, his whistle to his lips. He blew into it, a single sweet note that said *Ally*.

I broke into a fresh run, legging it towards him ungracefully, captivated by the song, which carried on, note by note, spelling the sweetest story, telling me how wonderful things would be if I followed... How beautiful life would be, how brilliant the places he could show me.

A furious scream broke through the song.

Panic overrode my captivation. I blinked and looked around. Several lesser roars, still impressive, though not so blood curdling, shot through the air. I looked around, but the Piper had gone. I hurried on, towards the sounds of the yelling. As weird as my day had been, I shouldn't have wanted to get involved in *more* oddness. But these sounds were coming from right by my house.

Skidding around the corner I saw a girl—and no one else, to my relief. She was having a hissy fit, kicking at the brick wall of the house three doors down from mine, swearing and cursing. As I started to back off, she kicked too hard and limped back with more melancholy swears. Something seemed to alert her to the fact I was there and she swung around with an impressive flick of her sodden hair, and I realised it was Alana. *Crap.* Her pretty hair was plastered down straight, so she looked utterly alien to the Alana who'd tossed her tousled hair at us all day, and her clothes were glued to her with rainwater, so dark I hadn't even recognised the patterns.

"Ally!" she said, stopping short, as out of breath as I was, though quickly the more composed. I was leaning on a gatepost just to stay upright, my chest heaving raggedly. "What the hell are you doing here?"

"I live here. What are *you* doing beating up my neighbour's wall?" I glanced around, but in the heavy rain her yelling had apparently been drowned by the thick double glazing, because no curtains were twitching, only steadily glowing with undisturbed light and television flickers. Did *anyone* else in this town ever bother to look out of their windows? "Dare I ask if you're okay?"

"I lost an argument," she snarled and looked away, as if too angry to face anyone right then. "I'm right, but it's not like he'll ever see it… Haven't you even been home yet?"

"I did, but then I followed the Pied Piper," I said, permanently brain-addled by the day's events until I felt I might as well just state the facts of the matter. I didn't expect her to understand.

"Are you an *idiot*?!" she shrieked at once, "What the hell would you do that for?! Do you not know *anything* about the Piper? Never heard that bloody story? I'll give you a clue: he wants people to follow him!" She marched up to me, grabbed me by the shoulders, and turned me around. "I'm taking you home before you do anything stupid like jump in the pond 'cause you thought he wanted you to."

I dumbly followed her a few steps before it occurred to me to ask—"How do you know which house is mine?" It wasn't like there was any real evidence that crazy people like my mum lived there—Dad wouldn't even let us have a single garden gnome outside.

"Never mind that. What's more important is making sure *you* are okay."

I stopped under our little sheltered mini-porch thing and fished keys out from the pocket of my coat. I looked at her suspiciously, suddenly thinking of vampires that needed to be invited to enter a house. "Who the hell are you?"

"Alana Larbie," she said, not letting go of the grip on my shoulder. "We go to college together now? I added you as a friend on Facebook, but you have been extremely tardy about adding me back."

I pushed her away. "No, seriously. Tell me the truth. Not, 'wait until you can talk to the Piper', or, 'you're imagining things', or anything like that, just tell me *what* is going on. How do you know about the Piper? Why are you even here?"

"I'm looking after you," she said, "Mr Brooke was an accident, totally unrelated to your story, but you had to go and get *involved*. Now I'm making sure the same doesn't happen to you."

"Protecting me from *what?*" I asked. "The Piper?"

"Oh, no, he's harmless if you aren't an *idiot* about it. So actually, yeah, maybe I'm protecting you from yourself."

"So what? What did that to Mr Brooke?" I asked, ignoring her persistent anger at me for following the Pied Piper's Piping… yeah, it was starting to sound pretty dumb to me as well. I thought of rats leaping off a bridge, children sealed away under a hill, and my stomach clenched. I guess it was pretty ridiculous to think that he'd have been playing me love songs just because he liked me. Boys never seemed to like me and I wasn't going to mope around wishing they'd see me, since I had a lot of better things to be doing. On reflection it seemed very unlikely someone as interesting as the Piper would have decided from a scant few glances to play romantic songs at me in particular.

Alana hesitated to reply at first, but then rushed out an answer that didn't answer anything. "Probably demons. I'm getting soaked. Can we go inside?"

I hesitated, but then nodded. I was freezing now I'd stopped running. "Okay." I turned the key and opened the door. For the second time today, wonderful central heating rolled over me and I stepped inside, dripping over the doormat. Alana came in after me with little of the polite hesitance that people normally had going into a strange house. She kicked off shoes that were almost full of water and wrung out the trailing hem of her shirt over the doorstep before she closed the front door, sealing in the warmth that had been jumping, lemming-style, out into the rain. "I think it's best we stay inside. Add me back as a friend on Facebook… Make your… turtles?" She rubbed her forehead and frowned, confused.

"What's Facebook got to do with it?" I asked, looking around for the stray turtle that would have led her to that comment. I was wondering why she was so adamant about us linking up on social media. It would be par for the course if it became a bit of the conspiracy that apparently was going on under my nose.

"Nothing… I just deleted most of my friends, so I kinda want to make up numbers again. Point is, the Piper is the least of your worries, so stop distracting him. Look, I'm trying to work out as much of this as you are: I genuinely knew nothing about you, whatever you think about me stalking you, until this morning. I barely know anything about what's going on in the wide world either: I'm making this up as I go along. The only difference is I've been told the part I'm playing. You'll find out your part in this in time; like everyone's been saying, he'll talk to you and until then I'm not going to let anything happen to you."

"I have a part in… what exactly?"

"Who's that, Ally?" Mum called from the living room.

"A new friend!" I called back, defeated. Although we weren't Facebook official yet.

"I'll go put the kettle on."

"There Sure Aren't any *Little* Green Men"

While Mum scolded Alana for not having a coat as she towelled her hair dry in front of the fireplace, I moved a stack of wicker turtles off the computer chair, in front of a desk crammed into the space under the stairs, and I curiously made my way to Facebook under Alana's glare. I have to admit I was a little smug to see Alana with runny make-up and genuinely wild hair in one of Mum's big ugly cardigans. Divine justice, or some such thing.

"Alana Larbie has added you as a friend," I read out loud, "two friends in common." I clicked. Tanya and Teb's faces appeared on the screen. Teb, of course, was not using her whole name, but went by the slightly easier "Tebster Magee" online. Because she *obviously* had Irish heritage. (It was a Great-Great-Uncle, Steve Magee, who went out to India in Colonial times to bring Western music to orphan children. You think we make all this nonsense up?)

I sighed and, now that Alana was officially my 'friend', went to her profile. She had a grand total of three friends, including myself. Even I had several dozen, as random people I'd talked to once at college had compulsively added me. Not like I talked to anyone except Teb and Tanya, but I expected someone's Facebook to contain a 1:453 ratio of people they'd friended to people they *actually* were on excellent terms with.

"See, now you're just looking like a creepy stalker," I informed her.

"My old friends all suck," Alana said. If she hadn't had a fairly active Wall with a couple of days' visible messages and her status updates peppered with comments from said friends, I'd have doubted if they'd existed at all.

All that was buried three months down in her Timeline though. Of late she'd posted little but a couple of quiz results and stuff which looked like she'd only been bookmarking it for her own use. A quiz about Tarot cards right at the top of the page caught my eye.

Since Alana was telling Mum about her experience of being the new girl, it was probably best I kept out of the conversation lest Mum find out about my snotty behaviour. I went ahead and started the quiz. I answered some questions about my favourite colour, tendency for mood swings, how lucky I'd felt this week and a random answer for my favourite character from some teenage fantasy series I'd never heard of. Somehow I managed to get the three of cups again. I scowled and closed the browser before anyone noticed and said something doomy and portentous.

"Do you want a cup of tea?" I asked the room in general, heaving myself to my feet and forcing a cheerful smile onto my face.

Dad came back from work a couple of hours later, conscientiously wiping his feet and shaking out his umbrella before he came in from the cold. Of course he had been prepared enough to have an umbrella on a day that had started bright and sunny. Mum swept down on him with a "Look, honey, Ally's made another friend… Maybe we didn't screw up entirely when we raised her!"

Dad carefully extracted himself from the hug to hang up his coat, as I called, "Well, *thanks*," out to the hall. Alana had cracked up with laughter and was temporarily out of action, except to look up at me with tears in her eyes to say, "I *love* your mum."

I sighed and went to lay the table. Mum and Alana were already bestest best friends. Mums clearly just know to make good friends with the one person you can't stand in the world, even dear lovely mothers like mine. We'd had a quiet evening making dinner and sitting about as Alana watched us braid more turtles. She had been curled in the computer chair looking up mythology on Google for most of that time. She was showing no signs of going and because my mum loved her now, I couldn't chase Alana out of the house.

I was feeling ready to pass out from exhaustion once we were sat with our plates of weird vegetarian goop and lumps (I'd long given up asking what was going into the bubbling pot, and just accepted that it was presumably healthy, and definitely very good roughage). Today it was also a bit green and stringy, and Dad was doing his careful fork-bobbing thing where he knocked most of it back onto his plate in an effort not to have any undignified dangling stringy bits, and thus was direly behind the rest of us as we polished it off hungrily.

"You need more sleep," he told me, spotting me yawning again. "Do I need to change the parental controls on the internet again?"

I shook my head, "I just had a really tiring day," I told him, trying to ignore the way Alana was staring back and forth between us with fascination, an odd, hungry look in her dark eyes. I wondered if she had a father at home. Her interest would quickly wear off if she had to deal with one all the time. They were extremely dull creatures.

His fork bobbed up and down, and a few globs of sticky green stringy stuff fell onto the plate, leaving a long trailing stalk between fork and plate. *Bob,*

bob, bob… I resisted the urge to hand him a spoon and tell him to get to it like spaghetti.

"Well why don't you get to bed early and maybe you won't always run late in the mornings," he sniffed, and, having knocked all but a single blob of green from his fork, daintily ate it.

"I will, Dad," I said, permanent insomniac.

"Ooh, unless it's a sleepover. Girls are allowed to stay up all night if it's a sleepover," Mum declared. She turned to Alana: "Are you staying the night?" she asked, a little too hopefully.

Alana glanced at me, biting her lip, probably nervous from Mum's intensity rather than a fear of overstaying her welcome, since she had already done that. "Um, if that's alright, Hester?" (My mum was great for getting on first name terms with people.)

I thought about Alana saying she was protecting me, and shrugged. "I suppose so," I answered for Mum. If anything strange happened between now and tomorrow, I would know exactly who to accuse for it, and could react accordingly. It felt *good* to have someone to blame for any weirdness. I'd spent the day hating the universe as a whole, and that wasn't good for directing anger––I could end up like Alana had when I'd found her—screaming and kicking everything in sight.

*

Dinner, dessert, popcorn while watching an old Tom Hanks film with my mum, who loved him unreservedly, and then the long-awaited shower… all passed without any weirdness. Alana was doing a tolerable job of being a normal friend. Of course, an average stay-over for Tanya would have had a thousand more mentions of the weird and unnatural things of the world. Alana seemed more than happy not to explain why she was here, *really*, but the dull socialising was so exactly what I needed that I couldn't fault her for just being a decent person to have in the same room as me. The thought of trying to open up the can of worms that had been the whole day's events seemed way too stressful right then.

The day wound up with me sitting on my bed, failing to blow-dry my hair in the mirror in the back of my closet door. Alana sat at my computer, looking through my iTunes library, making a playlist of epic proportions. The room was so small that with my closet open I couldn't see her as it made a full partition in my room.

"Your music is a lot more boring than I thought it would be," she complained. I switched off the hairdryer, and glared at my new levitating cloud of hair. This was why I *didn't* blow-dry it. I guess another day of odd hair was the price to pay for proving I couldn't?

"What?" I shouted, ears still ringing from the loud whirring.

She shoved the wardrobe door closed so she could talk to me around it. Her eyes widened at the sight of me and the corner of her mouth turned up, but she managed not to laugh. It still took her a second too long to remember what she had been about to berate me for.

"I thought your music would all be stuff, like… recorded by Amish people onto a wax cylinder in a barn?"

"There's another media player on the start menu—you'll find *interesting* stuff there."

She turned to give me a strange look, "Well, I'm putting it on iTunes," she insisted.

"No no no!" I said, jumping up, ready to slam my laptop closed if she dared.

"All right, all right!" she conceded, backing away as far as she could crammed into the tiny corner my desk was in. "You need to comb your hair while you blow-dry it, you know."

"I only have two arms," I protested, "Our hairdryer is too heavy." It was a monster from the seventies, dark green plastic and frayed of cord.

She sighed, double-clicked on her playlist, and turned the volume up so I could hear Coldplay over the hairdryer, then climbed onto my bed to help me.

A few minutes later I had a passably cool hairstyle. I stared at myself in the mirror, tipping my head back and forth to make sure that was really me looking back at me. As I tipped my head my hair rippled down over my shoulder in a silky curtain, slipped over my ear, and fell into my face. I blew on it, and it lightly fluttered away from my nose.

"Just wake up in time to put make-up on in the morning, and you could look great," Alana scolded, going back to my computer. "And never let anyone ever know you own such terrible pyjamas."

I pulled my pillow over my knees to hide the yellow pantaloons of doom and leaned over to see what else was on the playlist.

"You've chosen all the lamest mainstream music I own. Don't you listen to anything that hasn't been played to death on the radio?"

"*Lame?*" Alana said, "Coldplay know what they're talking about…"

"The music's so bland," I protested.

"But catchy," she argued. "Why's it on your computer if you don't even like it?"

"Teb, mostly. She only knows how to use iTunes so I can hide my *good* music elsewhere on the computer."

She pointed to a number on my screen—"Listened: two hundred and thirty times."

"Teb again," I insisted. "She practically lives here. Unlike you, who seems to *actually* live here after about five minutes. Are you homeless?"

We glared at each other.

To fill the awkward silence (I was getting very good at sharing these with Alana), Coldplay started singing about witches and ghosts. I tumbled off the bed and reached up from the floor to hit the skip button. "No weirdness." I insisted as I straightened up. Having dropped my pillow on the floor I'd made my room so untidy there were only a few spare inches of floor left that weren't under chairs or desks.

She grinned at me. "I found every song on your iTunes that references the supernatural."

I threw the pillow at her (that counts as tidying, right?). "You're a lousy friend."

She threw the pillow gently back as I flopped onto the bed. "I'm not here to be your friend… I'm here to protect you. And I figure as you're still in shock, listening to your favourite bands singing about quasi-religious, deeply impenetrable metaphoric happenings might ease you into it a bit slower."

"Well, those aren't my favourite bands, but… I've listened to that crazy hobo band of ex-preacher conspiracy theorists Mum likes a million times… It doesn't mean I was *expecting* my history teacher to go into demonic convulsions… Just because I have strange music doesn't mean I expect strange things to start happening."

Alana rolled her eyes; "See, even when you say it, you don't believe it. You're still trying to assume there's a normal cause for it. When we met I thought it was going to be easy because you were all, 'yeah, demons, whatever!' and now you're like, 'shut up Alana, there aren't any demons!'"

I stared at her, imitating Teb's favourite "oh my God you're such an idiot" expression as best I could. "Yeah, but… That sort of stuff doesn't happen. And even if it did, why would you, some random teenager, be protecting me, another totally random teenager, from it?"

She groaned. "Okay. What's *your* explanation for what happened to that history teacher? I mean, come on, we have all the Christian mythology about demons, right? Historical records of possessions and stuff, right? Witch trials? This is stuff you can look up in local museums, and find books on in the library. I did, when I found out about it all existing for the first time. The pond here was used for a load of witch dunkings. There's even a tombstone in the graveyard for the witch they accidentally drowned! The witch craze started here because there were all these demon-possessed people, and *that* was because of a millennia old story about the town pond being a portal to other worlds… Letting in things that shouldn't otherwise be here. It's not like the Piper is something I made up—we all know about him because of a certain incident. But not just that— he's everywhere, if you know what to look out for when you're reading old legends and stories and things. I researched him too, because when he found me, I was as dumb and confused as you are. I've been through this, Ally. I know how you're feeling."

"Unlikely. You didn't have *you* trying to tell you all this."

Alana's brow furrowed.

I gave up. She was going to keep talking, and I could only try and steer through the madness. "Well, what did you do… What *do* you do with the Piper?"

"Really? Not much. I know who he is, and he knows who I am, and he's given me some good advice in the past. We don't go jaunting about together or anything. All I really know about what he does I have to guess from what I've read; the stuff he's told me to do in the past isn't much. He tries to stop things like the possessions and witch burnings, to keep everything normal and safe. The only reason our world isn't overrun with the supernatural is because he stops them. Well. Sort of. He's *there*. People generally dealt with the witches and demons on their own. And fairy infestations usually clear up when they get bored. And all the other monsters are stupidly rare, he said, so it's not like we ever see them…"

"What are you talking about?" I said, throwing myself back with a *flumph*. Lying down made me suddenly feel really tired all over again, the dozen mugs of tea I'd consumed wearing off. The gentle, haunting music of Enya we'd transitioned to was making me sleepy, all her words blurring together with Alana's mad babble, losing their meaning.

"I'm trying to tell you, Ally, that you're an idiot if you aren't actually seriously considering that fairies stole Tanya."

"They gave her back," I yawned, exhausted and humouring her again because at that point it was clear she was not going to listen to me telling her that she was crazy any more. "What do I care?"

I heard Alana twitch like she'd almost stood up, because my computer chair made the alarming springy noises it does when its suspension is tested. But she subsided down into it again, and didn't say anything. I left my eyes closed.

"You don't believe me." She sounded disappointed. I could have almost felt guilty for leading her on: it was like my thoughts about the town all over again. Everyone thought Troutespond was weird, everyone thought I was barmy, and between hanging out with Tanya and listening to my mum talk you'd think I was. But it was all just talk. I was a normal human girl and Alana had clearly been getting mixed signals from my companions and family. Apparently just seeing Dad wasn't enough to convince her I was normal.

"I don't. You just invoked everything except little green men. There's a reason they keep books about that sort of stuff separate from the regular history books."

She shrugged and thankfully *didn't* find a way to include aliens into her mad mythology. "Well, it's okay. It doesn't matter if you do or don't believe me, because the Piper will talk to you on Saturday, and then you'll *have* to believe."

In the silence that followed, Jimmy-Three-Paws woke up and started sniffling around his cage. His scruffling noises weren't the usual comfort I found them.

"You know what, I'm going to go sleep on the sofa," I told Alana, sitting up. "You can have my room. Don't get crazy on anything in here."

"Well, that's good to hear… the amount of space you have in here I thought I was going to have to sleep standing up in your closet. I'm not a vampire." She stretched and flopped down on my recently vacated bed. I stared at her, still utterly unable to fathom her complete inability to realise how strange she was; then, because I'd already said it and it would look odd to keep standing around in my doorway, turned and went downstairs.

Cinderella and the Glass Flip-Flop

I woke up staring into the bug-eyes of a wicker turtle. It took me several minutes of wondering to work out why I was lying on the sofa, with all the prickly straw trapped forever more in the throw thanks to my mum's arts and crafts. It wasn't the best choice of bed. I remembered eventually that a terrifying girl who believed in demons was sleeping upstairs in my nice warm comfy bed, and I groaned. Not the best awakening thoughts, but at least more tranquil than the blare of my alarm clock... Aaah, Alana had to deal with that when she woke up. I grinned to myself. I'd definitely remembered to set it—I remembered the shudder of dread that had shaken me as I'd heard the alarm mechanism click into place. That kind of trauma is hard to forget.

I sat up and stretched, though I could see the sky outside was still only powdery grey-blue, dull and metallic, still deciding between which of the two colours it should turn. I wasn't tired any more, though. I operated on very little sleep and, having passed out early for my standards, I'd woken up early by them too and would function well enough until about one in the morning, almost a whole day away from now.

Was now the time for my strange early-hours adventure? Yes, I decided. I went to the hall and pulled on a coat and my flip-flops. Old habits die hard. Trainers today, I told myself, *trainers*. At the moment my weather appropriate shoes were stashed upstairs in my wardrobe, I guessed, as they weren't in the hall's shoe rack. I didn't like the idea of heading upstairs in case I woke Alana up and she stopped me from going out. This was just poking my head out the door, though. Flip-flops couldn't hurt, right?

I suppose I was semi-sleepwalking, and I'd forgotten a day of being warned that I needed to be protected, or I was deliberately ignoring Alana's warnings.

Maybe something was drawing me out of the house. Instead of just strolling down the road, perhaps with the intent of going to the corner shop and picking up something nicer for breakfast than more toast, as if drawn to do it my feet took a left turning towards the end of the street. Climbing over a fence at the end of the road was probably not the best idea, nor was walking up the field at the back of the houses to sit under a lonely tree bang in the middle of it to watch the sun rise, what with the spring equinox coming. I didn't know much about the fairies at that point, but I should probably have guessed somewhere in this string of actions that I hadn't done the most sensible thing. I mean, Mum rambled on enough that I could have drawn plenty of lessons on the theory out of it, even if I didn't believe in the practical side. I'm not completely sure I was actually awake at that point though, let alone up to using my brain.

The sun's light appeared slowly in the watery sky, creeping up from behind the hills on the other side of the valley in its usual "peek-a-boo!" way. It was after it started adding tints of gold here and there, and sending the remaining shadows into a deeper contrast, that I noticed the sparkles in the air. I took them for the little floaty things you find in heady air—cottony seeds, slow-drifting bugs, pollen dust, blossom and other things that trees shed all over the place. But as they rapidly increased in number and more drifted close by, I realised that there was no substance to them except the glow of reflected sunlight… Or maybe a light they themselves produced? I could see them drifting in and out of the shadows around the tree. They weren't going the same way as the breeze. In fact, a lot of them seemed to be cutting a rather clear line towards me.

I cautiously stood up, the little burst of adrenaline from my first panic of the day starting up my brain at last, overriding my dreamlike haze so that I finally remembered that I had been marked out by weird happenings. I don't think anyone had specifically told me that yet, but if nothing else, the Piper winking at me should have said everything. As it was, I at least knew in that moment that I really shouldn't encourage said weird happenings. For a moment I thought I'd got away with it, not disturbing the floaties in their serene movements. As I relaxed, though, they suddenly caught like a gust of wind had run through them, and swirled up around me Pocahontas-style.

With a "Waaaaah!" of surprise I fled from under the tree. If there's one thing to be said in favour of my lifestyle, it's that one does get awfully good at running in flip-flops. I didn't stop to see if the weird lights were still following me but stumbled down the side of the hill as fast as my legs could carry me, tripping and rolling the last half. I scrambled over the stile, dropping a flip-flop like Cinderella. I grabbed it from the other side and limped home as fast as I could, looking over my shoulder every few steps.

I let myself in, still panting. I carefully closed the door and let the silent calm of the house surround me, dark and quiet like the morning hadn't happened yet. I went to the hall mirror to check my appearance, wondering how obvious it was that I'd just rolled down a hill. From all the damp grass in my previously-snazzy hairstyle, I could see I had a lot of work to do to make sure Alana didn't scream at me when she woke up. I started slowly picking the grass out, running my fingers through my hair to flatten it out. Despite a large cowlick in my fringe I was quite impressed at just how flat it went. If magic existed for real, Alana had probably put a spell on my hair as she brushed it.

There was the sound of movement from upstairs, and I glanced into the living room to check the clock—seven a.m. now. *Who'd be moving around?* I wondered. Dad, probably. I didn't know what time he woke up in the morning, but it always seemed offensively early to me—he often mentioned having done some work that morning when we were in the car on the way to college, when I was still mostly asleep.

I heard his mumbly morning voice—"Ah, Alana, is it? Bathroom's free."

I sighed, and slunk into the living room while the bathroom exchange happened. Maybe I could get breakfast, I thought, and went to put some toast and the kettle on.

What *Can't* You Fix with Skittles?

I thought Alana was looking at me suspiciously when she came downstairs an hour later, looking so perfect and polished I had to wonder if she'd done it with yet more cosmetic magic—seeing as she only had the clothes she'd worn the day before, and the supplies of my bedroom, I couldn't understand how she looked so good. Her perfect make-up was back, and her hair was as perfectly tousled as it had been at our first meeting.

"Huh, didn't peg you for an early riser," she eventually said, taking some toast from the big plate I'd made while my mind still played over and over the odd light show I'd seen on the hill. The stack of burnt bread wobbled like Jenga bricks, but stayed upright.

"Sofa's full of hay," I muttered.

"Yeah, there's some in your hair," she said, leaning over and pulling out a piece I'd missed. "Go upstairs and brush it again, and I'll try and make you look presentable for college, okay?"

I sighed. "Yes, mum."

I fed Jimmy-Three-Paws something that wasn't toast, and changed from my crazy pyjamas into my jeans from yesterday (I had no argument with them now they'd dried out), and a long-sleeved shirt with a hooded jumper over it. I was taking no chances with being caught out by the cold now. I applied socks to make sure I didn't get lazy and put my flip-flops back on.

Alana fussed over my hair for the best part of an hour until she admitted defeat and gave me a wonky ponytail in under a second that looked better than any of the other fancy complicated hairstyles she'd tried.

"Face it, I'm not meant to look perfect like you," I grumbled, secretly pleased with how asymmetric and awful I looked that morning. If I was too cowardly to be a Goth or a full-blown hippie, I was certainly happy not to fit in by sheer dint of terrible dressing.

"Guess we'd better get going," she said, smiling though.

I followed her downstairs to where my family were sparkling at her. I think they thought she was a good influence or something. My mum made lunches for us and Dad. Alana offered to help. I mooched around unnoticed, feeling a bit useless.

"Oh, good, why don't you get in the car? I might actually be on *time* today," Dad said when he came in, straightening his tie. Which totally was to make me feel unduly guilty. He always left an extra half hour whenever he went anywhere and therefore my morning routine only stopped him from hovering uselessly about spending his money on extra cups of coffee before his office opened.

He picked up his briefcase, Alana our lunches, and we all got a hug from my mum on the way out the door. I had to give her points for acting normal around my 'friend'—she'd only been as cringe-inducing as anyone else's parents might be.

The short drive to college passed in silence, and we abruptly found ourselves standing on the pavement at the top of the hill, sucking in the cool morning air, though for once it wasn't acting as morning coffee to me, my mind having been active (as it ever got) for a good few hours.

I saw Teb standing at the school gates as we approached. I supposed she and Tanya waited for each other in the mornings. She certainly looked surprised enough when she saw me, and she came hurrying up to us, her pumps flapping as she walked—I took a moment to savour having the more sensible shoes.

She pushed a super-sized bag of Skittles into my arms. I looked down at the bright packaging and blinked.

"Um? It's not my birthday for months…" She really wasn't the random gift-giving sort of person, opposed to Tanya, who gave away almost anything that came to hand even if it wasn't hers to give.

"I know," she said, her expression extra-serious. "You can open them now, you know."

I did, mindlessly following orders, and ate a couple, after offering them around (both girls declined).

"Ally," Teb said, biting her lip, "Tanya's missing again. Properly."

The rainbow skittled across the pavement as I fumbled the vast bag of sweets.

"What do you mean, *missing?*" I hyperventilated as Teb led me into the schoolyard. This was my fault: it had to be. She had been trying to prove something to me. This didn't show me anything except that when she got home she needed some serious counselling about what was acceptable behaviour and what was not. Trying to frighten me because she thought I was boring was *way* out of line.

Teb cleared a bench of year sevens with a glare. She forced me to sit down, and handed me the now-half-empty bag of Skittles, pushing them at me a couple of times until I ate some. I numbly took a handful and shoved them into my mouth—the bright, tangy flavour shocked me right to the back of my head, and I could focus on Teb as she spoke. She did like managing me, but I felt grateful for it.

"She came home from college as usual, but when her dad went to get her for dinner she wasn't in her room. He looked all over, but couldn't find her—he called me first, and I told him not to call you—"

"Mff!" I protested, mouth full of half-chewed sweets.

"Because you'd have *panicked*, and I didn't want you creating more trouble than we already have. It was dark and pouring with rain: like as not you'd have run off into the woods looking for her and fallen in a hole, or dashed onto the motorway. Anyway, he was waiting to see if she was with any of us, but she usually says and your Mum made a Facebook update about how you were having dinner with Alana so I guessed you didn't know where she was either. And that's as far as anyone's got... The police are trying to trace her now, but there isn't much to go on."

I swallowed a huge citrus-flavoured lump with some effort. "But you didn't call me?!" I protested.

"Look, I'd have let you know, but I don't trust you not to hurt yourself," Teb said, taking me by the shoulders and looking me squarely in the eyes. "Or you'd have beat yourself up about it all night and got no sleep and found a way to blame it on yourself. Look at me and tell me you wouldn't have."

I sighed, looking down at my big bag o' Skittles. She was right—my speciality was huge freak-outs. This would have come right after my repeatedly weird day. I supposed sitting down to dinner to hear my friend had just wandered off again would have been the icing on the cake—instead I'd got a nice, relatively relaxing evening, perhaps because everyone had already worn out their "he'll talk to you later" lines by the time I went to bed. But the moment I heard this news... It wasn't that I was blaming myself unduly. Tanya had said "*You'll see.*" And now she was gone. I couldn't stress that enough. All the weirdness suddenly seemed to have been leading to this, and Alana had kept it from me.

Teb tentatively relaxed the pressure on my shoulders—"Are you okay? Eat some more Skittles."

I did, remembering how Teb had bought me Skittles every time something bad happened. I should have realised: she was mentally conditioning me to see them as soothing in a time of crisis. The sugar helped as well. After I'd managed to mechanically chew a few mouthfuls of them I nodded. "I'm good... Thanks for worrying about me." I felt kind of bad she'd go to so much trouble for me when there was more to worry about—though she seemed to think it had saved more trouble in the meantime... I'd not comment on that in too much depth. "So what do we do now?"

She grinned at me, "That's our Ally... I was thinking we could do all her favourite haunts; the woods, the library, the junk shops. The police are out looking for her, since she has such a great history of this sort of thing and I'm sure they remember all the trouble she usually causes if she isn't found quickly. I gave them some ideas of where to look, but they don't know her like we do."

"Well why didn't you tell the police the secret stuff we know?"

She gave me this look like *really, tell adults?* Sometimes she could be the biggest child of us all; maybe that was why she was so obsessed with acting like a grownup. "If Tanya's run off, she won't come out when some Bobby starts stomping around her hiding place. Remember that time she decided to live in my attic? She only came out and revealed herself when my little brother got freaked out by the noises in the roof, even though her dad already came around and checked after we told him she had been saying she'd like to live in an attic?" Maybe, on the other hand, she really did just understand me and Tanya better than anyone else on the planet.

Alana, who'd been lurking to one side, stepped forward, "I, uh, can I suggest something a little crazy?" She looked apologetically at Teb, who narrowed her eyes at Alana. Teb had zero tolerance for crazy, and I almost handed Alana the Skittles as a reward for her bravery in attempting to try unstoppable force versus immovable object. Because if anything was certain about this girl I barely knew, it was that she could spout some wackadoo theories at the drop of a hat.

"How crazy?" Teb asked, wisely.

"On a scale of one to ten, with grocery shopping at one, and Mr Brooke's breakdown at five, I'd put it at…" she hesitated. "Eight."

Teb tipped her head to one side, and regarded Alana suspiciously. "What's ten?"

Alana glanced at me, and I think she winked. "Little green men wandering the streets."

"Right."

"Right?" Alana was caught out, clearly forgetting that Teb was used to humouring Tanya. Teb didn't have much tolerance for silliness when she thought we needed to be serious, but perhaps she was so concerned about Tanya she would stop and listen.

Teb shrugged, "What do you think happened to Tanya, then?"

"That she's not wandered anywhere. She's been taken by supernatural forces…"

I groaned. Teb looked my way.

"If *Ally* thinks it's crap, then it *has* to be crap," she said.

I'd been more upset about Alana's delivery; Teb might have been reasoned with if Alana had built it up slowly, quietly pointing out evidence here and there, asking me to describe the stuff I'd seen… But to just tell Teb outright there was magic afoot? This was someone who thought Disney movies were 'too silly'. I wanted to defend Alana, but my attempt to explain it more rationally came out a bit biased towards the friend I'd known all my life instead of all of yesterday: "What is it now? Fairies again?"

Alana nodded. "You're always right when you're sarcastic, you know?"

I groaned.

Teb stared at me. "Has she been encouraging you to come up with mad theories?"

"A load of weird stuff's been going on… I suppose a six or seven on her wonderful new scale? The Piper—that guy with dreadlocks I pointed out to you? He's been turning up all over the place, at the mention of his name. I saw the freakiest light show in a field this morning…"

"*What?*" Alana wailed.

"Oh, and Alana here has been trying to protect me from it all, and failing epically."

"What were you doing wandering off into the fields?" my so-called protector demanded.

Teb was smiling now. "Oh, this is great, you two go together perfectly… Kidnapped by fairies? I know this is Tanya, but that's still pretty hard to believe, you know?" She reached down, took my arm, and hauled me to my feet, "See you, Alana… Ally and I have some searching to do. Call us if you bump into some trolls who have seen Tanya, maybe."

"Can't I come?" Alana asked, alarmed.

"No, you're a bad influence on Ally, and you've only known Tanya a day. The office wouldn't have given you the day off to look for her if I *had* asked, which I didn't because… You've known her a *day*. See you 'round." That parting was rather more pointed than the first casual 'see you'. Teb started dragging me back out the school gates.

I waved to Alana, who was fuming, and then turned to make sure I didn't trip over myself as Teb dragged me away down the street.

"You really don't like Alana, do you?" I asked, once I'd asserted my right to move my own feet without assistance.

"I dunno, I thought she was cool yesterday, but she started *clinging*. And now fairies? Does she honestly believe the crap Tanya spouts? I never thought *Tanya* believed most of it. And, I mean, since when do you make new friends that you like so much they sleep over on the first night you know them?"

"Er, well, she got to my mum."

"Right, right. But you're not always a total wet blanket; you could have told her to leave!"

I thought about the strange things I'd seen before Alana announced she was staying over, and realised that whatever else I'd felt, I had also felt a little safer with her under my roof. Also, I was a wet blanket.

"Where are we going?" I asked, to change the subject. Alana was doing something Tanya never had: making weird stuff an issue. How many odd comments of a far more incendiary nature had Teb brushed off because they came out of Tanya's mouth? And in maybe three short conversations Alana had shaken any ability Teb had to listen to her. I quietly sat on the fence, agreeing with Tanya or Teb without really believing either, but maybe Teb had thought I was on her side after all, and now it was three against one?

Teb reluctantly let go of the Alana argument, perhaps sensing that I was not going to openly say that I thought the new girl was a creep. "Tanya ended up in the junk shop last time, so I was thinking we could start there…"

Taking Stock

When we were a few minutes down the hill, having walked in silence most of the way back into the town, Teb spoke: "Are you okay, Ally?"

"I'm fine," I told her. I think I'd hit brain-overload time, and was utterly incapable of forming any new thoughts, so this Tanya-related madness was washing over me a lot more peacefully than it might have on a normal day. I'd only just recovered from losing her once in the last twenty-four hours: I had been annoyed enough to find her well and safe, and then her phone call… Right now, if she genuinely was hanging out with hobgoblins, I was tempted to let them have her for a bit.

"Did you get shocked into believing that Tanya's been taken by ghosts just now, or is this really something that's been going on for the last few days?" So Teb *was* still harping on Alana. Great. Couldn't we all just get along while holding wildly different viewpoints on the supernatural?

"Just yesterday, really. Maybe I went mad after the Mr Brooke thing, but yeah… This has been happening since before Tanya vanished. The first time. And it's not ghosts… Um, she said fairies. I'd maybe believe her, if I were you." Away from Alana and her sullen expressions somehow it became easier to take her seriously. Maybe it was just Teb's rampant disbelief making me more certain of what I *had* encountered that was weird. I was all for a rational explanation but I had crossed that line before lunch yesterday, and I didn't have a whole lot of footing left.

"Look… You saw the dancing girl yesterday…Right before Tanya disappeared. Didn't it strike you as a bit… odd?"

"That she didn't get frostbite? Maybe she's related to you."

"How she… well, disappeared at the end of the song."

Teb gave me a fed up look I got a lot when I didn't speak clearly. "What, Tanya? Like I said, she probably got bored of watching and sloped off to go to the shops. We don't have to *mind* her every second of the day, unlike you."

"No, the *girl*," I insisted. "One second Tanya was holding my hand and the girl was dancing, then the next… Neither of them were there."

"Ally… I know you've had issues with paying attention… Are you sure you didn't see a really interesting pigeon and look away? The girl packed up and left."

"You saw something *very* different from me."

"No, I saw something you didn't. That doesn't mean it didn't happen just because you didn't observe it. We went over this in philosophy: our teacher put the chair outside the classroom and told us it didn't exist, remember?"

"Well… I'm sticking by me *not* being crazy and I know Alana saw the same as me, whether she said so or not. I wasn't sure at first, but everything else she said since then…? Maybe the chair never existed after all." I was terrible at this metaphor business.

Teb sighed, clearly showing every intention of not believing *anything* Alana told her. I could tell that the conversation they'd had outside the school had damaged all the good standing Alana had forged with her… And perhaps it was the certainty too: whatever Tanya said, she always seemed to be mugging, laughing, going along for the ride. She posed questions and theories, and said "I bet it would be really weird if…" a lot. Alana stood there stoic and unmoving, radiating this aura of *this is happening and I'm certain of it*.

That thought of Alana seemed to be nagging at Teb as well: "And what part does Alana have in all this? I mean, Tanya was the one who suggested Mr Brooke was possessed by demons, and you never listen to *her*. I'm assuming the new girl has found a better way of getting to you."

"I don't know," I said. "She's coming up with way weirder theories than I was or Tanya ever did… And mum—I've just seen some odd stuff over the last twenty-four hours. It's made me a little inclined to listen to her, but not like a total idiot. I still only believe what I've seen."

"And what's that? We've established you probably just sneezed and missed the dancer you're so obsessed with."

"You were there for Mr Brooke's breakdown…" She flinched a little when I mentioned that, like she'd forced the memory away and I'd broken it out again. How could she have *forgotten* it? I still got his screams echoing in my ears if I stopped to think about it.

"That wasn't *weird*," she said, defying all logic. And when Teb spoke it was the belief that logic had better damn well listen to her and use her standard instead. "Not in a supernatural way. I mean obviously it was very disturbing for a class full of sheltered teenagers to see mental illness at close quarters, but these things happen. Some people were not meant to be teachers. You said it yourself:

that fan club was going to get to him."

"These things *were* strange," I said. "I saw Mr Brooke up close… He was not right but not in a… normal sort of way. And we all saw that dancer vanish and we just don't want to admit it. We'd happily pretend we had an epileptic black out for a second and missed her walking off, every single one of us, rather than just say she disappeared."

"I just find it hard to believe that *you* are saying these things: Tanya makes up all sorts of stuff and that's fine because it's Tanya and we get a good laugh out of it. You can't muscle in on that, Ally. I like you as my boring but weird friend." She was looking at me sadly, and I wondered if she thought that I was making this up… or going crazy. But I couldn't be cracking: this wasn't just my delusion. Teb was strange for being outside of it! "I'm not going mental!" I protested, a bit loudly and in a whining voice. I shut up quickly and looked down at my feet.

I didn't feel too convinced, though. I had almost been taken into protective custody a couple of times because of my mum when I'd been younger and she hadn't been so mellow. I think that was really why my dad was so unimaginative and normal—he'd spent years having to convince the world he could look after our family. Still, despite his efforts in that direction, I'd always been watching Mum instead, learning her crazy ways, much more interested in the brightly coloured world she painted (all over our hallway wall, at one point). I'd ended up openly embracing the idea of my looming nervous breakdown in my second year of university because I was so set on following in her footsteps.

Something that had been the punch line to my jokes about adult career choices suddenly seemed to be a lot scarier now I was seriously considering the existence of the supernatural, and their growing meddling in my life. But it was so *separate*. I could see myself called crazy, and I could see myself believing in the Piper as an honest-to-God mythological dude that Mum could summon with candles and oil and a half-assed spell, but I couldn't accept the idea that because I believed it I was crazy, which was probably a sign I *was*.

"Maybe I am?" I suggested, into the silence that had fallen between us. Teb would at least not poke too much at my mum, not *seriously*.

"It can happen," Teb said without sparing my feelings much, though perhaps she thought that she was being diplomatic. "But I think you know what you're doing still, even if you don't know why. And maybe that's what we need right now. We have to find Tanya, first and foremost, and if your weird brain problems get us there, then I'll just have to agree it was fairies until we find her and it turns out you've been hallucinating. Even so, I think I'd be rather more concerned about getting a counsellor to Tanya when we find her than you. This is the tenth time she's run off, and it's not like she's even unhappy."

"Why *do* you hang out with us?" I asked, not going through the old "But psychoanalysis bounces off of Tanya!" argument.

"Somewhere along the line I realised I wanted to be a psychologist, and you two will make perfect case studies for my doctorate."

"Name something after me," I sighed. "It's the least you could do."

"Don't worry, I'm on it," she said, with a grin. "And in the meantime… You and Tanya *are* fun to hang out with. I wouldn't trade it for hanging out with Jess Standerwick and her boring friends any day of the week, even if they do listen to real music…"

"So why do you *really* think Tanya's run off this time?" I asked, curious about how she was rationalising all this.

"I don't know… I think… We misplaced her pretty recently after that man was doing his busking thing…"

I stopped short. "And the dancing lady disappeared… dammit! Tanya disappeared as well! At the same time! He Pipered her off somewhere, same as the dancing girl, and then he must have realised he hadn't meant to do it, and sent her back! Maybe she hadn't known for sure that all this magic stuff existed before and that was the moment when she had it confirmed… I mean she never ever said that she'd *met* any elves or anything like that. So yesterday was as significant to her as, well, me, I suppose. Except I just got tricked into inviting Alana into my house and Tanya went off to play with the fairies instead…"

Teb groaned. "Do I need to get you an icepack for your head?"

"No, no, no, shut up, you were right, we need to go back to the junk shop. That's where he sent her when he returned her… That's how no one saw her get into the basement… She was Pipered into it! So that's where she'd have gone first to try to get back again."

"Okay, if you really think so, we'll try it your way… I don't believe you, but if you're tuning into Radio Tanya, maybe this will get us to her in a roundabout way."

"Okay," I agreed, riding on a wave of happiness that I'd *finally* made some sense of yesterday's events. All I had left to work out was, er, *why*. Maybe "all that was left" wasn't really the right thing to say…

*

The high street looked strange to me without the near ubiquitous smattering of student-aged kids with nothing better to do while they waited forty minutes for the next Bilsworth bus. It made the wide triangle of land between the shops and church unusually lonely, reminding us just how tranquil Troutespond was. It was worse than the summer holidays, when at least there were children running around everywhere unsupervised. I felt the glare of every old lady who hobbled past us—it seemed to be the time that they came out to play—but apart from them, and a couple of bothered mums with prams, there was an unnatural silence on the streets. Even the morning traffic had calmed down to the next-to-nothing our town got on a regular day.

The group of skateboarding boys from yesterday all whizzed past in a row, hats pulled low like that would stop someone from recognising them, and maybe assume they were sensible adults who just happened to be tiny lanky things with foul mouths who thought skateboarding was still cool. They whistled at us as they passed, and vanished down the road that led to the skate park. If there wasn't a community support officer waiting down there with a big van, doors open at the other end of the half-pipe, I'd eat my shoes. This was an ongoing saga we all got to read about in the local newsletters that were angrily circulated by citizens with nothing better to do.

We hurried to St Troute's charity shop, guilty to be out and about—even if we had been allowed by the college— and feeling tainted by the presence of kids genuinely bunking off. I was sure all the old ladies hanging out in the front of the shop were memorising names and faces to gossip intensely about us next time they were ahead of one of our parents in a post office queue. Mrs Potts certainly looked up and gave us very dark looks when we came hurrying through the ringing door.

While I caught my breath and looked around the dusty brass and ceramic contents of the shelves, unable to stop myself checking out any new arrivals to the shop, Teb composed herself and approached the old lady behind the counter with all the fearlessness she'd developed of the elders of the town after realising that being the child of immigrants and brown-skinned would automatically cancel out any favour she might earn for being a model student and good citizen who sometimes picked up other people's litter in the streets unbidden. "Hello, we've misplaced one of our friends… You wouldn't happen to have seen Tanya here, would you? About this tall, blonde, spaced-out look?"

Mrs Potts made a grumbling sound to herself for a minute, then replied, "You lost her yesterday, didn't you?" She addressed the answer to me instead of Teb. She sounded pretty annoyed I couldn't keep better tabs on my friends if I had to ask again *already*.

"Yes, her," Teb said, betraying a little relief.

"She was trying to get in here yesterday at closing time, all dressed up like she was going to a party," Mrs Potts said. My heart filled with happiness—Tanya had come back here. I was *right*. How often did *that* happen? More importantly, I wasn't *crazy*! Thank you racist old lady for confirming it!

"I haven't seen her today, though," Mrs Potts added. "I've been here since opening."

I groaned.

"Thank you," Teb said, and caught my arm before I could pick up a battered giraffe toy that looked like it was stuffed with wood. "Let's go," she hissed.

"Wait, I wanna ask a couple more things," I said.

"Um, *what*? We're looking for our friend here…" She wasn't used to losing her leader status on a mission.

"Look, I don't know how well you believe me yet, or if you're just humouring me, but I was right about Tanya coming back here… Even if she didn't get in, there's *something* in here that was calling to her, and we need to find what it was…"

For a moment she looked blankly at me, but then I thought she might be recalculating in her head, like a GPS when you take a sudden turning onto the scenic route, because she didn't pooh-pooh my ideas at once. "So we can use it as bait?" Teb suggested, and I sagged with relief that she had her expression normally brought on by Tanya showing up with a pirate map and three shovels.

"Maybe not that literally," I said. "But… we have to know what's going on in the first place to understand where Tanya is and how to find her… I'm not sure about Alana's explanation of fairies but something weird is happening…"

"Well I definitely don't believe all this fairies rubbish if you don't," Teb said at once, determined not to let me think she was yielding an inch on that point. "But whatever is happening…" she sighed. "I guess I'll have to go along with this."

I grinned, knowing just how much Teb had to put aside her personal beliefs to admit that things might not have rational explanations. Even I normally felt that way, however suggestible I might be on a day-to-day basis. If you stopped me on the street with a clipboard and a free cookie for answering your questions on life, the universe and everything on a typical day, I was going to tick most of the boxes that say "It just happens. Science, maybe?"

"It's really not that bad to be crazy, you know?" I said, putting a reassuring hand on her shoulder.

"That's alright for you to say. That's all you've ever known."

"Anyway, it's not bait I'm thinking of so much as information to help us."

"Okay, so what are you going to do?" Teb asked. She had on her amused face again, one eyebrow slightly raised. This was just like when she was telling me about the dance at the fair. She thought that I was being *funny*.

I'd show her. Initiate detective mode! But don't tell Teb I said it like that…

I turned around to see Mrs Potts still watching us suspiciously, wondering why we might have had a hushed conversation a few feet withdrawn from the counter. I approached her again, clearing my throat in what I hoped was an intimidating manner, the way our deputy head teacher does: "Hrrm-hmm-hmm!"

She just looked concerned for my health.

"Do you want a cough lozenge, dear?"

I shook my head. "Um, no. So… Mrs Potts," I said, leaning on the counter. "Umm…" My mind, busy trying to think of catchphrases from cops on TV or witty things to say, went utterly blank. "That is to say… remember when I came in here yesterday? What I bought?"

"Some dolls, wasn't it? I thought to myself, girl her age, still buying dolls, but then with your mother…"

"Uh… It was an antique collectable figurine, but that doesn't matter," I interrupted before she could ramble on and make me hate her too much to finish this conversation properly. "There was a recorder as well…" I suddenly remembered that it was still in my bag, and swung my heavy backpack onto the cluttered counter; Mrs Potts scowled at the huge clatter as my bag clipped a collection jar. Seeing as she clearly didn't like us anyway, I started unzipping my bag without bothering to go through my usual round of apologies and attempts to tidy up a rather lost cause.

Teb helpfully dived to pick up a few spilled pennies as I rummaged with as much dignity as possible, disinterring many old pens I'd thought lost forever in the detritus at the bottom of my bag. The old woman's glare bored into the top of my head. I almost felt it growing hot under the pressure. "Aha!" I said, emerging from the bag and flourishing the instrument. It was unscathed, a testament to its magical powers, I supposed. I was assuming that it had them because for the last two days I'd been running around bumping my backpack into everything.

Mrs Potts seemed to think it looked a bit too perfect as well. With shaking hands she put her glasses to her nose and scrutinised the instrument. "Are you bringing this back for some reason?"

"No no no! I just wanted to ask about it!"

"I don't give music lessons!" she snapped.

While I was fighting the urge to cry, Teb stepped in. "What I think Ally wants to know is stuff like, where did this come from? How long have you had it?"

Mrs Potts had probably been deliberately torturing me: I was sure I saw a look of disappointment on her face before she picked up the recorder and examined the price sticker I'd left on it.

"Seems it has been around for a good few years. We stopped using the round-cornered stickers back in 1983," she posited. "I'll have a look see if there's something in the books about it. Can you read the little number on the sticker?"

"Seventy-five pence," I confidently told her.

"The one in grey at the top," she said, patience vanishing quickly. She kept giving Teb furtive glances as if worried she'd steal something. I'd already seen her dismay that it was Teb who had handled all the pennies that spilled from the collection jar, though she had been the one to set the box upright and drop the money back into it, coin by coin.

I hurriedly reeled off the number which was in pale, faded grey against a brown background and all on a surface less than the size of a postage stamp. Fortunately, however dorky I might be, I'd never needed glasses. Because if I ever got glasses a week later I would need a new pair that hadn't been trodden on, sat on and probably drowned too. Somehow.

Mrs Potts tottered off into the back without another word.

"Oh dear," Teb said.

"What?"

She shrugged. "Whatever is going to happen next? I'm out of my depth here."

I thought she might be winding me up, but I still clung to her arm from fear when I heard the shuffling of old lady slippers returning. Mrs Potts had an ancient ledger in her arms, the leather cover worn thin along the spine, the sticker on the front as brown as the price label and much more splattered. She gestured at me to move my backpack and I hastily dragged it out of the way, sighing as pens and folders slipped onto the floor as I had forgotten to zip it up. She heaved the book onto the table with a thump. It wasn't bigger than most photo albums, but the old lady had arms like sucked lollipop sticks, thin and white and wrinkled.

She opened the massive ledger, licked her finger and slowly rubbed it against her thumb before turning back a page. She ran her un-licked middle finger down a column and said, "Hrm."

"What is it?"

"There isn't an inventory number here."

"What does that mean?"

"Well, so we can give sales reports, we number all the different places we get our donations from. Church donations are one, school fête and town fair donations are two, private donations are three, stock from head office are four, bequests in wills are…"

I felt *myself* growing old as she explained it. "It should be in here," she finally said after listing the twelve or more places people donated from. She twiddled the book and pointed to the entry. On one side was: "Stuffed armchair, Bequest Victoria Jotter, delivered 18th March 1974" some details of the number, and when it was finally sold. On the other was: "Tea set and tray, floral, Donated Mavis Smith, collected 24th March 1974". Between those two: "Wooden recorder". And its number. A line of empty boxes followed it across the page until "20th March 1974".

While Mrs Potts self-consciously began filling in the details of the sale, I looked at Teb and attempted waggling my eyebrows at her to signify something important to her. "That was today a few dozen years ago!" I hissed.

"You don't really think that's an omen, do you?" Teb picked up the recorder and was likewise examining it. "I wonder what happens if you play it?"

"I only know *Lightly Row* and *Mary Had A Little Lamb*," I said. "So probably not much, even if it is magic."

I was beginning to think that unless Teb possessed some previously unheard of detective skills, finding out where it came from was going to offer us no help whatsoever anyway, because I had no idea how to make use of the information we'd uncovered aside from being vaguely unsettled. Even if there had been a name, did we go chasing up some address or person who was in all probability a hundred years old or dead by now? What did we even ask when we found them? If they were a wizard?

"Is there anything else you want?" Mrs Potts asked, closing the book when I was halfway through reading the second page (there had been a taxidermied monkey here at one point. I had *missed* out). The shopkeeper was clearly growing impatient, and probably a little embarrassed that she or one of her underlings had mislabelled something, and the one time it happened was the only time anyone ever chased up the provenance of an item. "Is there anything you're going to buy or is that it?"

I sighed. "I guess that's it…" I glanced around at Teb. "Unless you think we should have a look down where I found Tanya yesterday?" Maybe fairies didn't exist and we'd just find her curled up asleep under the table with all the porcelain figures on it, strange but normal, and the concern of a psychiatrist. Teb's way of thinking was very contagious, because it was *comforting*. It was how the world was supposed to run.

"Okay, fine," Teb said, hopefully as unsettled by the date on the recorder as I was. "We'll keep on going with weirdness. But I'm warning you that as soon as some sort of logic comes along, me and common sense are jumping ship from your crazy boat."

I grinned, a momentary victory riding over the unease that had had me gnawing at my lip as Mrs Potts talked. Tanya had found a recorder—a *pipe*—that just happened to be in the basement, and it seemed like no one had put it there. Why had she given it to *me*? That was what unsettled me. She hadn't kept it for herself, but decided it was my destiny to own it. I never knew what Tanya was thinking, and at this point I'd have traded my tea intake for a year to have a peek inside her head. If nothing else I could use the view from her eyes to find her.

Teb followed me without any further complaint down the stairs. I quickly found the room with all the clay figures in it. They hadn't changed, the dancers still prancing around behind the Piper. I noticed that behind them loomed a large doll of Queen Elizabeth I, glaring down at the dancers with extreme disapproval. I think she was a loo-roll holder, since her cloth skirt was hanging limp around her porcelain legs.

There was no Tanya.

"What are you looking for?" Teb asked impatiently, looking about with the scepticism she always had in a shop where you could buy an enormous gilt-framed mirror for forty pence.

"Tanya was messing with these when I found her," I said, "I'm not sure what they mean though. There is a Pied Piper statue, obviously. I know who he is, and there are dancers—the first in the line was wearing white, so that means she was the one he disappeared…" I picked up the little model of the Piper and looked at it. It didn't resemble the man I'd seen at all, being all cutesy with red painted dots on its cheeks, sky blue eyes… It was dressed like a jester, not a grunger. But it was symbolic, nonetheless. And fifty pence. I resolved to buy it, just in case.

"And this is their pretty castle?" Teb said, examining the tableau behind her. She swung open the front of a big pink doll's house in the shape of something very turret-y and fairytale. Inside was a headless doll twenty times too large to play in that castle, pushing the rest of the tiny dolls into one room, and a teddy bear in a French military outfit sitting in the bathroom with a scowl on his face.

"That doesn't really look very symbolic of anything," I said, throwing a wild guess out there.

Teb leaned over and considered the scene for a bit. "Okay, so if Tanya's the headless doll, we can assume she's been kidnapped by The Sims, who are all French, which we all know she failed to learn in style. I suggest phoning the army at this point and they can extract her."

I poked her out the way and closed the castle doors. My eyes were drawn to one of the turrets, where on a little princess balcony for your Rapunzel doll stood another clay dancer in yellow. As I reached out to pick her up the unmistakable sounds of the Piper's tin whistle came to my ears. I looked over at Teb quickly. "Can you hear that?"

"No?" She tipped her head. "Hear what?"

"Come on, let's go," I said. I grabbed the dancer and hurried back the way we'd come, backpack grazing shelves of china and glass. I hesitated, glancing down at the sticker on the side of the dancer—"Can I borrow a few pennies?"

Pipered Off

The outside hit us cold and breezy after the stuffy, dead air in the junk shop. Coughing out the dust we'd picked up, I listened more intently to the Piper's music, and found that the sound was layered: I was hearing it through the ornament, and more clearly, though faintly, a carrying echo of the notes, coming from somewhere in town.

"I can hear it now," Teb said, ears perking up, "It's coming from down there, I think…" she pointed away down the high street, in the direction the skater kids had taken. "So what's the idea? Do you think this Piper will know where Tanya is?"

I shrugged, "It's by the by if he does for now… He apparently won't talk to me until tomorrow."

"Let me try, then," Teb said.

I stared at her, in awe of her brilliance. All this time being told he wouldn't talk to me, it hadn't occurred to me who else in the world might talk to him *for* me. I was calling Teb as my lawyer next time I was in need. She changed her aspirational over-achieving career once a week anyway: she'd been reading up on Law more than once in the past year. I had a pretty decent chance of that coming true.

Once we'd cleared Charity Row there were only a couple more shops before we were hurrying along beside the field where they were setting up for the fair tomorrow—tents slowly raising with shouts as they wobbled and collapsed, fences that were rolls of bright orange tape without stakes to run between yet, people testing speakers with feedback-filled coughing. Along a stage a woman in a cardigan was hanging dozens of paper plate decorations made by the primary school: I'd done the same when I was in baby school. Each one had a hundred paper oak leaves glued around the plate, framing a selection of leering or deformed faces as drawn by children who still thought noses were an L shape. Like Santa Claus, I was fairly sure the children believed in the Green Man wholeheartedly, and it would take some undoing to make them realise this was not a celebration level to Christmas in popularity out of a ten mile radius from this green. Our fairs every spring (equinox *and* May Day), summer, and autumn were the pride of the town, and about the only thing we ever did where people from the outside world came to visit. The summer one was where they pulled all the stops—usually because a fair in March was liable to rain out, and the Halloween/bonfire night celebrations were run by a different group, involving less participation in the form of shops and dancing, and rather more fire and explosions. I liked the spring ones best, though—they had a lot more fake mysticism to them, so Mum really enjoyed them, or enjoyed criticising them in any case. She made a point of doing arts and crafts instead of getting involved in all the fake-pagan mumbo jumbo like everyone expected her to, hence the living room currently full of wicker turtles. I didn't think her own personal mumbo jumbo was any more informed than theirs, but still.

Past the noise of the setting up there were new noises under the sound of the Piper's shrill whistle—the distant rumble of the motorway and the more jumbled noises of the skate park: clattering and yelling. The town council had given in and built one when the kids had started using the space around the war memorial as their playground. At first the council had tried to convince Bilsworth to fund one in their town to get the kids out of Troutespond entirely, but the larger town had steadfastly refused and then someone had ramped off a bench and knocked themselves out on the statue and that was that: the youth group that had been lobbying for it started building the park, stuck outside of the town borders where no one but kids had to look at it. The finished off-road from the motorway loomed over it, the bridge's ugly fat pillars sunk into the ground, a wide strip of bare earth beneath in an otherwise lush meadow. The small river that crossed the town ran between the back of the park and the motorway.

With the large amount of concrete and tarmac thrown around out here the whole thing was more industrial-looking than anywhere else in the town, a blight on the rural aesthetic (a comment I had heard grumbled in a town meeting). The pale concrete and dust from construction work were slowly creeping their way up the road towards the town. The motorway hid everything past it, standing in the way of the horizon. It was raised up on a tall embankment of newly-planted trees, the kind of forced green between neat lines of pale concrete that I associated with the end of times. Even the river stopped running a wild, unchecked course at this point, trapped in a narrow channel. Wild flowers did their best in the spaces of green, but there just wasn't room for them.

The river took a sudden turning under the embankment, vanishing into a dark tunnel with a loose grille over it. Every single person under twenty in the town had a different horrific story of what lurked under it, or how much skin they'd taken off a leg trying to get in or out (down to the bone while fleeing a fictional vampire road worker who never left when the motorway construction moved on was a favourite tale to spin on a dark night—it hadn't quite got refined to the sort of thing you'd find in books about local legends but give it another twenty years). I personally had stayed home when Teb dared Tanya and me to go in the tunnel at night. I regretted nothing, and Tanya had had the least interesting night of her entire life there, not even seeing a rat.

At that moment there were six skateboarders in the area, though only two were mindlessly rolling up and down the half-pipes—the other four, the smallest, brattiest, ugliest ones, were riding in wide circles in the middle of the abandoned-off-road that ended in the skate park. It was something to do with planning permission that had left this attempt at the road unfinished—there was a fat, but utterly disused, quarter-mile of tarmac that ended abruptly before a copse of trees, some way away from the river. The rest of the route to the motorway was a wasteland of old construction equipment, like barriers and traffic cones still lying around, and vast mountains of disturbed earth, some of which now had half-pipes up their sides.

Walking right down the middle of the empty road towards the skaters was the Piper. He was playing his whistle, dreadlocks swaying in the wind. Behind him danced a girl in yellow, a slender teen in a swishy swooshy gown, long black hair fluttering over her shoulders. The living image of the porcelain model that I had just bought. She was barefoot, but as she skipped and swirled I could see the soles of her feet were perfectly clean despite apparently walking at least halfway from town on a muddy road still damp in places from the rain last night.

The skateboarders were jeering, swearing, whistling and clearly intent on harassing the young girl, ignoring the Piper—giving him a very wide berth— but riding as close by the girl as they could without hitting her, trying to scare her. She seemed utterly oblivious. If she had looked at all scared I wouldn't have waited around to see what happened next, but charged right down there to help her. Possibly. The Piper did kind of frighten me, not to mention the bratty skateboarders.

"Oh God," Teb said. "Is he really the Pied Piper? The one from the stupid story with all the rats? He doesn't look like him, but…"

"I think he is," I said. I knew he was. This was long past it being an elaborate hoax or odd performance art. I was witnessing *magic*. I was tempted to take my phone out and take a photo, but I somehow just couldn't break my concentration on the scene for long enough to reach into my pocket and grab my phone.

Teb had more important things on her mind: "He's walking her down to the river. He's going to drown her, like the rats…" she moaned.

"Hopefully he'll take the skate-brats with her," I said with feeling.

"This isn't right. We have to stop it," she said. "She's just a kid. She has to be younger than us. Look at her!"

"We don't know *anything*," I said. "All I've heard so far makes him sound like… He has a purpose and he does it… I think if we interfere he won't hesitate to add us to that purpose… But I think whatever he's doing now… He has to do it. I think he already accidentally banished Tanya once… He brought her back, obviously, but what would he do if we *deliberately* got in his way?"

We watched their slow progress down the non-road. It was an utter wasteland, and a *very* good site for potential murders and disappearances.

Teb sighed, "Okay, let's keep back." She was biting her lip, terribly conflicted, but at the same time her self-preservation instinct seemed to have finally listened to the message that the scene we were witnessing was broadcasting loud and clear to me: *Stay away*.

The Piper took a sudden turn, over the verge and onto the land of the skate park itself. The two skaters who had stayed behind both reached the top of their half-pipes and stopped short, holding their skateboards and watching him from under their hoods. The Piper reached the middle of the biggest half-pipe and stopped. The two bigger skaters both stomped on their boards at the same time and rattled down to meet him. He lowered his whistle and the girl in yellow slumped, still standing frozen, like the music ending had cut her strings. We were too far to see her face. The other four skaters all whooshed into formation around her, stopping in a tight circle. One of them laughed, the only sound strong enough to carry on the wind aside from the music. It didn't sound half as nice.

One of the bigger skateboarders questioned the Piper. He smiled and raised the tin whistle. That smile was not friendly: the actions together were a clear threat. The second biggest skater looked over his shoulder at the shaking girl. The Piper stepped back and started playing again—a similar tune to the one he'd played yesterday in the town centre. The two big skaters (although I was beginning to think there might be more to them than barely-teenaged boys with wheeled planks of wood) stepped forward, took her by the shoulders and pulled her towards them.

They climbed the steps at the back of the big half-pipe, boards under the arms that weren't holding the dancing girl at the elbows. When they were at the top, the music reached its bright climax and they vanished.

I'd been looking for it—it didn't hit me half as hard as it had done before, but Teb went right into the "Urgh!" kind of vacant flinch while her brain reprocessed what it had just seen a few times. I was already watching the scene again as she furiously scrubbed her face with her palms.

"Was that… What was that?" she demanded.

"The same thing that happened to the dancing girl yesterday. Do you remember?"

"*No.*"

The Piper was coming back our way, while the four remaining skaters went back to innocent skater boy things like doing ollies and gobbing at (but never hitting) the river. So the brats had been in on this the whole time? Maybe they weren't even meant to be in school right now… Maybe they were…

"Teb, Teb, he's coming back!" I hissed, shaking her. She looked around, then her eyes fixed on the Piper.

"Please, go see if he'll talk to you—ask him where Tanya is." I pushed her forwards.

She rubbed her head tentatively, but Teb was Teb and so she didn't dither or look scared. Still, something in the shaking of her legs as she approached the Piper told me that she had all the confidence of a zebra who'd been told to go invite the lion to her birthday party.

A few dozen steps down the road, she stopped. He stopped too, and a weird, wonky smile appeared on his long face as they held their dramatic stand-off. He raised a hand in greeting. "Well met." He didn't even look at me. Right, because he wasn't talking to me yet. I sat down on the damp grass of the verge and pretended to be admiring the fluffy white clouds drifting by overhead. Nope, I wasn't involved in this conversation at all and you could never say I was. If I could whistle, I'd have done so. The world could be spared my hissing, spluttering attempts though.

"Uh, Mr Piper?" Teb said in a tiny shaky voice unlike anything I'd ever heard from her before. Who'd have thought such a sensible girl would have a fear of the supernatural? I would have happily marched up to him and demanded answers if I hadn't been advised to wait. "Do you know where our friend Tanya is?"

He tipped his head as he slid his whistle into one of the deep pockets in his faded grey jeans. I glanced away again as he looked back up. He'd disarmed himself, for what good it did Teb's nerves.

"She is well looked after," he said in a clear voice. He was probably speaking louder so I would hear as well. "You should keep out of this, Teb. It does not have to be your story."

And then he vanished, without any attempt to be polite about sneaking out of sight as he'd done to me the times I'd seen him. Teb froze for a whole minute from the point-blank range oddness, then bent over and threw up. I hurried down the road to her.

"Are you okay?" I asked nervously, putting a hand on her back, rubbing it gently as she got over the shakes.

"Urgh, I don't know… It must have been something I ate."

"What about the Piper?"

"The what now?"

"The guy… with the dreadlocks? That you just talked to?"

"Oh, God, I hope he didn't see. It's a good thing I managed to hold on until he left…" She looked around, couldn't see him anywhere and shrugged. "I feel better now anyway."

He had to be reprogramming her head. I couldn't understand her reaction otherwise. "What about Tanya?"

"Maybe I'm just stressed out from running around after her all the time. Come on, let's get back to town. She's not here, and I think we're meeting her Dad in a bit anyway. Maybe I should go home to wait by the phone and hope the police find Tanya before she wanders too far."

On the other hand, this was Teb. Perhaps she had decided magic wasn't real so intensely she'd gone into self-inflicted denial shock or something. She was the one with the interest in psychology; I wasn't equipped to explain it. Somehow, though, I didn't doubt she was strong enough of mind to convince herself what she said was true.

"Going back to relying on the police isn't going to make them magically be the ones to find her," I told her, taking her arm and leading her up the road.

"Don't care," she said shakily.

I thought about it. We were pretty far from a kettle, so tea was out. "Can I buy you an ice cream?"

Ritual Homework

As we headed back up to the centre of the town, Teb, recovered by then from sheer willpower and also probably the fact that she wasn't really sick, phoned Tanya's dad and asked if he'd like to join us in looking for his wayward daughter. He willingly agreed.

While she chatted with him, I wondered why the Piper had been so happy to make Teb forget him, but not turned that power on me. Maybe he only liked picking on one person at a time. Maybe Teb just wasn't cool enough to start getting cryptic messages about when he would talk to her all day long. And I was. That made less sense than anything else that had happened lately. Maybe it was just that she really didn't care a jot for finding out about him, and I'd been so curious as to come out and see him in the wee freezing hours of the night that he was slyly letting me in on the secret while showing me what happened to everyone else he happened to bump into, explaining why no one else seemed to really know about him.

By the time we'd walked back to the centre of town, Tanya's Dad was standing around at the war memorial waiting for us. Teb took charge again at once and told him her revised plan for finding Tanya, before I'd run off with the whole 'follow the Piper' idea. (Hadn't Alana said something about not doing that, come to think of it?)

Mr Pomphrey looked dismal despite Teb's assertiveness and absolute conviction that Tanya was just sitting under a hedgerow somewhere, humming to herself. I kind of wished she'd been left with some sense of the supernatural: it was cold and if Tanya had been Pipered off as we'd seen happen to two separate dancing girls, it was extremely unlikely a long walk in the countryside would show any trace of her. Maybe Tanya's Dad, being somewhat familiar with her ways, quietly suspected something more along the lines of the truth, though he was never openly admitted into Tanya's games. Mr Pomphrey worked half as an accountant, half as whatever other random helpful legal services one could charge people for—he had lots of qualifications and a degree in Sociology. Half the week he spent at dull offices in Bilsworth, the other half he spent working at home, and keeping as close an eye as he could on his daughter.

Like Tanya, he was small and a little weird-looking—a short man, balding behind a close-cropped hairstyle—and pixie-like in appearance with a pointy face he tried to disguise with a large moustache and little delicate hands he was always carefully moving around. He was a fairly normal guy when it came down to it, but my first impression had blossomed anyway, just from wild speculations about what pixie fun and games he and Tanya got up to on the weekends instead of the reported Monopoly marathons. I'd first visited her house within a week of knowing her, but that didn't stop me from imagining to this day them living together in a giant white-spotted mushroom.

"How are you doing, Mr Pomphrey?" I asked politely.

"Well enough," he sighed, British politeness stopping him declaring whatever depths of utter despair he had lately dived into. "It's still a shock every time…"

We nodded and "Mmm"'d in agreement.

A shout distracted me from the pleasantries: "Ally!"

Alana was hurrying down the road from the direction of school, not to very much surprise from me, though Teb had a rigid grimace on her face; Alana was officially not happening as far as Teb was concerned. I'd been wondering when Alana would join us. She hadn't taken Teb's "stay in college" message graciously. I glanced at my watch. It was barely half ten.

"Finally gave the teachers the slip?" I asked.

"Hey Teb, Mr… Tanya?"

Her dad nodded, bemused. "You can call me Paul, if you like."

"This is Alana, a new addition," I explained. Teb scowled. I could only imagine how Alana seemed to her if Teb couldn't be persuaded to see what I was seeing.

"Can I borrow Ally?" Alana asked, coming to a stop at our side, doubling over and puffing.

"We're here to look for Tanya," Teb snapped. "Go back to college. Or home, I don't care."

"So?" Alana said, "I'm taking Ally Tanya-hunting. We're just going a different way to you guys. Good luck!" Her hand clamped in an iron grip around my arm, and she started dragging me away.

"What the hell are you doing?!" I demanded, even as I waved resignedly to the others, accepting that there was no *real* arguing.

"Teb has no idea what she's doing…"

"And the Piper doesn't want me looking for Tanya," I said. "Are you just here to mislead me?"

She looked at me with some sort of new respect, or perhaps just annoyance I'd figured it out. "You really are learning fast," she said, "Yeah, you have this annoying habit of stumbling on things. Teb would have no chance of finding Tanya with 'normal' methods by herself, but with you there the scales might tip, so I'm taking you off somewhere you're not going to fall head first into the fairy world or get possessed by demons, or anger witches, or anything else."

"Was Mr Brooke actually possessed by demons?" It was a roundabout way of asking, "Can that seriously happen to me?" Again with the utter, terrifying certainty of the way Alana talked: I seemed to have drawn my lot to be on her side, but there was no way you'd get me to casually suggest the fairy world was as nearby and accessible as the local shop. I had always figured the reality we lived in sort of depended on it not being so: if it was, we would hear about it far more often. And as freaked out as I was by Mr Brooke's meltdown, as much as we'd joked about demons… It made me queasy to think that it *actually* happened that way, that I had stood inches from him and looked into his eyes and seen some sort of monster looking back at me.

Alana shrugged. "It happens. Not as much as it used to, but it does. I took the poor dear vicar up to visit him and got him all exorcised and back on his feet… The Piper sneaked the priest into the hospital in Bilsworth last night, and Mr Brooke's fine now, if with restored faith…"

"You say that like it's a bad thing." I didn't really care either way, raised agnostic/pagan depending which parent had control of bedtime stories, and with plenty of inadvertent Christian bias in the stories we learned in our apparently secular school… Maybe I'd just never been given the chance to get a good solid faith of my own, but it didn't seem such a bad thing for someone to have.

"Try going to a Catholic school," she sighed, "I wanted to punch a nun by the end of any given school day."

"But you think that demons exist…"

"And that doesn't mean God does," she snapped. Ah, she was a little touchy on that subject.

I shrugged. Didn't know, didn't care, and it had never bothered me. I mostly got annoyed by people who had strong opinions one way or another. They tended to want me to agree with them.

I tried changing the subject a little. "How about paganism?"

"Not too impressed by that either, from what I've seen. Just because you can sit down and have tea with the gods doesn't make them any better," she said with a shrug. "I just wanna be left alone by it all."

"Fair enough," I agreed, and we walked along in silence. Because continuing that conversation meant trying to come to terms with her suggestion that she had sat down and had tea with a pagan god at some point.

We passed St Fish's school, which Alana hissed at and hurried me past like she couldn't bear to be in its presence for any length of time. Groups of students in maroon blazers stood around in a small playground, looking bored. None of them glanced out of the gates at us as we passed, though I wouldn't have minded someone hailing Alana and confirming that she had some history there and hadn't just sprung up into my life from nowhere. It seemed half-likely the way things were going.

We were heading up towards the north edge of the town, towards the train tracks and the abandoned station, though there was also the turning to Tanya's road coming up. I wondered if Alana was going to do any detective work and needed me around to help her break into Tanya's house while her Dad was out, but when she turned off from the main road it was not down to Tanya's street. We carried on between identical little detached and semi-detached houses, missing Teb's turning by a single road, until we hit fields again. Alana nodded towards a stile and I climbed over it, jumping down into the meadow on the other side. It was a bit wilder than the field I'd sat in this morning but that just gave me *more* creeps, thinking if there were any more floaties in it, they'd be wilder in turn. Alana pulled me along towards the woods, however, and didn't stop to let me shiver.

"What *was* it that I saw this morning?" I asked. "Little glowy light thingies in the air… They came out about the time the sun rose."

"Fairies," she said shortly, focussing on picking her way along the path. I knew these woods as well as someone could without having a dog to walk, and we were circling around slowly, heading to the same fields at the back of my house, distanced by half a mile of woods. From there the trees carried onwards up into the bigger, wilder hills where we'd be less likely to stumble across fields and isolated little farms.

"Fairies," I repeated, just to be sure we both had the same understanding and I wasn't going to be really embarrassed when we encountered them again and I had the totally wrong idea after imagining Tinkerbell when Alana was thinking of, like… Some weather phenomenon or something. I don't know.

"Yes. Your basic pointless little woodland spirits looking for some attention. They probably like you because you've got magic smeared all over you like honey, thanks to the amount of times you've bumped into the Piper and listened to him play lately. They also like literal honey, if you're interested in catching some."

"Is going into the woods a good idea when I'm currently cursed?" I asked as we broke the tree-line for one last field.

"Probably. Nothing wants to attack you. They're all just curious. You're an interesting person. It's other people who are making all the complications right now. Namely Tanya."

"Does that mean you know where she is?"

Alana kept her mouth sealed in a firm line.

"What about Teb?"

"What about her?"

"Well… She's… difficult."

"I'm keeping her away from you as much as I'm keeping you away from her. Without your magnetic attraction to weirdness, she'll be fine," Alana said disparagingly.

"Why don't you like her?"

"Ally, I know you've been friends with her for about a hundred years, but there's something you should know about Teb if you were to meet her for the first time today. She's kind of a bitch."

"She's not!" I cried, and even as that was still echoing in the hills around us felt the need to add, "Much."

Alana shrugged and concentrated on picking around some rabbit holes before she spoke, having gathered her words carefully. "I am pretty sure she's lovely to you and Tanya in her own prickly way, but honestly, after one day of knowing you and Tanya I can see you're gagging for new friends. You're outgoing, friendly types. Teb clearly interviewed me, found me lacking, and is trying to eject me from the group. You wonder why you've only got two friends? I don't think there's anything actually wrong with you and Tanya certainly isn't lacking in friendliness. For all I know she acts out like this because Teb tries to keep such a tight lid on her."

We made it to the tree line and their roof of leaves closed over us, thankfully blanketing the shrillness of my voice, making this conversation feel more private and not like we were sharing it with every hill for miles. "That's not… Well, maybe she doesn't like sitting with other people, but she has others she gets along with. We can have other friends!" I complained, trying not to betray Teb while inadvertently remembering any number of people who had been turned away, even actively avoided, on Teb's orders. Tanya had a sort of stray puppy of the week for a while, particularly sensitive boys who knew computer coding, but any attempt to have them sit with us at lunch or take them with us on an excursion went over very badly.

"I'm sorry," Alana mumbled, clearly alarmed at how whiny I was getting. "Just… I like you guys. Even Teb! In a way. I mean, I can see what you've got as friends and I can see why you like her… I'm vulnerable here: I'm the new girl. I would like to be your friend. I'd even like to be Teb's friend. Don't you know how to stop her driving people away?"

I shook my head. "Maybe talking about fairies and demons in front of her is a very good way *not* to get invited back, though."

We tramped on in silence for a bit, into the shady green world of the woods, all twisty, muddy paths that sloped gradually uphill; I think I'd accidentally shut Alana up. She certainly didn't seem willing to keep poking at my safe little knot of friends. I wished I hadn't brought Teb up at all. I knew she was difficult, I knew Alana and her had got off on the right foot but then immediately found themselves on the wrong one anyway, but I'd never taken the time to analyse

Teb doing this to everyone we knew. For all Alana knew, this was the first time it had happened. Except she had been certain this was regular behaviour for Teb, and now I could see her reaching around me and Tanya, pulling us together and shielding us from the outside world. Protective mother bear, I thought. And we were her cubs. There was nothing wrong in that.

Except I did kind of like Alana, for all her terrifying, incomprehensible ways. Maybe it was my lack of experience in making new friends; she was so wild and different from what I knew, and it seemed so fascinating. I knew Tanya had loved her in about one second flat. And she wanted to be friends with us. Yet Teb's presence felt less like an unconvinced friend who needed to be bought muffins before she warmed up to Alana and more like as unsurmountable as the woodland terrain off the paths.

As we walked we had entered what was the real wilderness, known only to the bravest explorers from the town. Ivy crawled over anything that would stay still and brambles grew in thick clumps around ancient, bulging roots. Broken boughs from storm-damaged trees hung over the path, or lounged like fallen dragons in the thick undergrowth, cloaked in nettles and holly. None of the volunteers from the Council ever made it this far in their drives to tidy up the woods and make them walker friendly. There were no more steps on the paths, which had become in places more like the paths rabbits took, with the undergrowth, primarily nettles, pressing in close. Trees with fat branches leaned over the gullies, ready for generations of dangerous rope and tyre swings. If you hadn't broken your arm in these woods at some point as a kid you didn't belong here in the town. With the exception of Tanya, who'd fallen all the way down the hill when a frayed rope snapped under her weight but come out with only a few scratches and some serious nettle prickles.

There was a little standing litter around the more well-trodden corners, near the best swing spots and drains, but the bulk of the woods were untouched except by the most experienced dog-walkers and explorers and made for a much more tranquil, lost-from-civilisation walk. The only sound of life came from rustling in the undergrowth, crashing noises as squirrels darted from tree to tree, and a background track of birdsong. We'd played here almost constantly as kids, deliberately getting ourselves as lost as we could so we could be explorers in the Amazonian rainforest, or played games with the wood elves we imagined were there and looked like characters from that ancient old-school *Dungeons and Dragons* handbook Tanya had found in the junk shop and absorbed like she was a sponge for nerdy facts. Now the thought gave me much more intense shivers. Tanya *must* have thought of this place. If the junk shop hadn't helped her get into the fairy world, this was exactly the sort of place she'd wander off to.

I hadn't talked for a while, panting as we walked, wanting to focus on putting one foot somewhere in the vicinity of in front of the next. But we slowed as we got near the top of the hill. Alana didn't have Duracell batteries in that day either. The Catholic school might have had mandatory games and PE knickers that made us comprehensive students wheeze with laughter when we saw them, but maybe Alana had slacked as much as I did. She didn't seem the lacrosse type.

"Five minutes?" I panted, spotting a fallen log. I staggered over to it and sat, and Alana didn't argue, plonking herself right down next to me.

"So," I said, mopping my hair (frizzy again) out of my eyes. "For the sake of argument, fairies really exist then? And they're just little sparkly bits in the air? It's kind of disappointing. Not the six foot tall elven rangers Tanya painted them to be." I still had Tanya's games on my mind.

Alana shrugged. "No, what you saw are just the impressions of fairies over our side. They're a lot bigger and meaner in their own world. But each one is tied to something in this world, and sometimes they meet up and drift and dance out in this one. It must be pretty boring to be stuck in a tree all day."

"Right… Are those dancing girls fairies?"

"Pixies of some sort, I think." Of course they were. Silly Ally, not knowing what a pixie was!

I gave her my best serious look. "They're not little floaty things." I was tempted to burst out laughing, but Alana looked so deadly serious I couldn't get something to spark. With Tanya she'd be biting her own lip, chortling by the end of the sentence… Maybe it was the ultimate bluff: she was laughing because we didn't know it was real, and while she laughed she convinced us further that it wasn't.

Alana was having none of it: she continued like she was reciting the Wikipedia page. "No, that's the actual pixie, here in our world in the flesh. There are plenty of doorways for them to cross over through. The fairies love to find an excuse to come into this world. We can't just fall through the same doorways into the other world normally, though. They're very well-defended and the Piper will catch a lot of people and send them home long before they see too much. Like, there's a door here but nothing usually ever gets through it… If Tanya came here, she'd have just run around the woods until she gave up. She probably went through a much newer, weaker portal down at the other end of the town."

I hadn't guessed, but it was always nice to have some more unsettling information. "So why are we up here?"

"Well, it's about as far from the pond as we could possibly be. I've seen how out of shape you are—I'm guessing you can't run all the way back down there."

"If she jumped in the pond, wouldn't the Piper have followed her?" I asked, thinking of St Troute's reported heroics. Not that I had much evidence other than Alana's hint that *someone* liked the statue and was still making magic recorders. And the fact that St Troute's symbol was a whistle at all. If he and the Piper were one and the same…

"About the time we lost Tanya he was leading you on a wild-goose chase around the town," she reminded me, heaving herself back to her feet. She offered me a hand, and I let her haul me up as well. We carried on along the close-cut and less-trodden path. "He had no time for rushing off to save girls.

And anyway, he was tied to Troutespond for seventy-seven years last time he climbed into that pond—he's gotta be a lot more careful these days. And Tanya knows that myth, so she wouldn't have jumped in the pond."

"So that's his story?" It was fairly disappointing. I already knew enough about St Troute that it felt too obvious once Alana had casually linked them. It lacked mystery when we were taught the story in school from a young age.

"He'll tell you himself," she said. "How impatient *are* you? The fair starts at ten am tomorrow, and you will probably sleep in that long…"

"It's not even eleven now. If you won't tell me what happened to him, then tell me what happened to you? Something did: you can't have just been reading about witches and suddenly had the Piper on your doorstep, or Tanya would have been Pipered away long ago."

"I'm not special. He just specialises in second chances, and telling me to help you is my chance."

"Is that why you're stalking me then?"

She didn't say anything in response, and I let it drop so I could catch my breath a bit. I was getting rather nervous to ask just what it was that Alana had done. Regular misbehaviour tended to get only regular second chances.

We carried on walking, while I looked out intently for Tanya despite Alana's scepticism. The police might soon be stomping through these woods if they took Teb seriously (who didn't?), and the untouched feeling might not last. Nor the chance of Tanya staying long if she heard them coming.

The paths led uphill, tiringly so. "Do we *have* to go up this path if you're only trying to lead me away from civilisation?" I gasped as it turned to rough steps cut into the path and shored up with logs. "I'm sure there are flatter routes to get equally lost on."

"Don't recognise where we're going yet?" she asked smugly.

"No!" I panted, right as the familiarity kicked in. We were approaching it from another, far more difficult angle, but… We passed a long, fallen, mossy stone, taller than I was, mostly buried in the hillside, a tree's roots crawling all over it. A once standing stone that had rolled a short way down the hill from its friends.

"What's the story here, then?" I asked hopefully. Alana may be pretending to not tell me anything, but I felt like I was grilling her with all my skill as an interrogator. Um. Maybe I should have been a bit more wary of what she was telling me and wondering what she wasn't saying.

"It's just your basic ritual spot to the gods of the sun and moon, and a good calendar before all these trees moved in and blocked off the view of the valley. Maybe the fairies use it to get between the worlds but, like I said, we can't." Alana gave the nearest stone a friendly slap. I flinched like I had in the church when we'd been loitering near St Troute's final resting place. Nothing happened.

I huffed in response and decided to leave talking until I had my breath back, looking about and re-evaluating a landmark I had known a great deal of my life with fresh eyes. It was a mostly-collapsed stone circle of dubiously Neolithic origins, and not very impressive or important as stone circles went. Even the Druidic population of Britain paid it little heed. It was only preserved because the forest itself was of special scientific interest due to some rare birds. That much I knew from Mum and Tanya. We picnicked up here sometimes in the summer. It was a tranquil spot where the forest seemed hushed and the cares of the world slipped away. All that remained of the circle as it had been in the past were the big table stone in the middle, a big fat, square thing, and a couple of the tall standing stones on one side. The rest had been knocked down the hill, fallen over on the spot or vanished years ago.

The very top of the hill was a little dryer than the rest of the ground, but there was still nowhere good to sit except on the table stone itself. Alana pulled herself up onto it at once, but I was rather more wary, and lent against it as reverently as I could.

"Who are these gods, then?" I asked, looking around, almost expecting mad cultists to come out from behind the stones to start chanting. Or sacrificing us.

"The Green Man and the Lady of Winter."

"Oh, but… But people dance to them. That's what they celebrate tomorrow. We have those big floats that go down the street with them on. The paper plates!"

Alana slapped herself on the forehead. "Well, *duh*. It's nothing so mysterious and secretive you need to be inducted into a secret club before you learn the first thing about it. People wouldn't waste time worshipping gods who weren't there… Or maybe it's that the gods themselves wouldn't come here if they weren't going to be worshipped."

I pulled a face to show I'd understood none of that.

"Well, anyways, they're the old pagan gods from around here. All the barrows down in the valley were for their worshippers, you know, like the one the church is on top of. Everyone in the whole valley used to worship them, but only Troutespond was secluded and strange enough to keep the faith through the centuries, even just as folkloric traditions, as they faded out everywhere but here…"

"Maybe St Troute protected them?" I asked, not sure how the Piper operated. He didn't sound like a particularly Christian sort of person, whatever his links to the little church that Alana had implied. Or, you know, the name he apparently used.

"Maybe he did," Alana nodded. "His protection on the town is strong enough that it probably extends into the fairy world. Maybe he only did it accidentally, but this would be a good place for them to hide nonetheless. There's a protective bubble around the whole place."

I tried to look wise and understanding, but I'd heard a squirrel move in the trees and had been watching it for most of her explanation.

"So now what?" I asked, half hoping she'd say something oddball and crazy and fill my day with excitement. I mean, we were here now, weren't we?

"Well, there's some Literature homework you could help me with?" she suggested.

*

After over an hour of discussing magic and religion in *The Tempest* and scribbling notes I had to say it.

"Alana…" I ventured. Something in my worried tone made her realise I wasn't about to point out a useful line from the play for her to scribble down in the margin. "I really do not understand you. You know that? I mean even more than all the other things that I don't understand at this current moment, or even the rest of the time."

"What do you mean?"

I assumed she was asking about my first point, not for a translation of that ramble.

"I mean… What are you doing here? At my college, writing the same rubbish essays as us? I don't understand it on so many levels. You're smart—and despite never having even opened *The Tempest* and not going to the Globe with the college because you weren't there yet, you're still owning this essay. People like you don't get kicked out of a prestigious sixth form for something as trifling as trifling with trifles.

"And then there's the fact you want to do homework at all. You've shown up spouting stuff about fairies, and you actually seem to believe it right down to the core, and maybe it's true and all this stuff I've seen is real and you've known this for ages and you just *live with it*. I mean, it's real? We're actually going with the idea that Tanya has been kidnapped by fairies and for some mystical reasons no one can explain to me until tomorrow… we can't go and rescue her or whatever until then. How could you ever make yourself care about Shakespeare at a time like this? I love the man, but I'd skip an opportunity to go to the Globe to see Hamlet if I had to pick between it and saving my friends from fairies…"

Alana pulled a face. I was amazed she hadn't kept on taking notes while I talked because that was long-winded even for me, but *aargh*, occasionally I needed to vent everything on my mind.

She took a moment to reply (I felt a little guilty for not saving up some points and turning it into a more structured discussion). "Well… Like I said, it's good to unwind when you have nothing better to do with your time. The job I do for the Piper… Like I said, I got in trouble. I'm paying it back, but it's not all car chases and explosions. Sometimes it's just being in the right place at the right time. There is a lot of waiting about." She nodded, as if pleased with that answer. I felt it begged a great deal more questions: I had to accept that she believed she was in on this big secret, that she knew the Piper personally. That was easy, but she outright *worked* for him? It explained a lot about her, but if I hadn't been so desperate for her answer to the first round of questions I would have interrupted her then and there for more. I could see she was working up to the next thing she had to say, though.

"For another thing, I could do everything I do for him in another city, another country, really. Much as I love this town for its weird ways, I don't love my home."

I carried on not saying anything because I didn't want to ruin her opening up, so there was a lengthy pause there. When she realised I actually wasn't going to ask anything she carried on. "I can't wait to escape and go to university, that's all. It's been my goal to get out of here for a long time. And *nothing* is going to yank that out from under my feet. So right here and now I *care* about how an Elizabethan audience would have interpreted Caliban or whatever this essay is about."

"Er, not that."

Alana shrugged. "Close enough." She self-consciously shuffled the pages of notes she'd accumulated to show that she did have some redeeming academic qualities. It could have been the end of the discussion, and we could have gone back to pretending to be normal students who just happened to have a stone circle study group. But I couldn't stop myself from asking dumb questions all afternoon.

"You work for the Piper. How does that happen?"

"He tells me something that needs doing, and I go do it."

"No, I mean… You said you were in trouble."

"Drop it, Ally. I'm paying it back and helping you. What else do you *have* to know? I'm not a bad person."

"So you're only here—hanging out with me—because he told you to?" It seemed important to know if she really *wanted* to be here: not just doing the homework, but doing it with me. I couldn't help feeling we'd be very good friends if I wasn't worrying about everything else.

"If I was stalking you, well, you wouldn't know it. I do want to be here for myself as well as because he asked me to."

I was so flattered she would admit to *wanting* to be friends with me after the introduction we'd had that I pretty much let that all slide.

"So… am I ready for any straight answers about what's happened to Tanya yet?"

"Um. To be honest you probably are. But after all the suspense the Piper spun for you, it seems like a bit of a waste to just start explaining everything now."

"So you're not going to tell me anything because it will mess up his attempts to drive me crazy for the last day?"

"Well, that and if you have any follow-up questions I'd be completely unable to answer them. I'm not an expert."

"I thought you knew everything," I said with a disappointed pout.

Alana laughed at that one.

"I know selective details that allow me to do my job, which I am still very new at. To be honest, this is my first big assignment. In any case, he hasn't shared much with me: you've seen the way he works. I feel I almost could have ended up here without his intervention. After I got expelled it was blatantly clear that home-schooling wasn't going to work for me. In any case, I couldn't tell you exactly where Tanya is right now, nor who she was having a tea party with."

"But she's somewhere and having a tea party?" I demanded.

"Yee-ees. Maybe. Probably not an actual tea party. It's not Alice in Wonderland."

I groaned. "I was going to say you should talk to Teb. She was really shaken up when I tried to get her to talk to the Piper for me… But when you say stuff like that, maybe you'd only make things worse."

"Oh *Ally*." Alana smacked her forehead. "I let you out of my sight for half an hour… I'm *assuming* that was when you took her to talk to the Piper, because even you would have trouble fitting in any more stupid acts in the remaining time…"

"Heh."

"It's not something to be proud of! Freaking out Teb and getting chased by fairies are *incredibly mild* compared to what you might have caused when you wandered off. I thought you knew already that Teb was being kept out of it; you saw her after the dancing girl vanished. I can't believe you'd be so stubborn that you'd talk her back around *out* of that enchantment."

I endeavoured not to look embarrassed. Alana scowled, clearly thinking that I wasn't taking this seriously enough. I'd just wanted the validation earlier.

"Well anyway," she continued, still shaking her head, "that explains why Teb has gone off me *so* quickly. Her reaction to the paranormal will get more adverse each time she's exposed, because she isn't meant to see any of it."

"You know, she encouraged me and Tanya to be weird. Why is she so unsuited to finding out about this? When we went to the shop and then after the Piper she was really beginning to warm up to it all. Without the supernatural to blame, she'll be remembering all the times she pushed Tanya into harm's way for fun. She'll be blaming herself now. Isn't it kinder to tell her that forces beyond anyone's control are involved?"

"I don't think anyone can be blamed for Tanya."

"Oh… But when the Piper spoke to Teb he didn't say much but he said, 'this doesn't have to be your story' or something like that. Can you… interpret that? Is that why…?"

Alana grinned. "You ask him yourself tomorrow."

I groaned and slid from the huge rock to sit on the ground.

She wasn't going to get any more essay help from me.

None of This Explains the Turtles

I felt surprisingly relaxed by the time Alana let me go home, at a reasonable time of two-thirty. It was before college really ended but late enough that it didn't feel strange going home and taking advantage of my day off. Maybe it was just the places I'd hung out with her—my house and then that day in the woods—but for all the nonsense about fairies I was only just beginning to get a handle on, I felt more chilled out with her than I did with either of my friends. Teb made for mental sparring and Tanya was too busy being weird to let me relax around her. Alana, on the other hand, seemed to want to be as normal as normal could be when it was wrapped up in some deep mythological crap.

I had thought over a lot, as I sat and talked her through Shakespeare, and I'd decided that there was one missing piece in the puzzle that I *could* try and slot in before I got my promised talk with the Piper. There was someone who knew a lot more than I did, maybe even as much as Alana... There was the slim chance they might actually be as informed as Tanya was. Someone who'd been reading the books and joining the dots and *knew* what was going on. I would have my answers.

As soon as I got in I made a beeline for my mum's wicker nest of turtles, where her fingers were dancing to a Celtic punk band singing about cursed pirates. I hit the stereo's power button as I passed, and flopped next to her as she protested mildly.

"Look, you made me mess up the head! You know how hard that bit is."

"Sorry Mum, but..."

"Hey, you'll never guess what. When I went to the One Stop to get some more milk for my tea, the lady in the line in front of me went into some sort of fit," she said, "Knocked all the lottery tickets to the floor. Screaming about her demon lover and stuff…"

"Really?" I asked, alarmed. Yeah, I *still* hadn't taken the idea of demons that seriously until right now. Unlike fairytale people and creatures, the idea of something like *that* existing was going to take a bit of head-wrapping-around time. And I was going to start sleeping with the light on.

Mum nodded, "Mmhmm! She's only a year older than you… No fit age to be the teen mum of the Antichrist!" She was giggling as she said it, but the way Alana was always taking *my* sarcasm seriously had finally sunk in, and now I felt the roles had been reversed with my mum being a bit too flippant about it.

"Look, possession or not… I want to talk to you," I said seriously.

"You know, I'm always here for you to talk to… Is it about love?" she asked hopefully.

"No!" I protested, swallowing hard, and took the plunge—"It's… I want to know what happened to you… When you… At university. You ran away…"

I'd never asked her a thing about it, mostly because Dad had warned me so strongly against ever mentioning it. He seemed to have this idea that it would have her stripping off and dancing away over the countryside but, as flighty as she was, since she had summoned the Piper for me, I had begun to think Mum was made of stronger stuff and knew her own mind, maybe holding back from Dad how much she really knew, and I was willing to risk it. I was still terrified once the words were out—don't get me wrong, I'd spent my whole life fearing her mental state like nothing else, but it was now *important* that I knew, and I thought *I* could at last handle the truth as well. I had to know if she was really truly in on it.

She smiled at me. "I'll go put the kettle on for us." She stood up in a rustle of skirts and a waft of her spicy orange and lavender perfume, and she skipped into the kitchen. The kettle clicked. I fiddled with a turtle for a while as the crescendo of the kettle peaked and clicked off. Mum came back, handing me tea in my favourite big spotty mug. She set her own down on a coaster that she had crocheted herself, picked up a turtle and a pot of orange paint, and started filling in the shell.

I sat with my back straight, leaning forwards, cradling the tea close to me. Until she'd handed it to me I'd barely even noticed that my fingers were bright red, nearly frozen off during the day spent sitting outside in chilly air. There was a pause as Mum stirred her drink, fished the tea bag out and threw it in the fireplace, where it made several loud crackling noises. She sat back, her hands wrapped around the mug, and looked me steadily in the eye as she spoke.

"Well… You've got to remember I was young once, Ally. You know me. It's not like I had some hippie transformation at university. I'd always been a little wild, not like you. I was much more trouble for my parents. Don't get me wrong: I'm glad you're a good girl… But I was not really like you even when I was small. University was my big excuse to do everything rebellious I'd never have got away with under my parents' roof. I fell right in with the hippie scene at university, and I was in my element organising protests, going to music festivals and I admit that, as I wasn't at the same university as my poor square boyfriend, I wanted an excuse to be going to parties and drinking or smoking whatever was going around…"

"Mum!"

"It was the eighties, I blame it all on that."

"Pfft, you couldn't even manage the seventies?"

"I was a little girl then! Eighties or nothing, kiddo."

"You aren't a real hippie," I protested.

"Don't say that to my old university friends," she said warningly. "Want to hear this story or not?"

We grinned at each other.

"Well, carry on then," I sighed, pretending to be defeated. Like I'd *oppose* her telling this story.

"I survived first year with decent grades, considering the lifestyle, and for the summer I was due at a big music festival, open air, thousands of people, hit acts and many of the niche artists we listened to. I snuck away from under my poor normal boyfriend's nose, hopped on a bus, and met my friends who were all, 'Woo! Camping in the woods! Woo!' and we all smoked a few and went to find the music…"

"I can't believe you're saying it so casually," I said, product of years of anti-drug education in school.

"Don't worry, if you came out screwed up, it's not 'cause of anything I took when I was younger," Mum assured me.

Her suggestion I was screwed up anyway wasn't much of a comfort.

"So we followed the trails of people before we hit the fields where the stages and solid crowds of people were. There were these wide fields in the middle of the woods, huge stages set up, and what felt like a million people all crammed together. Actually maybe it was literally a million people… The portaloos certainly looked like it may be. Anyway, we made our way to a place where there was just enough space to spread out one of our blankets; we all sat down and started smoking again… And that was where I first saw the Piper."

I groaned.

"I don't know why you've taken so badly to him," Mum snapped, "He's some sort of super powerful agent of the higher powers of the universe, so you'd better respect him when you get to talk to him!"

"He's rude," I muttered.

"And so he should be in his line of work! Well, when I first saw him, he looked different to how he might to you—and even me now. He needs to be an outcast, wherever he is. So to us, in that particular location, he was even more of a square than my Danny is…" she giggled. Oh help me, my mum had a thing for businessmen. "Really ugly, he was. Really unwelcome as well. People were staying out of his way, even at a festival where there was hardly room to stand, like they were a bit scared of him. There was a big circle around him. I would have expected them to be jeering him or something for looking and standing like he did, but I think he looked more scary to those who would have taken harder against him…"

"He's not that ugly," I said, confused. And rather understating the case.

"Really? Face like a boot, to me. I went right up to him, though. I mean, there was space to dance around him, for one thing. But I also felt sort of bad for him, being all on his own and ugly and not fitting in like he was. So I gave him these flowers I'd picked as we walked to the festival, and he pulled a freakin' *clarinet* from his pocket," she coughed, perhaps avoiding making some sort of joke, and continued, "and he played a couple of notes on it. I thought he was mute, or something, and that was his way of saying 'thank you'. But now I know he was testing me. There were so many high people there, crazy dancing people in long, bright dresses… Giving away flowers and kisses like they were air."

"He thought you might be one of *them*?" I asked, having seen two strange dancing people in bright clothing now. I'd have been dumb not to make *some* links. Mum had never been as pretty as the fairies or whatever those dancing girls were (and I took after her in the long face and hooky nose department), but she certainly would have had the rest of the look down.

She nodded happily, "Uhuh! Greatest compliment I've ever received! And, I suppose, the worst, depending on your opinion."

"I don't see how this leads to you being declared unfit for work," I said. Lots of washed up hippies presumably had found nice normal lives to fit into after this scene was over and they needed to turn to dentistry to pay their bills.

"That's because I've hardly told you the story yet. Be patient," she tutted. "We enjoyed another day of the festival—saw the Piper around a bit, listened to loads of music to make hardened music fans jealous, and a load more stuff that I have no *idea* whether it applied to his line of work, or what we'd just taken, or both, but I was having a very surreal time. I had an incredibly long conversation with a chair at one point. He had some very neat ideas about Kant, but I thought he was a bit of a tosser. Maybe it was a person who just looked like a chair. Hm."

I sipped my tea to mask my discomfort: I was beginning to get very fearful of Dad coming home early. A single line of this conversation was clearly all that needed to be overheard before he knew exactly what Mum was telling me. I wondered how much of it she had even told him. Imagine my dad knowing about the Piper!

"But our second night camping in the woods we were all so happy and peaceful. Somehow the whole group made it back and we all sat around a camp fire that it had taken us over an hour to create and light… *And* we had matches. Not a proud moment for hippies… Although come to think of it, someone not far from us set fire to their own tent, so maybe we did quite well with just stopping to stare at the firewood, or being too entranced with the matches to actually light the thing…"

"I'm glad this story isn't about how you burned all your hippie friends to death in a fire."

"I haven't done telling it yet!"

"Oh God, *Mum!*"

"I'm *messing* with you. I never burned up anyone."

"I have no idea what to expect here… For all I know you did!"

She shook her head, waited for me to take another gulp of tea, and continued. "Once we had that going, we all took something that one of the guys had bought at the festival. Don't know what it was, but it *really* got to my head, more than anything else had, and I ended up having a really strong, scary trip. I went to all sorts of places in my head, but eventually I came down a bit to find myself still in our tent, and I could hear the Piper playing. I'd spent the last few hours thinking I was a pixie, so I guess what he was playing called me as well, because I couldn't stop myself from sneaking out of our camp and running off to find the source of the music without a second thought. I was still high, but I remember all this perfectly. Maybe I *was* sober again. It's hard to tell when strange things like that are happening."

"Tell me about it… I thought you'd put LSD in my orange juice yesterday morning."

She smiled. "I wasn't sure this had even happened to *me* until I came across hundreds of references to very similar stories… The trouble is the Piper changes faces so much there aren't many things that these conspiracies agree on, including how the Piper looks, but they can agree he is there. It takes dozens of stories to work out the pattern if you're starting from scratch."

"So getting drunk or high is a good way to bump into him? Are you sure you didn't do something to my food?"

She just laughed. "He does seem to spend a lot of time sort of… yelling at drunk people to get off his lawn, if you get me. Anyway, my story?"

"Yeah, carry on." I was hooked.

"There was an old stone circle in the woods, not far from our camp. Pretty much like the one here, but bigger and in much better condition. A lot more well-known, which was probably why the festival people had wanted to be near it. And also why the people who owned the land had put huge barriers around it, like that would stop it from getting vandalised. People had been breaking into it for three days by then, so the fence was broken, and there were blankets and litter all over the ground. There was a clearing around the stones so they were in a meadow, except there was a big old tree bang in the middle of it. The Piper was sitting at the foot of the tree, playing, and all the weird dancing girls we'd been bumping into all day were there—there must have been fifty of them—weaving a big loop all around the stones, like the dance you'll do at the fair."

"I am *not* dancing at the fair," I groaned.

She gave me a firm but smiling look. "Yes you will."

I shook my head. "So the Piper was there? Did he see you?"

"Not right away. I really wanted to go out and join them, but I was so scared——I knew somehow that I wasn't meant to be there—wasn't one of them, no matter how clear it was in my head that I was a fairy at the time. So I stayed back, clinging to one of the stones, hiding behind it and stopping myself from running out and joining them. And then his song ended."

She took a deep breath, with a hint of a shudder to it, and downed the rest of her tea. She did her compulsive check of the dregs, but didn't see anything interesting because she had used a teabag. I realised I still had a mostly full mug of tea and took a sip before it could go completely cold. My hands were shaking as I raised the mug: this was what had happened to Tanya. I was sure of it.

Mum continued, a faraway look on her face, staring up at the ceiling light in its homemade patchwork shade. "That song he played was one calling the dancing girls back—back to where they belonged. And whatever I was supposed to be, my mind was convinced it belonged in a pixie. I had hit a similar note to them in his song. I saw them disappear... And I went with them.

"I didn't know how the wood was supposed to look at that point—I'd seen it in so many different guises that day. But now it was very, very different and clearly wrong... I can't describe how strange it was—it started even with light itself, before you could even see how the rest of the world had changed. The colours were so intensely beautiful, and if the Piper's playing had been a siren call before, it was nothing to the singing that filled the air now. There were fairies all around me, calling me, begging me to come play with them. I was going to go, even though I had never been so scared in my life. And then I saw the Piper—the *real* Piper, how he looks under all the glamour..."

"What's that like?" I squawked before I could stop myself from interrupting.

Mum shook her head impatiently. "I can't describe him, though I think you can see it in him better already than I ever could before I saw him then, in this... fairy world. He was more beautiful than all the colours in the woods even though he was all in black and white. And he took my hands, and said, 'You should not be here,' and the woods went back to normal. But I wasn't—I'm still not. I can see the magic that hangs in the air—I can read auras, and sense ghosts, and follow ley lines and find meaning in the shape of the stars. Being able to actually *see* it all faded fast, but I can still feel it everywhere, waiting to be read."

"So that's how you always know..." I waved my hand vaguely. "Everything?"

"Ha ha, sweetie, that's being a mum. Being able to feel the pressure points from the Other Worlds is pretty useless for parenting."

"I remember less of the months that followed my trip to the fairy world than I do of that one brief moment itself—most of what I know that I did I was told about later, and the rest is like it hasn't happened; there's just a gap in my memory for the whole time, and I see it in third person when someone tells me that I was seen by a farmer here, chased by the police there... I led them on quite the wild-goose chase before they finally pinned me down!" she giggled. "Then they had me sectioned because I was still a little hysterical."

"Ah, this is about where Dad's telling of the story started off." It never had made much sense: I had assumed a nervous breakdown, and the arts-and-witchcrafts stuff had come when Mum had been trying to entertain herself on the road to recovery. I wasn't sure this explained everything, but it filled in a lot of obvious gaps.

Mum laughed. "Maybe that's because I wouldn't tell the rest. I got very possessive over this story! It was my little secret for years. I told it to my therapist and she told me that's what I *thought* happened, but..." She shrugged. "Some things you know were real. Until we got an internet connection I never really shared it with anyone. You can find forums for anything really if you look hard enough, so I've got some support since then from a few rare people who might have seen real things like I did."

I didn't need to hear about the conspiracy theory websites we sometimes found her browsing. The parental lock was probably for her as much as me. Anyway, I didn't care about these other peoples' stories. "So were you... ill... for long?"

"I'm not completely sure how long I was *out* for. The first real memories I have afterwards are unintelligible blurs of wandering around the nut house they put me in. Well, it was a modern private clinic, not very spooky from the outside. It was the worst place to put someone who had just had my awakening though. I was distressed because of all the negative energy there, and all the ghosts who lived in the walls. I finally realised that the only way to get away from all the bad feeling there was to pull myself together and act normal. I managed to convince them after Danny came to visit me. Your father is such a normal, boring man, bless him. A real anchor..." She got a faraway look in her eyes, and I had to clear my throat to get her to continue.

"So they let you go?"

"It didn't take long for the doctors to see that he made me more normal, calmed me down. They decided that I should be allowed to go home with him. I mean, we grew up next door to each other, and he was still studying in the same town, so it wasn't like we would be apart again. I've never *wanted* to get away from him since then. He finished his business degree, we got married, and that's officially the last of it."

"But you made us move here," I said. "Troutespond is so weird. Didn't you think, if you were trying to be normal...?"

She nodded, her mysterious smile creeping back; "Your father let me choose any town near where his company had an office... We both liked the look of Waitingshire; it's quaint and we're on the same side of London as our families, and then our town was up to me. He didn't want me to be bored or unhappy. I couldn't resist picking a place where I had a high chance of meeting the Piper again... Somewhere really weird, where the normal rules don't apply, and mythology is everywhere. I had already looked up all the big festivals, all the ghost stories and conspiracies and so on, trying to find the strangest place in the country and Troutespond seemed the nicest place to go that fit both our criteria. I guess I wanted to thank the Piper if I ever got another chance to see him… But I think he knows already."

"*Thank him?*" Everyone thinking that you had suffered a mental breakdown hardly seemed like something to be grateful for.

"For all the trouble he's given me, I wouldn't give up the few minutes of what I saw for all the normality in the world. It made me who I am, and I love that person."

We were silent for a few minutes, and then I said, "Tanya was taken to the fairy world by the Piper yesterday… I think exactly the same thing happened to her."

"She's always been otherworldly. You know, mind often away with the fairies… Maybe for real. Hearing the Piper's call awoke her spiritual side harder than any sitting around with my incense and cards has ever done, and she responded too strongly to it."

"So what if what happens to you happens to——?"

Mum shook her head, "No, she seemed normal enough on the phone last night. She just needed a more dramatic awakening than most people. You know Tanya—she can't do things by halves. And she found her way back again, you say?"

"*Mum.* You are not going back into the elfin realm."

She shook her head, "No, I think that would really break my mind. I think that if I hadn't been as high as I was then, I'd had done even more damage to myself."

"I can see why the Piper's been warning me not to follow Tanya," I sighed. I felt helpless suddenly. I'd spent the afternoon in a blissful state of mind because I had finally realised that I was not going mad. If Alana said fairies existed then they existed, and it was the most wonderfully freeing feeling. I could see all this weird stuff but pat myself on the back and say, "It's nothing personal, Ally. Anyone else in the same situation would be seeing this too."

And now I was hearing the more I looked at it, the closer I was walking to having a breakdown anyway. A *real* one, not all my ridiculous teenage hysterics. Mental ruin waited for me if I was to make a move, but all I wanted was to look after my friend.

Mum scooted along the sofa, and gave me a hug.

"Don't look so depressed, poor Ally… I think it's wonderful that you're finding out *everything* the world has to offer… So many people walk through all this with their eyes downturned, and never see it for themselves, no matter how it might dance in front of them… Maybe you just caught it from me—it was a few more years until you were born, but I think it was still something you could catch from me—and you're more receptive to this sort of thing, or maybe it's just because of your inquisitive nature, and this town's reputation for unending weirdness, but… I'm *happy* you're going through this."

"It's scary," I said pathetically, "My friend's been kidnapped, people are going into demonic fits, and I've got someone sent to *protect* me by a force so powerful I could never have imagined it existing… This doesn't feel like an ideal life."

"But you're still excited, aren't you?" she said softly, "You're looking forward to the fair tomorrow like you've never done before."

I couldn't really lie to her—and now I knew she could read me like a big-print pop-up book.

"I want to find out why the Piper's singled me out," I said. "I want to be involved in this, even if it does scare me… I'm not made for the dull life as Dad's daughter. I'm very much… Mini-Mum."

She looked at me with this big wobbly smile, tears appearing in her eyes, and then she gave me such a tight hug I almost spilt lukewarm tea all over the sofa and her stack of newly-painted wicker turtles.

"Ack, okay," I said, squirming free.

"Let's paint these turtles," she said with a clogged up throat, "I still have hundreds to do, and the fair's getting awfully close."

Zombie Nightlights, Anyone?

With towering stacks of finished turtles lying around us, I went to bed early like it was Christmas Eve, in the hope of making tomorrow come sooner so I could meet the Piper and *fix* this issue once and for all.

But instead I lay awake. It wasn't even dumb 'going to stay awake all night because that's how I roll, baby' like usual, when I found myself still with eyes glued open at three in the morning. It was stuff that would have kept anyone awake. Well, you know, anyone whose best friend had been kidnapped by fairies and had been told by their mother about the time that *she* had been abducted by fairies, leading to a total and utter mental collapse, like this was somehow meant to be a reassuring conclusion to the story instead of "hey look, now we can all get fixated on making straw turtles together!"

I didn't *want* to end up crazy like Mum... The more I thought about it, the less she had actually reassured me. She would like it if I could stay home forever and be her best friend, never head off to university and leave this strange little world we lived in behind... Making turtles with her was great part-time but I had my own life too.

Also, Jimmy-Three-Paws was rattling away in his hamster wheel, which, come to think of it, may actually have been a much greater cause of my insomnia in general than I'd ever really noticed before. There is probably a reason that most people don't keep a hyperactive nocturnal pet with a squeaky wheel in the same room that they try to sleep.

I fought with my blankets until they let me sit up (I'd been tossing and turning for a while and had managed to knot them around my arms in an unbelievably complicated way). I looked out of the window. It was still just a view of the usual white streetlights and stuff. The lack of any sign of the Piper put me off right away. Something told me that he was not going to be there tonight. Why would he even come when everyone had been making such a big deal about how I would talk to him tomorrow?

If I hadn't gone completely bonkers by then.

How did I know that the way this had sprung up so suddenly in the last couple of days wasn't just me *already* being bonkers? Maybe Alana was just an imaginary friend? Of *course* Teb would be completely sceptical and ignore her and leave her out of her plans, my twisted imagination filling in the times they had interacted. Tanya, being the sort of person that she is, would merrily encourage me by talking to Alana and humouring me. Part of me couldn't even tell if she was always having a massive joke at our expense somehow on a normal day-to-day basis anyway.

Oh God, had I killed Tanya? Crept out in the night and murdered her, and then Alana had chatted to me all night and given me a head full of false memories so I could tell myself, "You're not crazy! You didn't kill your best friend!"

"Oh Jimmy, what am I going to do?" I groaned, getting up and leaning on my dresser to look into his cage.

He broke off from his scrabbling and scurried up to the edge of the cage. He wuffled his nose at me as if to say either, "You're not a mass murderer, Ally!" or possibly "I ate all the big crunchy ones and now it's just the flat muesli bits! Refill pleeease!"

"No," I said. "Eat it. It's good for you."

He wiggled his nose at me one more time. "Fine. Be like that." And he scampered back to his wheel to pound it even faster, like a teenager throwing a strop and slamming doors.

"Idiot hamster," I said, to make myself feel better about being bullied out of my own bedroom and to pretend it was my own idea. "I have to get out of here."

Yes, I was going on another midnight jaunt. If the Piper wouldn't come to me, I would force his hand. No, I really hadn't learnt anything.

*

I tried to be a bit more prepared by wearing a coat and real shoes. I got outside and realised that, yes, I had forgotten to take my keys with me. It was always one of the three.

"Brilliant," I sighed. I ought to tattoo the list on my arm. Except then in the summer I might keep compulsively putting a coat on and then pass out from heat exhaustion. Being nervous reduces my IQ a considerable amount.

Oh well, I hadn't left the house to mope on the doorstep about locking myself out. I was escaping from being stuck in my room, a state with a bedroom of that size equivalent to being locked in one's own head. None of this would happen if I was just allowed an internet connection after midnight.

One thing about Troutespond after dark: it was without fail completely dead. It wasn't just my own street that looked one slowly shuffling corpse away from a horror movie. Even tomorrow, once the fair was over, all the visitors would be out of here as soon as possible, if only to get as far as Bilsworth where all the hotels were since our two B&Bs would be full. The pub closed by nine or ten because the dear old couple who owned it wanted to go to bed, and that, really, was your choice of nightlife here.

I wandered slowly down the street, breathing in chilly one a.m. air and puffing out steam in exchange. The sky was clear, which didn't help the temperature very much, but at least meant that I wasn't going to get rained on while I was briefly homeless.

The most annoying part was that if Tanya hadn't been murdered or kidnapped by fairies or whatever had happened to her this time then she would still have been awake, or at least have woken up and let me into her house with good grace and probably a mug of cocoa with extra marshmallows. Teb was a good girl who went to bed at a responsible time and then became an extremely grumpy person if disturbed. She would probably tell me to go away (but with not such nice words), no matter how dire the situation. And I had no idea where Alana lived, and was creeped out by her more than enough to not really want to look either. I wouldn't have been surprised if she'd been sitting on the wall outside my house to make sure I didn't get any more ideas about nighttime wandering into my head, but perhaps she had underestimated me.

So. I'd been told that the Piper would eat me if I summoned him (or something like that), which would ruin all the nice build-up we'd had going about when he was supposed to talk to me tomorrow. I couldn't even call him up for a chat or something. Even if I promised not to ask about Tanya? I looked hopefully about, but he didn't appear. And with that I had exhausted my list of good ideas for instantly finding the Piper.

I resolved to do a little more investigating. I knew that a couple of nights ago Tanya had been wandering around the town looking for fairies, and if I was awesome at anything that week it was finding fairies. Maybe they only came out in the witching hour? It was worth a try to have another go at retracing Tanya's steps in the proper time.

My mum's story of the Piper sitting at the stone circle playing with all the dancing girls around him kept floating into my mind. I wondered if the same may end up happening here. I had made it down to centre of the town by the time I had worked this out, so I really couldn't be bothered to backtrack and walk all the way up the hill in the dark to see if the stone circle really was a doorway between worlds. And anyway, there was an eerie glowing light that was coming from behind the church, giving it a strange, slightly green backlight. That *totally* had to be worth checking out.

Unless zombies glowed in the dark. Did zombies glow in the dark? I had already walked up to the fence around the graveyard, so I guess I was just going to have to find out the hard way.

I mean, you'd think you'd have heard about it if softly green-glowing zombies wandered mindlessly around the graveyard at night here, but then this place was (quite possibly literally) dead after midnight, so who would have been around to see it and tell the story?

As I climbed the fence I tried to remember if there had been anything in the local news bulletins about upstanding members of the community being found in the street with half of their head gnawed off and big bite marks on their brain.

I was almost disappointed when I found the graveyard completely zombie-free.

However, the pond was glowing, a blobby sort of green shape at the bottom of the little hill the church was on. Tall grasses made a spiky black silhouette around the side closest to me, while on the far side the water lapped over a large stone at the water's edge, leaving a faint tide line of phosphorescence when the water drew back. The surface of it was attracting dozens of the little glowing blobs like the ones I'd seen up on the hill this morning.

"Maybe they're just, like, fireflies?" I said out loud for the comfort of a human voice saying sensible things, since Teb was unavailable. The floaties didn't do the polite thing and answer. I mean, I had this idea of fireflies swarming around the lantern set on the porch of a home in Louisiana, looking out over a swamp as a grizzled man sits in a rocking chair, corncob pipe clenched between his teeth. Maybe I was just being horrifically stereotypical about the existence of fireflies, but I don't think I'd seen so much as a glimmer of a glowworm outside of the TV screen.

The ground squelched a little under my feet as I got to the bottom of the slope and crept towards the pond. "Er, so… floaty… things?"

They carried on gently swooshing about over the water, ignoring my attempts to make first contact.

"Have you seen my friend Tanya anywhere?"

If the floaties had a way or the intellect to respond they didn't use it. At least this time they didn't try attacking me.

I knelt to get a closer look at them, taking advantage of how they seemed utterly uninterested in me. I was guessing that they weren't fireflies, whether those were native to this country or not. Even as I leaned closer to the floaties I still couldn't see a thing about them except for the glowiness: not a single leg or feeler or whatever other body parts a firefly had.

"Well that's pretty interesting." Sitting at the side of the pond, just watching them, made me feel a lot more comfortable about these fairies or whatever they were existing. They were cute little glowy blobs. How could I possibly have been scared of them before?

It was kind of odd though, how the water also had that luminescent feel to it as if there were more lights moving beneath the surface… Were there floaties down there too? I leaned over further to look. No, I felt *drawn* to look. I bent more and leaned right over the water, clutching the long grasses either side, ignoring the floaties completely. My mind was set on getting to the bottom of the mystery of how a pond could look so pretty when in the day it was a grey murk with a garish yellow prawn cocktail crisp packet floating in it like an extremely bad attempt at an origami duck.

In fact these waters felt really quite different from anything I'd ever felt before now. It was like being around the floaties but a million times stronger. Like that horrible sinking in my stomach in the moment when Mr Brooke and I locked eyes before he began screaming. It was listening to the Piper's music. It was magic.

And, I realised, it was sucking me face-first into the pond.

"No, no no!" I said, and pulled myself away from the surface of the water, which had ended up worryingly close to my nose somehow. I fell back onto my bum… but, as muddy as I now was, at least I hadn't been sucked through into the land of the fairies. I even thought that I could hear disappointed gurgling mumbles coming from under the surface of the water.

I picked myself up and carried on backing away with a bit more style, going through a routine of brushing myself down, pretending that this had never happened, whistling nonchalantly and other things that people did in cartoons.

As I passed the church doors, animated things on the brain, I remembered something that I had learnt from Disney's Hunchback of Notre Dame as a kid, which is that you could go into a church and if you asked nicely then they couldn't make you leave again and you'd be safe from anything that wanted to hurt you. More out of curiosity than anything I went up to the doors of St Troute's and gave them a push.

To my amazement one of the doors creaked open. Clearly the mild people who lived in Troutespond were so non-threatening that the dear old priest never worried that they would sneak in late at night and graffiti on their favourite pews.

Or, as with many things in my life, some mysterious creature had come by and unlocked it for me because they wanted me to go in there, probably just to further my descent into madness.

As I slipped in through the door I remembered another fact that I probably should have recalled before this point. Empty churches at night were really creepy.

The room, with that unfamiliar dull streetlight not so much pouring as trickling in, was lit exactly the same blue shadow-intense way as a fake night in a film set when they are pretending it's pitch-dark. The pointed windows made long pale arches across the ground and pews, pale red flecks in them from the stained glass. Deep shadows striped the floor between them, heightened by the shadows already cast by the ancient pews.

I remembered vividly a lecture that I had heard at an archaeology summer school that Teb had dragged me on, all about where you could find dead bodies in churches… There were far more around me than I could probably count.

If everything went suddenly zombies then I was going to be seriously outnumbered.

But then, hadn't Alana said all sorts of odd things about St Troute? He certainly didn't seem bad, though I wasn't sure about the rules for skeletons raised by necromancy when the bones were 100% proof relic. Perhaps voodoo magic didn't work on saints?

By that logic I decided that I would probably be safest if I went over and sat next to St Troute's tomb. Maybe there was a zombie-proof radius around it?

So I plonked myself down on the cold stone floor next to the bench-like tomb and idly patted it. "Good zombie saint. Stay!" I told the stone, but would most likely have got *roll over* from that command if anything. The echoes in the room sent my voice back to me, revealing how nervous and high it had become.

Absolutely nothing happened, which I had to take was a very good sign.

The March weather was not the sort of horrible coldness that gets everywhere like right in the dead of winter. Once I had got between four walls in the surprisingly un-drafty building I didn't feel the need to shiver quite so constantly as long as I kept my hands tucked inside my sleeves. Perhaps I had just hardened up from leaving the house so badly dressed so many times. In any case, it suddenly felt viable to stay here until the sun was up and I could justify knocking madly on my own door until I was let in.

It was funny, as I sat there I could hear the Piper playing again. Not loudly and not in any way that made me think he was close by. It was more like a distant impression of his music, like when you put a shell to your ear; you know that it isn't really the sea but it is something that sounds an awful lot like it… So I put my ear against his tomb because I was working on the logic that it was like a sea shell, and it did seem like however bad that logic may have been, the faint pipe music did get louder.

And then… well, I don't think it was anything too disturbing, but I began nodding off. I know, I know, I should have been all, "OMG! He's putting me under a spell!" like you probably are now, but actually what happened is that it seemed all distant and vague, like this magic was only an echo of him… A memory of some music that I'd never heard before. And then I fell asleep.

*

I woke up at a time much closer to the one I'd bookmarked as "time to return to civilisation", but not so late in the morning the elderly priest would stumble over me on his way to morning prayers and wake half the town up with his girlish screams (don't ask how we know what they sounded like; just blame Tanya and move on). As if the Piper had known just how horrified I'd be when it finally sunk in where I'd spent the night, and why he'd kindly given me half an hour extra just for freaking out.

First I pried my face off the cold stone of the tomb, my first conscious thought being a pang of guilt about drooling all over a saint. Then that thought avalanched into "Crap! He put a spell on me last night!" and I hopped about checking that I still had the same number of limbs that I'd had when I fell asleep the night before. I did, but it was initially hard to tell because they'd all gone completely numb from being lain on in awkward ways in a chilly room. My nose felt thick and my arms and legs heavy even after I'd jumped some life back into them. As I sneaked out of the church I could tell that I wasn't going to be feeling awesome later in the day… My fingers were actually sort of blue. Another thing to add to the list of stuff that I'd thought only happened in cartoons.

A swift walk home warmed me up a bit more, and I was just feeling a bit stupid and very tired when I rang my own doorbell a few times. I hopped from foot to foot in the dawn light. A lamp came on in the bedroom upstairs, then the hall, and finally my dad opened the door and looked blearily at me. It turned into a stern look when he realised who was there.

"Ally?" he asked blankly. "Aren't you in bed?"

I guess I got my utter thickness when tired from somewhere. I got the insomnia from Mum, but she could stay up three nights in a row and not even be yawning. I was permanently a dullard because of the bad hours of sleep thanks to Dad not handling it well.

"Maybe I was sleepwalking?" I suggested, taking advantage of his less than coherent state.

"Hmm, yes… Yes. Well, come on in and warm up." He shuffled back to let me through: I slid past him at once and put my hands to the radiator. It was off, much to my disappointment, so I started up the stairs.

"Just remember your key next time you sleepwalk," Dad mumbled as he followed me.

"Uhuh," I replied, and though I woke up in my own bed wearing pyjamas once it was a proper attempt at morning, I don't really remember anything else past that point.

Ally G—Town Fool

It is always worth getting a ringtone that you don't mind using as your alarm clock when you are friends with Teb. Much later in the morning, with the sun shining down through the crack in the curtain, the merry strains of the Banana Phone song began blasting out of the tiny speaker. I sat up with a "Wah!" of horror and began hurriedly searching my bed for the offending item. I found it shoved into the pouch of my teddy bear hot water bottle cover and just as it was trilling, "Ring ring ring!" again I answered my phone.

"Huuuh?"

"Morning Ally! Looking forward to the fair?" Teb. Of course.

"Muuuh."

"Get down here and learn how to talk… There's a news van here to cover the fair, so we're going to go make an appeal for Tanya."

"Oh god… Why?"

"'Cause she might have wandered further than Troutespond! We need more people looking for her." I'd forgotten Teb had this weird idea that nothing strange was going on and things could be resolved by mundane means. It made things very awkward considering I had now fully climbed on board the weirdness train. I wished the Piper had thought about that. I was barely competent at social situations as it was.

"Guh. Kay." A master of conflict resolution when I was half-asleep, I hung up on her, slid out of bed, and stood in my square inch of floor looking for clothes. I'd show up and smile for the cameras if it kept Teb happy. I just had to show up not looking like a scarecrow. New jeans, three-quarter-length—the old ones must have been put in the wash by my mum when she realised how much mud I'd trailed in the door that morning—and a... jumper! Aha! It was shop bought as well, not like the lumpy concoctions my mum produced. That automatically put me on the more snazzily-dressed side of the scale. I tucked it under one arm and trailed downstairs, in my flip-flops as a ward against the freezing kitchen floor, to find the living room empty of turtles and of my mum. There were layers of TV guides, paint splattered and glued to the coffee table, that dated back to Christmas. I stuck them in the recycling as I flip-flopped to the kitchen to down a glass of orange juice.

My phone rang again as I was contemplating toast versus cereal, scaring the life out of me.

"Come on, Ally! We're already down here!" Teb's voice echoed from my phone into the kitchen. Then in a hiss she added, *"Don't leave me here alone with Alana."*

She made me so panicked I grabbed my school backpack from where I had left it on the sofa and I was halfway down the road, blinking in the morning sunlight, before I realised I was in my pyjama top and flip-flops, my jeans kidding me into believing that I was dressed. And I had no reason to take my backpack since it only had folders and notebooks in it. I dragged the jumper over my head and groaned: my house keys were in my coat pocket, safely in the hall. It was fine: I'd spend the day out until Mum was ready to go home. But I wished I had the coat for reasons other than the keys in the pocket.

"Oh, screw it," I muttered, and carried on down the road. Not worth breaking into my own house for some decent shoes and a warm jacket. I'd managed not to be trapped outside wearing my bright yellow pantaloons: this was the important thing. I reflected on how it was so often my fault that I ended up in such impractical clothes. But Teb's this time. Definitely Teb's fault.

I spotted the news van on the side of the road as I approached the centre of the town, parked next to the ice cream van and causing a considerable overlap of curious onlookers and ice cream clientèle. Teb and Alana were standing around in this crowd looking impeccable, if glaring at each other. I realised I hadn't brushed my hair, and spent the rest of my walk running my fingers through it, peeking into the windows of parked cars to use as impromptu mirrors. A few drivers still sitting in their cars glared back at me.

"Ah, just in time, they're going to film our bit soon," Teb said, skipping up to me, hairbrush in hand. She attacked my head with vigour, producing hair bullied into submission almost as effectively as when Alana had charmed it. "They said they love a good missing girl story... Well, I mean, obviously they don't love missing girls, but..."

I looked over to where the small news team were loitering: two blokes beside the van, one with a camera and a cagoule, the other with a cheap suit and galoshes. Did we come with a severe weather warning, or was this just standard practice when city-folk were sent deep into the provinces to report on the bizarre local behaviour? The way the men were looking at us I felt we'd be lucky to escape without our faces being beamed onto the local lunchtime news with "Village Idiot" beneath them… I could only be thankful that Mum was distracted with her stall today, although there was always iPlayer. And she would *know*.

Teb dragged me back to where Alana was standing and we exchanged awkward greetings. I didn't want to get too into a conversation in case I blurted something about my nighttime wanderings, and she seemed pretty distracted giving the news team back the mistrustful looks they were pointing our way.

Finally the man in the long waterproof came over, hefting his microphone like it was his sceptre of office. Alana ducked out of the way. "Can I have your names for the interviews, kids?" He gave me a glance.

"I said she was coming," Teb said, linking arms with me. "Ally's a star."

He obviously decided it would be easier to humour her and not use any footage with me in for the sake of getting the story.

"Name?"

"Teb…" Teb trailed off, without trying even for the fourth syllable, let alone the seventh, "It's spelt 'Teb'. Tee. Ee. Bee."

"Surname?"

"Magee," I said helpfully. "Tebster Magee." She glared at me. It totally wasn't, but we'd been using it as an in joke so long I figured it was about time the rest of the world knew. I grinned at her.

They filmed her looking worried and saying how she missed her friend. They cut filming less than halfway through her little speech, which was about five minutes long and sounded like she had prepared flashcards the night before. As she carried on asking an imaginary audience to keep an eye out for Tanya, the reporter dude looked at me, "Name?"

"Ally G," Teb cut in, switching gears from tearful to malicious so fast I was almost knocked over. I hadn't realised she'd even noticed the camera's red light turn off.

"Really?" the reporter said flatly.

"No," I scowled.

"Oh, what do I care?" he said, "Write that down." The cameraman, his trusty servant, did so. I groaned. Teb looked smugly at me, as I hastily corrected it to at least "Ally" spelt right.

I found the camera staring at me alarmingly close up, my reflection in the slick lens looking like I'd slept in a pigsty. I swallowed nervously as the light flicked on.

"Reaction on hearing your buddy had vanished?" the reporter drawled.

"I, uh, wasn't too surprised," I mumbled, "I mean, uh, she always was a bit weird…"

"You think she might have run away then?"

"Well, I think she can look after herself pretty well. She's not the sort to get herself kidnapped," I replied, irritable now that I'd accidentally badmouthed my friend, possibly to the nation, and given them a sound bite which made me sound like one of those callous onlookers who was ten degrees separated yet suddenly claimed to be their best friend, yet had nothing nice to say.

He went through a couple more stock questions in a lacklustre way, then I thankfully found myself released from the pinning eye of the camera.

"Thank *you*," he said, flicking the camera off, before I could babble on and try justifying myself. That was a statement of "I think *someone's* going to look like the attention seeking acquaintance on the lunchtime news" if I'd ever heard one.

"But she's been my best friend all my life!" I protested, to no one in particular since he was looking around for Alana.

"Where was the other girl who was here?" he asked.

Teb and I glanced around too. There was no sign of Alana: the space she'd been loitering was conspicuously empty. Teb seemed happy enough that Alana didn't want to butt in on our fifteen minutes of fame, and shrugged. "Guess she was worried she'd look ugly on the news. She must have gone into the fair."

"We should head that way too," I said hopefully. I didn't like the TV people, suspecting that they had been mocking being sent to cover local trivialities and we were only confirming their suspicions about small town people.

"I guess. I gave them Mr Pomphrey's number and there's not much else we can do. He's a lot better at organising Missing Tanya campaigns that we are, after all."

I felt a pang of sympathy for Tanya's dad: if she really had been taken by fairies then there was nothing he could do; Teb really shouldn't be encouraging him when for once perhaps he could just put his feet up and let someone else worry about her. Tanya had put her poor father through enough.

Anyway, now it was time to leave these newsreader men to it; I wanted to find Alana and ask her why she'd sloped off (probably some sort of mysterious business was afoot), and there was another very big reason I wanted to get into the fair. I started tugging at Teb's sleeve while she stood fretting in sight of the newspeople.

Time for face painting, expensive handmade cakes, and a meeting with a powerful mythological force.

As we walked through the gates in the temporary barriers ringing the field, I looked up and saw the ribbon-bedecked stage bang in the middle of the field, the band setting up, the local troupe of Morris Dancers limbering up in front of it.

"Oh no," I said. At some point we were also going to have to dance a little dance.

Invite Only

The rest of the town green had become a sea of tents, with stalls laid out in every free space in between, and was soon to be populated with herds of people moving through it all. The booze, authentic-ish medieval ales and meads from a brewery somewhere up the road, had yet to start flowing however, so only several dozen people were in sight at any given angle. It was busy for Troutespond, but nowhere near as mad as it would get when the tourists would finally find the turning on the motorway and start pouring in—I still vaguely recognised most people around at that moment. Many of them waved at us, and several asked if we'd had any luck finding Tanya yet. Teb shook her head and looked miserable. I realised that I'd forgotten to be worried about Tanya—the fact she had set Teb and I up to dance and then disappeared off to do her own thing was rather more on my mind.

"It's not until twelve, so we have some time to look around," Teb said, stopping by a chalkboard with a schedule for the day written up. Her eyes lit up. "Hey, they have owls here!" She grabbed my arm and hauled me off to stare for a disproportionately long time at a massive owl the size of a fuzzy doorstop, with massive beacon-like orange eyes. After that she let me drift in a more aimless way through the crowds.

There were stalls of jams, and mugs, cheese and breads, beers and roast pork, jewellery and notebooks with magnificent covers that made the jewellery look half-assed, ornaments and weapons. Teb got distracted by the pretty amethyst earrings, and I spent far too long wondering if it would be practical to buy a quill pen and ink when my handwriting barely qualified as a scrawl. Scrawling had style. Maybe spidery scratchings instead… When Teb came over with little stones dangling from her earlobes she slapped me on the back of my hand and I dropped the feather. "*No*, Ally. That way leads only to a path of ink stains on everything you own and broken quills."

I sighed.

We spotted Mum's arts and crafts stall, surrounded by turtles. They looked amazing in the sunlight, finished and sparkling with varnish. Mum waved madly at us, and we went over—"I've sold twelve already! Do you want to buy one?"

"I have three," I protested, but she glared, and so we both forked out the pound fifty required. Unlike the junk shops, this fair went for the throat—outsiders were coming to buy things here. Mum's prices were insanely reasonable. So was she, I supposed. I'd seen some other handmade arts and crafts go for a small fortune on the other tables.

"Seen the Piper yet?" she asked me.

I shook her head. "I'm keeping an eye out."

"Maybe he's stuck in traffic," she assured me. I saw her glance at Teb: I hadn't told her that Teb was being far less useful than she thought she was. But I also knew Mum didn't think the Piper was the sort of person who got stuck in traffic.

"What was that about?" Teb asked, as we walked away.

"Just someone she knows, who's supposed to be here. They have a bit of a history. University days, hazy music festivals, that sort of thing."

"*Seriously?*" she demanded.

I shrugged. Teb seemed currently incapable of remembering the Piper for what he actually was, and so she didn't press the matter. I suppose Alana was the one I should have been sharing that with, but I hadn't seen her yet either.

We bought bags of fudge and trudged around looking at the free entertainment—there were a lot of dancers, but they were students from the primary school, and I didn't think the Piper was going to be bothering them as they skipped around in cute little outfits with all leaves sewn on them, asking for money for local charities or advertising upcoming events. Let a little girl dress up as a butterfly and prance around and she will happily do any amount of menial work. The grownup entertainers were still a bit stretched—a clown had shown up, and we gave him a wide berth, but many of the musicians and Morris Dancers were presumably still sitting in hot vans stuck in a motorway traffic jam, and a CD of Celtic music was being piped endlessly around the field on huge speakers to make up for the missing musicians. I was keeping a sharp eye out for the Piper, but hadn't seen him yet. The selection of younger people was slowly turning from the participants and bored family members to seriously cool indie teenagers and young adults from out of town, but I reckoned it would be midday before any really serious goths showed up, and until then I could reasonably assume the only dreadlocks in the fair belonged to the Piper.

A lot of the stuff on sale appeared every year at most festivals, so we didn't give the stalls much attention after our first rush through and went right to the farm show to look at the cute pigs.

"Goats are *really* freaky looking," I mused out loud, staring into the weirdly rectangular pupils in one's eyes. Teb petted one that was trying to munch her bag. The tent had plenty of entrances to vent the animal pong around us, but it was still a little eye-watering. The suspiciously dirty hay underfoot didn't help.

"I know," she said, "Kinda like that guy we keep bumping into in town." She looked troubled, but I was more concerned with his reputation than Teb's mental well-being. I knew exactly who she meant even if she didn't.

"He's not that bad looking."

"Goth goats… Now there's a thought," she giggled, clearly not listening.

"I wonder where Alana got to?" I asked, leaning down to pull Teb's bag out of the goat's mouth. She was missing out, I reckoned.

"Who knows?" Teb said darkly. "Who cares? She's your weird new friend."

"She wants to be your weird new friend too."

"Ally, she's a complete stranger who's really creepy. She thinks magic is real. It's like… Tanya and I joked about it all the time, but she just feels like she totally missed the point. She's probably one of those girls who practiced witchcraft to feel edgy. Remember the special assembly last year where the school told us that there were kids trespassing on the graveyard at night and doing weird rituals?"

I cleared my throat: I hadn't got so far as *rituals*, but if the town had still been on high alert like it had been last year, I'd have been nabbed as a desecrater.

Teb continued like I wasn't trying to pretend I hadn't been weird. "Well, they never mentioned it again, did they? I bet the police just went to both schools and said it was happening, but they caught the culprit over in St Fish's and never needed to follow the story up at our school, otherwise we'd have heard if someone got done for killing cats. Well, she's been expelled from St Fish's and is mental. How do you know we haven't got the Satanist in our group all of a sudden?"

"We can't know without asking, and if it was her she wouldn't tell us. Teb, she seems really nice and genuine, if you give her a chance…"

"*Why* would she say stuff like that about Tanya then!?" Teb shrieked. The goat baa'd in surprise but she was clutching it, a bit manic with her stroking.

"Um."

"What do you mean *um?*" Teb demanded. "You're acting all mellowed out and unconcerned, and it's really freaking me out! I expected you to flap around like a headless chicken until Tanya came back! I got you *Skittles*. And instead Alana says 'Oh she was kidnapped by fairies' and drags you off, and I have this awful headache just trying to think about it. I want to know what's going on! Do you know?" She looked at me with this utter horror that I, Ally Guardian, might be more informed on a situation than Teb.

"Not yet," I said.

"What do you mean, *not yet?*"

"Well… He hasn't talked to me yet." I gave her a maddening Tanya smile, hardly able to resist laughing at paying back the weirdness on someone else.

To my horror, tears sprang into her eyes. The goat tried to pull away from her more insistently. She looked angrily away from me before I could see any tears fall, and kept patting.

"I'm sorry," I told her, gently prying her arms from around the goat. "People keep reassuring me there's nothing wrong with Tanya, and I trust them. Even Mum didn't seem worried, and you know she *loves* Tanya. If you aren't going to listen to Alana saying she's fine, then, please, listen to my mum."

Teb was silent for a minute. Having let go of the goat she headed over to look at the rare pig breeds. I trailed after her and leaned on the railing around the pen of an adorably rotund spotted pig. Actually, it looked a little like Mr Plebsy. I lost my admiration of it.

Eventually she looked over at me, eyes still tearful. "I really don't know what to think… I'm just not good at this. I need the world to be made of facts. I can't take the idea of fairies kidnapping my best friend. It's just… *not supposed to happen.*"

"Yeah, I don't think I managed to convince you before."

"And you're just like, 'Meh, she was taken by fairies, so what?'… It's not healthy. For any of us. You're going to have to give me more time to think about it. Before?"

"Before what?"

"You said before."

"Oh, well remember when we went to the junk shop to look for Tanya?"

"Yes, Mrs Potts said she hadn't seen her, and then we went down to the skate park to ask the kids if they'd seen her since they were always out and about at weird hours?"

"Nope."

"What do you mean by *that?*"

The Piper was probably not going to be pleased considering the trouble he went to making her forget the first few times, but… "Er, I'd sort of convinced you she'd been taken by fairies and we were investigating that lead."

"And how would *you* do that? You can't talk your way out of a wet paper bag."

"The Piper."

"The who now?"

"The dreadlocks guy we've been seeing around town. Um. I've seen him a bit more than you have." A moment of inspiration hit me and I hefted my backpack onto the railing, now we were away from goats who might try eating it, and pulled out the recorder with a little more success than the day before. "Tada!"

"You took up music lessons? When?"

"*No,* this is from the Piper!" I clumsily span it in my fingers, and then a mad whim took me and I raised it to my lips and blew a tuneless single toot.

Every single animal in the petting zoo looked my way, every *baa*, *cluck*, *oink* and adorable miniature Highland *moo* shutting up as heads turned.

"Oh my *God*, I can't take you anywhere!" Teb tugged my arm down so I wouldn't be tempted to play another note. "Stop freaking out the animals before we're kicked out!"

They were still watching me: all the pigs had come trotting right up to the railing, and I had to move my backpack, nervous they might take too much of an interest in me. I slipped the recorder back into it and let Teb drag me from the tent, back into the sunlight.

"You don't remember?"

"I…" Teb massaged her forehead. "Maybe? I don't know! I can't remember any *fairies*."

"Well if you're thinking of Tinkerbell, there weren't any like that." That she knew of.

"So what is going on?"

"I'll be honest, I really don't know. I mean, I know *something* is going on, but I've not been allowed in. We were as dumb as each other just yesterday. I'm going to see the Piper soon. Everyone's been saying he'll talk to me here, so I can get my answers and find out what happened to Tanya." This was exactly what Alana had said to me yesterday, right down to admitting she didn't really know what was going on. Maybe seeing the Piper led one person on to the next, and tomorrow Teb would be taking someone under her wing and confidently explaining that something weird was going on, she didn't know what but involvement was not optional.

"Can I come with you to see the Piper?"

"I don't think so. It seemed… Invite only. He's been actively trying to remove you from the action."

She looked away. "Right. Of course. You've got your special new club with Alana and this bloke. You don't need me."

"Of course I do."

"For what? To make you feel better that there's someone less informed than you out there? You say he's had to *alter my mind* to do that? I'm not stupid. If something… *magic* is going on…" she said the word like she was forcing it up from deep inside. "Then I can't remember it because he's scrubbed my brain clean. Does he think I can't handle it? I can handle ten times what you can! If he'd singled *me* out, I'd know everything! He has to *stop* me. You're so muddle-minded he can show you anything and you won't know what to do with it. I could already have *found* Tanya. Argh! I can't believe you were keeping this from me!" She made to storm off, but I hurried after her, not particularly eager to let her go off alone in case the Piper found her first.

"Okay…" I said, panting as I jogged along. "Look, I'm certain he's the only one who can help her… I'll tell you what he says… Whatever he decides to do. I won't let him scrub your mind again. I'll tell him you can handle it. I'll let you in on everything… I *tried* already, Teb. I told you about it yesterday and we were investigating it together and it was only because of him you don't know!"

She slowed, then stopped, to my relief. She nodded. "Okay… You tell me *everything*, mind. I won't let you keep me in the dark again. I'll… I'll leave notes to myself, like in *Memento*, so I know I have to ask you about it again."

"Just don't get any really ill-advised tattoos."

She cracked a bit of a smile at that. I was so relieved I impulsively hugged her. She looked up at me a little concerned, like "What was that for?", but then she smiled.

We stood about awkwardly for a moment, then heard someone calling over the music for the dancers to meet up.

For the first time I saw the fear in Teb's eyes.

"Good luck," I said to her. Funny how with everything else going on, we still had the time to be worried about making fools of ourselves in public. The human brain is a weird thing.

Well Met

We gathered in the middle of the field. I could just about see my mum's stall—she waved to us. Thankfully we were too far away to catch the presumable "Good luck sweetie!" she was likely to have yelled our way.

A woman wearing a full medieval dress and hat ensemble hurried over and handed us a collection of ribbons and garlands to wear. She looked down at my flip-flops and frowned. "Are you sure you want to dance in those?"

"Ally's pretty good at wearing sandals," Teb put in for me. The woman was too busy to really fuss about it, and hurried off to help the next group of people.

I got to work tying the skirt of trailing ribbons around my waist. This was the dancing session where anyone could join in: a man with a stage voice and a tambourine was standing close to a microphone and warming up the crowd—I knew from a dozen festivals past that he would teach us the dance and start us off slow into a nice simple skipping about pattern. The rest of the Morris Dancers had arrived and were warming up, bells clinking gently as the old men did their stretches. Some of them were looking at us with laughter in their eyes, at our pathetic contribution to the pagan dancing.

Alana was not exempt from this madness, and as we were heading into the dance I spotted her being herded towards us. She was scowling.

"When did Tanya find time to sign me up?" she demanded, pre-empting any attempt to ask her where she had been as flowers were rammed over her carefully tousled hair. "How did they know it was me? *Why am I here?*"

I grinned at her. She narrowed her eyes, but settled down to a sulk.

Soon enough we went through the barely-funny but joke-filled initiation process for dancing, and we were making gentle rotations around the grass in front of the stage. It was terribly dull, and there were people a lot worse than us drawing the mockery of the taskmaster with the tambourine; out-of-town people, embarrassed dads, confused ditzy teens. It might even have been worth remembering if it was *me* stumbling around getting laughed at. Alana had too much dignity to do it badly, although her school probably hadn't forced the learning of pagan rituals in PE class quite as much as ours had, being Catholic and all.

But as the allotted half an hour of dancing passed, the music sped up and the shouted, "One, two, one-two, in-out, go left!" etc. that the man called to us grew faster and more complex. We fell into each new pattern easily, and even those who'd stumbled about self-consciously to begin with were dancing fluidly. The faces that flashed by were quietly thrilled. There was a certain extra edge to the music—a new instrument playing along with us... I'd have guessed a cheap tin whistle, making the most amazing noises musical instruments were capable of.

After that, my memory is a blur. I hadn't been drunk yet in my life, so I didn't really have anything to compare it to, but it was how I imagined it would be. Colours were bright, and in my mind the impressions were of fluttering ribbons, twirling skirts, the towering maypole... And the smell of the damp earth, rain coming, the pounding of the dancers' feet on the ground almost as if I were under it and listening to the shoes beating on the grass like rain on my roof, knocking against it with a steady rhythm of falling feet.

I was barely aware of the dancers around me, but I do have a weird, and rather certain, impression that dancing next to me for most of the time was a girl with blonde hair in bunches, a green frilly dress clashing with her bright ribbons. It *couldn't* have been Tanya. It had to be the odd daze I was in, making me see things... Putting her face on another girl's body that looked just the same. And her clothes. Her mannerisms. Her laugh.

Oh, what do I know? The fairies were clearly pretty strange, and worked in mysterious ways. I let it happen without question.

When the piece was over and everyone was applauding I looked around, like waking up, and saw the Piper stepping down from behind the band. He caught my eye and waved. My heart skipped with excitement.

"Go." I spun to see Alana behind me. The shock drew me back to the fact there was a real world, even if she was urging me on to finding out... whatever there was to know about something very *not* real world. I hadn't realised she was standing so near to me. I hadn't really realised anything that wasn't music and ribbons in the last twenty minutes.

"Did you see Tanya?"

"No. Seriously, don't miss your chance to talk to him."

"Right. Right."

"I did," Teb said, coming up to us. She looked as spooked as I felt.

"You did?"

"Tanya… She was dancing with us. I only just realised… I mean, I saw her. But it's only just occurred to me that I should have grabbed her when I saw her…"

"Ally," Alana said, jabbing me in the side with a Morris Dancer's pole she'd picked up somewhere. "Go *now* and talk to the Piper."

"Okay, okay," I said, and hurried the way I'd seen him walk, shedding ribbons and flowers as I went, trying to make myself look somewhat normal again. I wouldn't have been surprised if someone told me there was a spell on the flowers, which had made me half-mad during the dance.

Back out in the main part of the fair, alone, and looking for the Piper, the whole event took on a surreal edge that it hadn't had before. More than a little of that was probably still my daze from yet another dose of the Piper's music. I was pretty sure he didn't normally show up for the fair and participate like that, because I'd never heard anything like it before. I had to assume that he was making fun of me. I'd lost him again, which pretty much confirmed it.

More people had arrived now—it was reaching the level of "packed out" as midday settled in, and the smell of hot dogs and burgers and the hog roast filled the air, the noises of music and people and events blurring together. I prowled through it all, determined to find the Piper. I kept away from Mum's stall, feeling weird about it, like she'd embarrass me in front of the Piper. Very mature of me.

I fell into the feeling of the fair, the music pounding around and through me as I slid unnoticed between the crowds, making slow circles of the field. The fair lost any individuality of sights and persons and became an endless mass, a single organism that I was interacting with only on the most superficial level, people I hardly saw going on with lives of an insignificantly irrelevant status. All I was ready to see was one man, with dreadlocks and a cheeky smile that was aimed at me.

Somehow, he still managed to scare me stupid when he suddenly stepped out in front of me from behind a new age candle and incense stall. He looked the same as ever, but a lot closer than I'd ever seen him, and he was smiling at me. I reverted suddenly back to normal scared Ally when close enough to count every piercing on his face.

"Eep," I said.

"Well met," he said.

"Eep," I agreed.

"Shall we find somewhere quiet to talk?" he asked.

"Eep."

I followed. He worked his way through the crowd, leaving me to skip and stumble after him to a small, unlabelled tent, where he held open the flap of the door for me. I paused outside to look around, but I could see no one was watching. Not sure if that was good or bad, I ducked inside. Stacked around the edges of the tent were crates of candy-floss making materials and a portable machine with a huge sugar-caked bowl. I compulsively sat down on a crate. He stepped in after me, the tent flap falling shut behind him. The interior of the small tent grew suddenly rather dim and dingy… Kind of like being underground…

I started to my feet at once. "Oh no! Have you Pipered me away?!"

For a moment his expression was utterly blank, shadowed in the gloom, and then he burst out laughing, a totally hearty, normal sound, like you might hear crashing across the room in a crowded restaurant. The kind of laughter that makes everyone at all the other tables turn to see what's funny, and usually involves breadsticks and nostrils or some other irreverent behaviour. He sank down onto another crate and pulled his tin whistle out of his pocket, but he only spun it between his fingers rather than casting a spell on me.

I maintained a deeply suspicious glare, though his guffaw (I'd met few laughs that deserved to be described as such but this was probably one) was so infectious that I was almost smiling despite it being aimed at me.

"You're not scared of me, are you?" he finally asked over his last few chuckles, when he was getting to the point where he wiped his eyes. "*You?* You're the one following me everywhere!"

"N-No!" I stammered. I sat heavily back on my crate and re-folded my arms a couple of times. "Not at all! I've only heard all the stories about you running off with all the children in a town… And you made my mum crazy! And what's happened to Tanya? And why are you here?! What are you doing in our peaceful little town, messing everything up? *Why weren't you allowed to talk to me until now?*"

He rearranged his face into a more serious manner, though I could see a snicker still lurking behind the surface; his eyes sparkled inhumanly bright and mirthful. "In which order would you prefer me to answer those questions?"

"Whatever you like," I snapped, determined not to look cowardly. He was just some guy… Just some weirdo who'd shown up here with a whistle and a bright grin. I could class everything else as March Madness and not worry about it. "No, wait. I want to know I'm going to be able to even leave this tent and use the answers you give me… I have to ask: the whole Pied Piper thing. What happened there?"

"Can I just say that they were really obnoxious people?"

"So you did do it?! Why on earth should I trust you at all?"

"I was only doing my job. The rats in the town weren't any old plague. The town had an old god who was awoken from centuries of slumber by some idiots practising witchcraft. He decided that he wanted a century worth of sacrifices to make up what he'd missed, but all of his followers were dead: the witches who brought him back had no idea who he was and what they were doing. They thought he was a demon, and the rest of the town had become too Christianised to remember the old rituals and send him back to sleep. So he brought a plague of rats upon the ignorant town. He was working up to a more wrathful response.

That was him flexing his fingers before the punch. So I stepped in and stopped him."

"By sacrificing loads of kids to him?" I was going to have to calm down and stop shrieking before fair security came by, but at the moment it seemed a bit hard to take a breath properly. In the shadows of the tent he seemed to have no edges, the dark colour of his hair and shirt blending in with the shadows behind him. His long legs were outstretched, and his one white boot (the other was black) was stretched out and catching a thin line of sun where it fell through the crack between tent flaps. The battered shoe glowed a little in the brightness, and made it all the harder to peer at him, until he was almost just a shadowy mass with a glimmer of pale eyes.

"It's never as simple as that," he told me. "And the sacrifice is not what you are thinking: you are imagining cartoon Aztecs on a pyramid with a bloody knife in one hand and a human heart in the other. Where do you think fairies come from? This god had lost his entire following and was going to keep causing trouble until he had some attention, so I brought him a new court. None of the children died… Considering medieval hygiene they probably lived much healthier, interesting lives as servants to that old god than they would have playing around in street muck and eating badly-stored meat."

I stared at him with my mouth open, hardly able to believe a word he'd said. He shifted uncomfortably.

"Come on, it was the middle ages. People expected different things back then. I worked in very different ways."

"And that's what's going to happen to Tanya? She's going to become their 'sacrifice' now?" I demanded, going back to something I had firmer footing about… I could have nightmares about his story in my own time.

"I didn't expect you to understand why this is happening. I'm frankly amazed that you followed as far as you did. I would not have spoken to you at all if there had not been a greater purpose in doing so. But this is about the deepest workings of an ancient and mysterious magical force in the universe, one that has existed since man first began to shape thoughts. By now it is so tangled that I am amazed that I understand it. I should go: I must have talked to you enough by now. Forget me, and your friend."

"No! Wait!" I wailed, leaping to my feet to block his attempted break for the exit. "I might not understand now but, well… I want to know! I will try."

He looked down at me with those mysterious grey eyes, which now more than ever looked almost alien. But then he hesitated and, in a sudden repeated display of his good humour, he smiled, showing all his crooked teeth. "Maybe there will be an easier way to explain this situation with your friend. And it is nowhere near as bad as the situation in Hamelin."

"Well go on then, explain. Before I go completely crazy."

His smile faltered a bit as he led me back to my box. He sat beside me instead of across from me, and suddenly his expression was one of a doctor examining a patient, wary about giving too much away, staring hard at me. "Alana tried to calm you about Tanya's disappearance yesterday, and at the time you seemed to have forgotten to be worried about her at all."

"Everyone was telling me not to."

He nodded, pleased with my answer. Perhaps I'd just given Alana her first job evaluation. His concern had definitely faded. "Your friend Teb was correct to try to keep you from panicking. At the time…"

"Wait, why *are* you keeping Teb out of it?"

He looked at me with deep confusion. "It is standard practice. Besides, I hoped your friend thinking that everything was normal would help convince you."

"While Alana was busy telling me that ghoulies and witches were real in the other ear? That's a pretty mixed message."

He winced. "Look, I have my reasons for keeping Teb away, but it seems that perhaps, as with Tanya's disappearance, her involvement will be inevitable."

I interrupted my own interruption to get back onto the subject of Tanya, my memory jogged and my priorities set rather higher now I'd established I wasn't getting a clear answer about Teb. "Yeah, about that. The way everyone's been going on, it sounds like you know exactly where she is and it'll all be better now we have this talk?" I pointed out accusingly. That was only half true, but what were the last couple of days about if not people foretelling that, when Tanya was gone, the Piper was who I had to talk to? How could the situations be unrelated?

"I can't," he replied and my stomach dropped. His voice was sharp—almost too harsh in the still air of the tent. The noise and bustle of the fair suddenly seemed a million miles away. "And she is in trouble."

"Oh…" The world spun around me in a blare of adrenaline that made my ears roar. "Why are we sitting here? We need to go save her!"

He caught my arm as I tried to jump up again. "She is in no immediate danger. And it is beyond my power to intervene. But not yours."

I lowered myself back onto the crate and pried his hand from my arm. "Yours… But you're… I don't know what you are. Are you an angel?"

He laughed again. "Just stories and legends. I am also balance. Light and dark." He gestured, for lack of other clear Pied Piper markings, at his one-white, one-black combat boots. "My job is to keep everything a plain grey; to stop the world spiralling out of control. There are few beings of pure evil or pure good, and so mostly I just stop everything else from getting too uppity about their position. Where Tanya has gone she has not upset any balance, nor is she encouraging anything to behave as it should not… yet. Most normal humans would have created a complete mess in the time she has gone, but she is fitting quite comfortably in with the fairies who have adopted her."

"Typical," I commented.

"The Lady of Winter has taken a particular interest in the unexpected visitor, and wants Tanya to be one of her handmaidens. This in itself would not be bad;

it may just have been another of Tanya's strange adventures, and I have a general policy not to intervene in personal heroics or soul-searching quests except as the most carefully distant guide if needs be. But the time it would take for Tanya's attention span to run its course is too long: there is a deadline she does not understand. Spring will be awakening. Within the day. In fact, the dance you did has begun the process. And when the Green Man is awake, the Lady cannot remain so. She will go into a seasonal slumber, leaving all her 'possessions' with her husband. This includes any human captives she may have with her. And trust me when I say you do not want the Green Man to be given a pretty young human girl."

I thought of Tanya as the silly little girl who had once climbed over her garden wall to get at her neighbour's strawberries, not knowing about his huge bull mastiff dog. She still had a bite-shaped scar on her leg. Was this the same situation? Tanya with her face smeared in a happy oblivion of strawberry juice, too caught up in her joyful crimes to even hear the monster approaching? I shuddered.

"What's going to happen?"

"The pagan aspect of summer has slept all winter beneath the town… *Traditionally* on his awakening there would be a sacrifice of sorts to appease him and to ensure a particularly good summer harvest. This hasn't been done for a very long time in these parts, but that won't stop the gods hungering for one. Unlike the sleeping god in Hamelin who felt neglected, the yearly rituals here are more than enough appeasement… if there are no other offerings. But here, Tanya will seem to them the perfect candidate for a summer sacrifice, especially as she has given herself completely willingly to the Lady already. When I took her back home, the time before she found her way back into the fairy world, they were more upset with me removing her, and I found that I had actually unsettled the balance within the world by taking Tanya from the fairies. They were expecting someone to be given to them, so…"

"You took Tanya back?!" I jumped to my feet and pointed accusingly at him.

There was still humour in his eyes as he sat still, looking up at me, but it was rather darker. I didn't like the twist to his smile any more. "No. I thought perhaps you had been marked for a reason and tried to take you to them instead. You were so slow to follow me, though, and while I was leading you away Tanya found her own way back and the gods settled down again, so I let you be. Alana was quite vocal about it afterwards…"

"And Alana really does answer to you? She's not some crazy internet fan girl who just says she knows you?"

He was smiling at me in a way that seemed sort of pitying and amused. Oh help me, he thought I was strange. The weirdest person I had ever met in my life thought he was more sensible than me. I could have cried.

"Oh. Wow." I sat down again, almost missing the crate—I bruised my hip on a sharp corner. I stared at him. He gave me a small smile. I meant to say something else, something non self-serving, a query about Alana, or why he had told Teb to butt out, it wasn't her story. To say Tanya's case was still urgent, wasn't it? But what came out was, "You were going to *sacrifice* me?" Who just happily confesses to almost sacrificing you to some ancient gods? Well… Someone who didn't see it as a problem. He was hardly rushing off to save Tanya either, the way we were still sitting around chatting.

"It's not… A fatal sacrifice. And it wasn't my original intent at all. This is all very confusing, isn't it?" He smiled at me a bit sheepishly. He didn't fool me. I faked a smile back though. I was too worried not to. What was to say he wasn't going to change his mind and steal me away after all?

"'Confusing' isn't the word for it…" I said, frowning at him. "You don't just tell people that you were going to sacrifice them and expect them to move on from that in a few words! If you were banking on me being extremely easy to manipulate and confuse, you picked the wrong ditz. I can follow extremely convoluted strings of thought. I just take a long time to work out concepts… Such as *why* would you even think sacrificing someone who had never seen a fairy in her life was a good idea."

He winced. "Maybe that one is something a lot of people would get stuck on, actually. Well, I clearly underestimated you, Ally. I guess the only reason I'd tell you that is because… well, I'm trying to apologise for leading you away. I wouldn't have brought it up if I didn't feel bad about it. I feel like I should do you a favour as an apology."

"Oh, you don't have to," I said, blushing. Dammit, he had managed to swing me back around to his side with soft-spoken confessions. He was obscenely likeable.

"I *want* to," he said. "Do you understand?"

"Er…" I shook my head.

"I can only *help* you by doing you a *favour*…" He said it slowly and loudly this time. "Do you want Tanya back?" he asked in a lower voice.

"Oh! Oh! You *can't* do anything unless I ask you to?"

I saw him wince like he had almost slapped himself on the forehead with frustration at me. Hey, like he said, it was very confusing. Tanya wanted to be there, we didn't want her to be. Apparently the fairies didn't have a problem with it, or whatever rules the Piper followed and, since it wasn't a kidnap, he had no ability to stop it or something? Would Tanya change her mind if she knew she was going to be sacrificed? Or, since this was Tanya, wouldn't she?

"Um. Okay. Let's go get Tanya back! What do we do?"

"First we need to de-curse you. If I sent you to the fairy world as you are now, demonic possession afterwards would be the *least* of your worries. You're all softened up like a sponge after this week. The longer I chat to you, the spongier you get."

"I can definitely feel my brain filling with holes where reasonable answers to my questions should have been."

He gave me a mysterious half-smile, like, yes, of course he wasn't going to have answered anything properly and even if I spent all day crafting a proper inquest I'd still come out confused. I should have guessed 'talk to you' wasn't the same as 'answer all your questions'. "How are you going to fix me?" I asked, thinking that my nervousness now was perfectly justified.

"Stand up," he said.

I did, and he stood as well. He walked right up to me so there was barely a foot between us. He was tall—I had to look up at him.

"Eep?" I said. This close to him I felt like there was something unnerving about his eyes. They were very, very pale grey, with hardly a dark ring around the iris. There was almost no colour at all to them.

"Will you allow me to lift the spell the fastest way I know how?"

"What's a slower way?" I asked, finding it unaccountably hard to swallow. I had to ask; I felt like he was about to ask me to sign a waiver.

"You sit still in a circle for an hour while I play soothing music at you. You must absolutely not fall asleep even for a second or I will have to start over. Frankly even in one attempt we don't have much time."

I pulled a face. "And the fast way?"

One of his large hands touched my stomach, slowly spreading out, settling against me. I studiously examined the design of screaming faces in faded grey on his black T-shirt, until his other hand gently fitted into the small of my back. I gasped in surprise at that contact, and looked up at him, face burning, heart thumping in my ears, to find him smiling at me closer than ever. I got one good long look into those shiny grey eyes, and then they closed, taking mine with them, and all I could do was jump a little when his rough lips brushed over mine. I felt the bumpy, cool touch of the several lip piercings he had, and then he kissed me properly, his lips ridiculously soft compared to the metal. At that point his hands were about all that was keeping me upright, as I discovered just what it was like to kiss someone with a pointy stud through their tongue. Surprisingly pleasant. And very, very amazing, as first kisses go.

A yell of alarm utterly failed to burst out of me. I was sure Alana or Teb was lurking close enough that a cry of "This crazy man is assaulting me!" would have them running to my rescue. But what I actually found was that rather more time than I expected passed (what part of this was faster than the sitting still method?) and I was still standing pressed against him, lips smushed against his, his arms around me… And no instinctive reaction to jerk my knee sharply upwards had occurred. Cursing my terrible reactions, I stepped away.

I felt a lot better than I had done before the kiss. The fuzziness that had clouded my thoughts and made me think that some very odd things were perfectly acceptable had lifted, and I was beginning to feel rather angry.

I didn't dare meet the Piper's eyes again. "Take me to Tanya now!" I demanded, not moving at all because I wasn't sure if he'd Piper me off somewhere or we had to walk. I almost fell over from the violent action of not going anywhere, and subsided, blushing.

"I believe Alana is talking Teb into accompanying the two of you on the rescue mission; you should go out and meet up with them."

"Aren't you coming?" I turned to look at him, a hopeful expression in place.

He smiled mysteriously. "I may see you there."

And with that I was ushered out of the tent and left to blink in the sunshine, dazzled. When I turned to look back into the tent he was no longer there, though there was only the one entrance.

*

Teb was standing outside, hands on hips. "I'm coming with you," she said firmly.

"Whu…?" I asked, having failed to process any speaking she did while still getting over my "Argh! Teb!" moment, and the fear she'd instantly know what had happened in the tent.

"I'm coming with you."

I looked around for the Piper, but by now he may as well have vanished off to Mexico to deal with some troublesome ghosts. I don't know. I'd never be able to catch him for more advice, that was for sure.

"So you're all cool with it again?" I asked nervously. "I mean, you know *where* we are apparently going, and why?"

"I remember. Alana said I had a choice to make if I wanted to know about this or not." Alana was standing behind Teb, eating candy floss on a stick and looking rather smug: I didn't want to ruin it by telling her that I'd probably done all the hardest work on winning Teb over to Team Fairies. She gave me a knowing nod.

"You said yes, of course."

Teb nodded at me. "I've decided I *do* want to know. I like knowing things. And if Tanya's already there, I don't want to miss out on it. I couldn't still be your friend if you all had this amazing conspiracy theory and I wasn't allowed in." Teb gave Alana a sidelong look. "I still think I need to see some of this with my own eyes. It hardly seems fair if I am the only one who doesn't remember anything strange. Though if Tanya really is inches away in some magical fairy land then we have officially wasted police time."

"*You* have," I reminded her. "I did my best to keep this between us."

She scowled at me.

"It's just… The Piper was trying to keep you away from it, like I said… I'm worried it's the same as my mum. She went crazy when she saw the same things Tanya's experiencing. That's, well… how it happened."

"I'll be fine," Teb snapped, "Do I look the sort of person to be affected by a bit of weirdness? I think you'll find I have *really good* hair. People with really good hair don't go crazy 'cause they see some weird stuff." She tossed her ponytail over her shoulder with an irritable flick of her head.

"I don't think having a stiff upper lip and impeccable taste in clothes means

132

you are immune to magic that wrecks your brain," I argued.

Alana waded in: "The important thing is that we're now allowed to go get Tanya, and we have a small window to do that without causing any fuss with those who have her. So shall we get going?"

Teb and I deferred to her leadership: it was almost as disturbing as seeing magical things to see the uncommon sight of Teb letting someone else lead the way. Alana pointed vaguely with her candy floss stick and set off walking, and like ducklings we fell into line behind her.

Real Names

Skipping along, Teb seemed to be channelling Tanya in her absence. She'd missed out on most of the story so far, so I summarised: Tanya's whereabouts, some sketchy outline of the surrounding politics with the magical beings involved from my already half-forgotten conversation with the Piper, and a couple of the major events she'd missed. Alana wept a little to hear of the incident where I may or may not have fallen in the pond and been trapped in the fairy world for the rest of my life. All the time we blindly followed Alana across the noisy, crowded fair and through a gap in the hedge. She finished her candy floss with expert timing and threw the little wooden stick into the hedge as we passed.

I realised where we were going almost as soon as we reached the main road—unless we were walking to the motorway itself, the skate park was the only landmark left to visit this way.

"Do you know what's so special about this town?" Alana asked, out of the blue, after we'd trudged along in contemplative silence for a minute.

Teb and I looked at each other but neither of us came up with a witty remark off the hoof, so Teb said, "No?"

"Magically, I mean. I figure if the Piper is letting me talk freely at last then I should tell you all the bits and pieces I know which are useful."

Being a sometime teacher's pet, I cast my mind back to all the stuff Mum blah'd on about, and tried to come up with an answer—"It's something to do with ley lines, right?" I asked.

"Yes, the lines as they've been figured out by mediums in the past tend to… unravel a little in this area. The stone circle doesn't fit in with any of the others, and people who don't know the area seem to think the skate park is influencing the ley lines somehow, so they just throw their notes on Troutespond out of the window and say there's nothing here, because why would a patch of land with no history whatsoever as far as they can tell be twisting their attempt to magically link everything?"

"The skate park's as weird a spot as the church or stone circle?" I asked, my mental map of the town being attacked with an imaginary pencil and ruler. They did seem to all be about the same distance from each other.

"See that little grove of trees?" She gestured a patch of darker green in the middle of the wasteland of long grass and weeds, a tiny spot of the woods that had somehow avoided the flattening of the earth around this end of the town.

"Yeah?"

"The Green Man's court is in there. The big old oak tree?"

"Literally?"

"No, it's just a tree, moron."

"Aww," I said, still tracing on my map, "The school's outside that area." So much for having a cool excuse for all the various problems school life threw up—missing homework? Pixies did it. Vending machines not working? Pixies did it. Teacher's car gets egged? Pixies did it... "How did Mr Brooke get possessed by demons then? Isn't all the weirdness contained in the triangle then?"

"Demons are everywhere," Alana replied darkly. "They don't need pagan magic to find you, though getting involved in it is a sure way to encourage them. As is religious mania."

I decided that maybe I didn't want to ask her any more questions. But Teb was still curious, partially in denial and perfectly happy going along with this new game.

"So what's the point of the triangle? What does the stone circle do?"

"Alana said it was a safe place," I put in.

She nodded. "There's magic connected to it, but it can't affect us here... Unlike where we're going..."

"Which is?"

She pointed ahead of us. The skate park was only a few dozen yards away now, and the noises of it on this first warmish day of spring were loud and obnoxious: clattering and yelling and swearing in childish voices that revelled in not having parents around. The skate park was heaving with skateboarding idiots—or possibly pixies. I didn't even know any more. A couple of them were making long trips up the road to roll down the hill backwards on their boards, because apparently the park itself didn't offer enough opportunities for broken necks. When these two particularly moronic skateboarders saw us coming they started furiously skating back our way. They stopped in front of us and picked up their boards, looking for all the world like tweenaged ugly little boys, with too-big shirts and shorts and chunky trainers on skinny ankles, one tall, with a beaky face, his cap worn backwards, one short with a piggy sort of face, a hood pulled low over his eyes.

"What are you doing here?" the piggy-faced one said to us in the most insolent voice I'd ever heard. They *had* to practice to sound that pissed-off about nothing—maybe they played online games and shouted down their headphones when they weren't skateboarding. All I knew was they were acting like they owned the place.

"Shut up, you brats, and let us pass," Alana snarled. Teb and I looked at each other and raised our eyebrows.

"Now now, who's been more disagreeable, of the two of us?" Beaky said with a grin, the words sounding strange out of his previously obscene-even-without-swearing mouth. There was a change all about him: the hands-in-pockets slouch vanished and there seemed something more businesslike in his dislike of us.

"You guys swear at me every time you skate past," I pointed out, "Or make hooting noises, which is just as disagreeable."

"Just a sign we like you, babe," Piggy said, with a leer. I think it was a joke, but I shuddered and edged over to stand behind Teb, because I had a feeling she could probably kill him for me. She looked like she wanted to.

"Just take us to the doorway and leave us be," Alana snapped, "Ally, don't encourage them."

"I wasn't!" I protested.

Beaky laughed at me like, "*Snerk snerk snerk.*" It was a pretty unattractive sound. But he gestured us with a wave of his arm and hopped onto his skateboard again. Piggy followed and they rolled back down to the maze of half-pipes and concrete bumps that was their domain.

Alana gestured for us to follow. "When you talk to the fey, keep it straightforward and simple, and don't accept anything they give you, even the time of the day. And don't give them anything in return! If it's a choice between talking to them and not talking to them, *clam up.*"

We carried on down the abandoned off-road. I thought it was a really sad thing that, should everything go tits up in the fairy world and we ended up all sacrificed to some ancient god, this sad reject piece of concrete should be the last thing I saw of my own world. Why oh why couldn't we have gone to the church or the stone circle, both beautiful and symbolic in their own ways? Would this skate park one day be as significant as those two sites were? Well... That depended, I supposed, if the claims of it as the new fairy hotspot were picked up on, and random druids showed up to worship here. I don't know, it could happen.

"What are you giggling at now?" Teb asked.

"Skateboarding druids," I chuckled.

"Not going to ask," she commented.

I think we were just nervous as we reached the curves, hollows and plateaus of the skate park. The skateboarders all looked so normal—I don't know, maybe I was expecting them all to look like a super-deformed Puck now, all wicked fairy faces, but maybe it was the Piper's "correction". Perhaps I would have been seeing them as a lot weirder now they knew I knew what they were. I grinned, pleased I'd not got into the terrible endless "they knew I knew that they knew that I knew…" loop as I was wont to do, then got a headache from thinking that anyway. They certainly knew we were looking for fairies, though.

"Are you absolutely sure that there is no better way to get Tanya back?" Teb asked nervously.

"One hundred percent," Alana said.

"Okay. I don't know when I started believing you guys, but it was way too recently for this."

"And that is why I spent two days with the lower divisions of weird stuff," I said smugly. "Dipped my toes in the water, got used to it and all."

Teb gave me a scathing look for my attempt to be more worldly knowledgeable than her.

We reached the skate park itself, stepping onto the hot, graffiti-splattered concrete, feeling the eyes of the skaters on us. Some of those boys *had* to be just ordinary guys from the town—some of them looked genuinely confused to see us, or else stared because we were older girls, and ones in skirts and with good hair (for the most part), rather than the ripped jeans and grungy styles of their crowd.

"So, how does this work?" I asked as we were led between skateboarders, many of them nearly colliding with us as we passed. We were heading for the largest skate ramp, the one where the dancing girl had vanished yesterday morning.

"You'll see when you get up there," Alana said, our tour guide through insanity. We climbed up the steps behind the biggest half-pipe, finding the crude concrete steps almost more graffitied than the slopes themselves. Dents and worn corners indicated they'd taken their toll on young knees, or that the boys had been pounding them into submission in an unconsciously safety-conscious way.

From the top, the view was surprisingly good for an elevation of only about eight or nine feet—I could see the town looking down on the valley, houses like crumbs of brick lining the fold between here and the looming hills that overlooked us to the north. Somewhere off to the north-east the stone circle nestled, but I wasn't sure from here which hill it was, as the trees swallowed the tops of the hills completely. The point of the church stood up against this scene, and I tried to work out that if this was one corner, that the other, then the stone circle must be up there… Did that make my house bang in the middle of it all? The thought made me shiver.

As Teb joined me at the top of the half-pipe a brat skated over from the other side, suddenly rattling up to us, flying a few feet in the air. He flipped himself in mid-air so he and his board landed the right way up for the return journey. He hooted with laugher, and I realised it was Piggy.

"Just ignore them," Alana mumbled.

Piggy came shooting back our way. Alana reached out and shoved. The pixie thing bounced back down the half-pipe, landing in a mangled heap at the centre. His board made it halfway up the other side, then came rattling back down and bumped into him.

"Is he okay?" I asked, leaning tentatively over to look down the half-pipe.

"He'll be fine," Alana snorted, and sure enough the brat was getting up, shaking limbs experimentally to make sure they all still worked and dusting himself off. After that, the half-pipe we stood at was given a very wide berth, some of the more probably human skaters still looking very confused about what we were doing there and why we were casually assaulting their friends.

"Right, where were we?" Alana asked, and held out a hand, apparently to Teb. She looked it very suspiciously.

"What's that for?"

"Think you need a bit of help, that's all," she said.

"Oh really?"

"Do you have the first idea how to get to the fairy world?" Alana asked.

"Turn counter-clockwise three times while reciting its true name?" Teb suggested. Alana stared at her. Teb sighed. "I'm not dumb about this sort of stuff, just because I don't believe it. I couldn't have stayed friends with Ally and Tanya without picking something up, and we used to play this game when we were kids... Tanya's idea, of course."

That made me shiver even more... From Alana's expression, we'd been playing a *very* stupid game. Did I have to have words about this as well with Tanya when we got her back?

"So what's the true name?" Alana challenged, perhaps hoping that Tanya would have made up one.

Teb closed her eyes, did a step around, her lips moving over some barely-audible word, and she *vanished*.

"Huh," I said, as amazed as anyone else.

Alana looked at me.

"Sheesh, I don't know it," I said. "We played that game when we were five or something."

I wasn't just impressed with Teb's memory. I was also freaked out. Because the empty patch of concrete where she had been a second before now told me very clearly that I couldn't not go. It wasn't just Alana standing there with her hands on her hips, amused and impressed with Teb as much as annoyed with Tanya. It was the fact that Teb *and* Tanya had now popped off to some other dimension and I had been left behind. I was always the last to pick up their fads, the one who finally started saying "wicked" (meaning "great") weeks after Tanya had finished her phase where she used it in every sentence. The one who got a colourful beaded braid in her hair the winter after Teb and Tanya came back from their separate summer holidays with braids without ever discussing it.

But I always followed them in the end because we were friends and friends did everything together. Even inter-dimensional travel.

Alana was holding out her hands: I reached for them and that was the last I saw of the realm I'd grown up in for a while—staring blankly at the grimy concrete where Teb had been standing.

"So That's When Spring Comes Early, Huh?"

66Ally? Ally! Open your eyes!"

I didn't. Teb was using her nagging voice. I didn't like the sound of it. Now that I was here, the whole concept of being in fairyland seemed way too big and scary to comprehend. Somehow it was all so much easier to understand when it was happening in the safety of your town… I was *longing* for random demonic attacks on my teachers, just so long as it happened in the school I knew like the back of my hand…

"No." What would it even look like? It *felt* different. I'd gasped for a moment, convinced I was going to die as the air pressure changed and I had to take an unexpected breath, but now it just felt temperate and still. It wasn't hostile, but that just led me to worry that the sight of it was where the fear lay. Would we be tiny, blades of grass towering over us, a rampaging herd of ants approaching? I couldn't hear anything. Or would we be in some sort of glittering kingdom of waterfalls and elves who looked like that guy from *The Matrix*, and here was I wearing flip-flops.

"Come on, you've been here for a whole minute already! Just look! You're wasting the experience!"

"Have I?" It didn't seem like much time had passed since Alana had said the words and carried us across. My panics usually happened a hundred miles an hour in my head: I felt like I'd barely caught my breath, and they were badgering me to look. I didn't feel any different, but Teb seemed to be here with me. Unless it had just been a trick of the light when she vanished…

"You're being silly, Ally! Look at where you are!" Was that excitement in

Teb's voice? I'd not heard her utter more than a dry "Yay..." for a long time.

I cracked an eye open just enough to register that the bright sunlight had vanished. I hadn't just screwed my eyes so tightly shut I was blocking it all out. We appeared to be underground, the sky black above us. I squished my eyelids back together. No thanks.

Except... Except, I dared to open one eye a tiny little bit, because that hadn't felt like the right word. We *weren't* underground. We were still standing in exactly the same place. But the world was far from the same. I closed my eye again. I needed a bigger run up to convince myself that this was really happening.

"Oh Ally," Teb sighed.

So I looked.

We had been standing at the top of a sturdy concrete structure with scraped up wooden boards lining a perfectly U-shaped scoop. Now, though, we stood atop a blueish, moss-covered pile of apparently loose stones opposite a similar ridge, forming at best a rough V shape between them. You'd only get broken legs if you tried falling off this with a skateboard (even without Alana's help). There were other columns and heaps of stones all around us. Together they added up to make an approximation to the skate park and surrounding mountains of refuse left behind from the road that never got built.

Looking beyond that, as I dared to widen my eyes a little more, was the road that *was* built. I barely saw the motorway when taking in the view from the town normally. But now it *was* the view. The huge embankment, already a long ridge of scar tissue from one side of the valley to the next, now seemed to reach almost to the sky. As much as I tried to see it as it ever had been, it kept on insisting that it was the edge of the world, that it was a towering wall of bare black earth.

Being hemmed in frightened me more than I could say; seeing the world looking completely different from how I knew it made my dizzy and unsure. I turned to Teb. She was a beacon of normality. There was her purple T-shirt that I'd seen her wear a million times before. The little flick at the edge of her fringe that refused to stay behind her ear. The impatient look on her face.

"Oh *come on*, Ally," she complained as I shuffled a step towards her and tried to bury my face in her shoulder. "Are you a complete child? Look at this! It's incredible!"

She pushed me away, grabbed me by the shoulders, and rotated me to face west. "Look there, for example!"

"Don't," Alana advised from behind me.

"What do you mean?" Teb demanded, as I tried to make sense of what I was seeing, looking despite Alana's warning.

At first I didn't understand. It was a pretty dull view as far as the town was concerned: unless you squinted to try and make out the school, there was nothing even in this direction except for the road that vanished around a hill on its way to Bilsworth. Woodland covered most of anything you cared to place your eyes on, even blocking out the view of the motorway embankment. It was pretty much the same here, though the trees were deadly still and a dark, matte blue that was almost as black as the sky above.

Then I realised what was different. Even in the same open space as us, what became a meadow on the other side of the abandoned road was a breakaway copse of trees, an annex of the woods bang in the middle of the long grass. It was just one of those parts of the background usually: a dozen trees that someone from the council came and mowed around once a year so the dog walkers weren't eaten by lions mistaking it for the savannah.

But here, in this strange dark version of our world, the tree in the middle was monstrously huge. The branches were snaggling and fat, hung with streamers of lichen and ivy. All the trees here were dead, or still nude for the winter. But the big tree was not: tiny green buds had appeared all over it, and their bright green shone through the murk as if they were giving off light.

The whole world didn't seem to have much in the way of light sources. It was lit with a black backdrop, yet the ground itself was lit well enough to make out every detail. It felt like the strange brightness the ground takes on when a wall of storm clouds approach towards the sun. But when I looked over my shoulder, the sky was just as night-time dark, the ground offensively daylight against expectations.

The air itself was empty, though. It seemed only a short way above us was the dome of the sky, and for once it really felt like that. The surface was inky-black. Across it wandered fat stars, none of them a void of light-years away. They swirled lazily about, lava lamp style, oozing through the darkness. Some globs of glowing celestial stuff seemed almost as big as the moon, but they all gave out less light than the furthest twinkling star in our own sky. They seemed to be responsible for the blueish tinge everything had here, though: I'd actually discovered a light source weaker than those streetlights outside my house.

"Oh god, it's starting," Alana moaned behind me. "We have to get out of here!"

"What's starting?" Teb asked at once, eager as a puppy.

"Where are we getting out of here to?" I asked, since Alana clearly didn't have enough complicated questions to answer.

She seized on mine. "Right, Tanya's clearly not here. It's a wasteland. Let's get somewhere else in case she's there."

"Ooh," Teb said.

I turned to see what she was watching.

We were not alone here after all. Small, humanoid (I guessed) things were making their way in a snaking line through the long grass down to the grove of trees, too far away for me to guess what they looked like. The trees had already sprouted a great deal more buds, and on the biggest tree in the middle there were now leaves.

"That's really fast," I commented.

"What are those?" Teb asked, pointing to the cavorting line. She turned and began picking her way down the side of the stones without waiting for an answer from Alana: she preferred to look at things with her own eyes than listen to people's opinions. A real scientist, that girl. Unfortunately for us right there and then.

"Don't go that way!" Alana hissed.

"I'm just getting a better look!" Teb called as she dropped to a crouch to save herself from slipping. "Something is happening… What's to say Tanya's not there? She loves being at the centre of attention."

"She's not!"

"How can you know that?"

Alana didn't have an answer.

Teb dropped down to ground level and set off, arms swinging. I recognised her mannerisms of steely resolve. She wasn't just determined to find Tanya, or even curious about what else she'd see on the way. Her encounters with the Piper had shaken her up to the core; she had been scared stupid of him and I think maybe she had begun to remember how she felt, if not the incidents themselves, as Alana and I had told her what she'd missed. Teb didn't do well with being told she was wrong, or being made to jump, or questioned when she thought she had the answers. Now, seeing it with her own eyes, she was determined not to be frightened of anything: she would accept it all and that was that. Nothing would make her feel that way again.

Come to think of it, that mindset could really get her into trouble… I lurched after her.

"Uurgh, something else is the centre of attention!" Alana hissed, mostly to herself and far too late to scare Teb, who was picking her way across the rubble already out of earshot of everything but shouting, making a break for smoother land.

Alana followed me: it seemed inevitable we were staying with Teb. This was not going to turn into a mission to rescue *both* of my oldest friends, and that was that. Tanya could wait if Teb was being weird though: she had the past form which assured me she was coping, wherever she was. I mean, the Piper had let her stay a whole day unattended…

"What are those things down there?" I asked Alana when she had caught up to me and we were scurrying after Teb. "I'd think since Teb is barrelling towards them in full rampage mode I should probably have a heads up. Am I about to meet fairies? What could possibly be so bad? They're fairies, right?"

"Pixies and goblins of various descriptions, for the most part. The fairies are the little floaty bits in our world," she replied as we plunged into the long grass. It came up past even my head… if Teb hadn't already beaten a path through it I'd never have made any progress. I had to do a double-take at the trees to make sure I wasn't suddenly tiny like I'd been imagining: no, the grass was really just seven feet high.

"So this… *isn't* fairy land?"

"Broadly it is, yes. But no one cares what the fairies do here. They come from here and that's all the connection they have with it. We just call it that because it sounds twee and adorable, and therefore is easier for our brains to cope with. There are much, much bigger fish here. They just consider the fairies an untapped power source or place to recruit new goblins from, to be honest. No one is having a tea party. A serious mythological event is about to go down instead. We do not want to get too tangled up in it for long, or we may lose our chance to save Tanya."

"What? What's happening right this second?"

"Spring is," Teb said in a weird whispery voice rather like Tanya's.

We abruptly fetched up against her, standing in the long grass. Teb had bent a stalk to peer at it. Colour was visibly creeping up the dark blue stalk, slowly bringing a more natural, lifelike green to it. Even the blue darkness around us had begun to go turquoise in the west.

"That doesn't sound too bad," I said hopefully, really hoping that this colour change—and a bit of welcome light perhaps—was all they meant when they kept on saying that.

"Trust me, it's bad," Alana said. She'd stopped a few paces behind us, doing the folded arms and irritated head tilt of a teacher on a field trip who is getting closer to shouting but right now will try and wheedle Tanya to get out of the mammoth display now, please, before any security guards come. She even had the little hopping from foot to foot motion down.

"Why?" I asked.

More rustling came from around us—more than Alana was making—and then two goblins stepped out and looked suspiciously up at us with beady, inhuman eyes.

"Waaaugh!" I cried, and backed behind Teb.

"I think you're about to get a nice demonstration," Alana sighed.

The creatures had something of woodland animals to their looks, but in the least cute way imaginable. One had a mottled beak and round dark eyes, yet shaggy fur and whiskers, moth-like feathery antennae, and a lanky, literally pigeon-chested body with clawed hands on the end of long arms, bare furry feet at the end of feathered legs.

The other was snoutier with keener eyes, fangs protruding over its fleshy lips. Bat ears trembled atop its bristly head, and its body was heavy and somewhat badger-like, though twisted upright so it could walk. It wore baggy three-quarter-length trousers and oversized trainers. And both clutched skateboards.

"Oh my. It's you," I said.

"Who?" Teb demanded.

"We met them a few minutes ago topside."

"We came to see what you were doing," Piggy said.

Beaky laughed: "*Snerk snerk snerk.*"

"Come on, there are two of them and they're smaller than us," Teb said, eyes a little too wide, all her curiosity about the goblins satisfied, thank goodness. "Let's go."

She tried to take a step forward, but Piggy grabbed her with a clawed hand. Whether she was worried about badgers spreading tuberculosis or if he was frighteningly strong, or even if he put a spell on her, she relented. I was certainly not going to try fighting them. I looked to Alana.

She shrugged miserably. "You blundered into this one."

"*Teb* blundered into it. I just followed."

"So what now?" Teb asked the goblins.

"We have to take you to the Green Man." Beaky turned and, clicking two bony fingers at us to follow, set off through the long grass, slashing it aside as if it were nothing.

"Oh *no*," Alana groaned as we followed. Piggy had taken up the rear and given her a firm poke in the back to start her moving.

"What's that?" Teb demanded. "The Green Man? Who's that? Isn't that the name of the pub down near the One Stop?"

"He's in charge now," Beaky said from the front of the queue.

"If we hadn't dawdled…" Alana groaned.

"Why?" I asked.

"He very literally just woke up. Or was born. Whatever. Five minutes ago this was all blue and we'd have been in the Lady's jurisdiction."

"Is she better? Should we have been captured by her instead?" Teb suggested sarcastically.

"No, but she has Tanya. Getting captured by her minions would have led us straight there, and we could have only had to enact one daring escape today. Now we have to deal with all this."

'All this' was the scene taking place beneath the trees. Beaky had led us to the grove. As we passed through the undergrowth around the edges we could see what was happening beneath the canopy, now rustling with green. The air stank of summer. It was like being dropped in the deep end of a swimming pool full of grass cuttings and flowers and hazy air. The choice of flip-flops suddenly felt a lot more seasonally appropriate.

It seemed the goblins had prepared for their own fair that day. The trees were fully green by now, almost summery in the lushness of their leaves. But only recently swamped by the natural decoration were miles of green streamers, so numerous that the undersides of the trees at least must have felt as green as summer while they were still bare. Long ribbons hung still in the quiet air, and each tree was linked by a dozen crisscrossing lines with fake leaves sewn of green silk spaced at close intervals.

Compared to the bold designs, the real leaves seemed fragile, almost crystalline, if that was possible. There was no bright sun to shine through them, yet they held a sort of inner glow like they didn't care. I'd already long had the impression that science didn't come here often for a picnic. I was amazed we were still stuck to the ground by gravity, though I had to do a double-take to check, so dazed was I at everything going on around me.

Even the bare earth had long carpets in green and gold spread higgledy-piggledy over the dark mud at the base of the tree. They bucked and sometimes just plain hung over the huge roots, but points for effort, I suppose. And over those carpets danced dozens of feet.

Pixies or goblins or whatever seemed to have serious hyperactivity issues. All the ones we'd met had been constantly dancing or skating. The ones clustered around the tree, their strange bodies taking all sorts of horrible animal shapes, were no different. They capered in no obvious order, but the longer I watched them the more uncomfortable I felt. They were clearly doing something purposeful; they were carrying about branches and leaves and handfuls of moss. They tumbled all over the place, but eventually these bits and pieces made it to the far side of the tree.

"What are they doing?" Teb asked after we had stood and watched for several minutes.

"Wait and see," Beaky told her.

"After dragging us over here you may as well explain what's going on," she grumbled. I knew she didn't want to look surprised at whatever happened next.

"It's almost begun," was all Piggy would say, and even that got him an elbow to the ribs from his bony friend when he tried gesturing at a particularly large huddle of goblins.

They would have drawn the eye anyway. They were carrying the largest object we'd seen so far: all the bits of tree before that point suddenly looked like twigs in comparison. At first I took it to be more branches. The object certainly was mossy green and brown, ivy hanging from it in long trailing curtains. But the shape beneath was far too regular, and I suddenly remembered that room in the museum in Bilsworth that Teb would always dare me to go in, and I wouldn't. Because the walls of that particular room were lined with hundreds of stuffed animal heads, shot by cruel local hunters in the Victorian period and donated to the museum by some rather disturbed families on their deaths. There were many pairs of antlers displayed on shields, sans the deer's head they had been ripped from. Just the memory of that room made me shudder.

"What are *those* for?" Teb demanded shrilly. Maybe she had been scared of the room too: maybe that was why it had been so important for her to make me terrified of it.

"Shush!" Beaky said, much more harshly than he'd spoken before.

The gaggle of goblins carried the huge antlers away behind the tree.

I glanced at Alana, wondering if she might have a clue about what was going on. But her face was rigid, and I couldn't have said if it was from uncertainty or fear.

We found out soon enough, in any case.

A huge groan shook through the ground. That was followed by a roar which made the groan seem like a warm-up. I clung to Teb, but she scornfully pushed me away. I transferred my death grip to Alana, who was much more scared and therefore compliant. I just wished it wasn't our previously in-control tour guide who was the one frozen in fear.

A ripping sound came next. This time nothing shook but the tree: newly sprouted leaves came falling down, still glowing softly as they settled on the muddy carpets.

And then he stumbled into view, the goblins clustered triumphantly about him, chattering with delight.

"Oh. My. God." Teb said.

The man who had emerged, apparently from the tree, was definitely not the sort of man you would take home to your parents. Well, my mum might be unnervingly cool with him. But…

He was eight or nine feet tall, and I was left in no doubt that he was the Green Man that I had heard so much about. While genuinely bare skin was a rare thing on this naked giant, what we could see was indeed the same hue as the leaves around him. But soft, dark moss grew all over him, and oak leaves sprouted across his body, following the lines of bodily hair, running down the sides of his arms, his chest and stomach… His long hair was a curtain of ivy and oak, and his beard the same. Leaves even seemed to tug at the corner of his mouth, as if he could open it and spew more out. The antlers had been rammed onto his head without much care: amber blood oozed around where they had recently been joined to his scalp, and a trickle ran, shining brightly, down his green forehead, soaking into his mossy eyebrows. His lower body was barky: his thick legs, lichen-splattered and with ivy twisting up and down, creaked like branches in the wind as he stretched and tested his strength. His legs bent strangely, ending in huge deer-like hooves, living wood. Part satyr, part tree, all newly-awoken god. I really can't emphasise just how big he was.

"Oh gosh," Teb said. I mentally high-fived the Green Man for being able to shake her, even when she seemed firmly avowed never to be shocked by something again. Though even I was failing to remove my gaze from the leafy, huge man yawning and stretching, looking like another tree in the grove, yet rather more phallic in places.

Alana tugged on my sleeve. "We need to give these goblins the slip and get away from here," she hissed in my ear. "I *really* don't want to get noticed by him, thank you very much. I am only a tiny person."

"Right," I said, mesmerised.

"What's wrong with Teb?" she asked. "Can you fix her so we can get out of here?"

Teb, blushing madly, had actually taken a step *forwards* on seeing the Green Man.

A hand waved in front of my face. "*Don't* tell me you have a crush on him suddenly as well," Alana groaned. Since when did I have a reputation for falling for the weird men?

No, the Green Man was *designed* to be insanely attractive, in a mad, animalistic way, and I had probably just had objective appreciation of the male physique ruined for ever for me, but I think I agreed with Alana—without sticking around to see if he had a nice personality as well, I was *not* going to be going over to say hi any time soon. Did I mention he had massive horns? Antlers, I mean. Don't look at me like that—I'm doing my best to describe him without describing, eh, *him*. God, I'm only a naïve teenager. Please can we move on from this subject?

"No!" I replied, a bit too late. "I mean, um, Teb's the one you should worry about. She's unstoppable."

"This is what the Piper meant when he told me to look after 'those girls'... That's what he said. I thought he was just lumping Teb in with you because, well, *Tanya*, and you were determined to run off and poke everything... I never thought Teb would need managing like you."

"You mean to say you could have left me alone for the last few days and stalked Teb instead?" I replied, thinking wistfully of peace and quiet.

"You know, there is a solution to our problems," Alana said, ignoring my apparent unhappiness with her company for the last few days. "You won't like it but it will give us time to go get Tanya, and free passage around the fairy world."

"What?" I asked.

"Leave Teb with him. I mean, look at her."

She was taking more baby steps towards him; she'd turned completely away from us so I only had the back of her head to go on, but the rest of her mannerisms didn't seem to be suggesting fear any more. The Green Man's minions were likewise gathering around him, goblins appearing from between the trees in their dozens: many of them were rather more regularly formed ugly green pixie things, mostly kind of human-shaped and styled, with huge dark eyes, sharp teeth and indeterminate gender, than the grubby mix-and-match creatures that were the skateboarding goblins. He seemed to be greeting them, if the low rumble of an alien voice was an indication.

I looked to Beaky. "What are you going to do with us?" I asked.

"Present you to the Green Man as a gift, of course."

"When?" Alana cut in.

"As soon as he's ready to have guests."

"Does he need to get dressed first?" I asked hopefully.

The two goblins laughed hard at that.

Maybe the sound drew the pixie over, or maybe it was just time to meet the first petitioners to this awoken king. A goblin with spikes like a hedgehog and a round, beady-eyed face waddled up to us on stumpy legs. It narrowed its eyes at us, peering above half-moon glasses perched on an upturned nose. It pushed the glasses up and gave us another look when that didn't make us any more obvious. "What are these?" it demanded of Beaky at last.

"Gifts, for the Green Man." Beaky gave Alana a smack on the behind to emphasise his point. She swung around and socked the goblin full in the face, knocking him over.

"Run!" she shouted, grabbed my arm, and legged it. I was dragged after her, panting and stumbling and concentrating on not flinging a flip-flop fifty feet away into the long grass.

Dealing with the Dancer

We got to the top of the hill, about where the town green should have been, before Alana stopped, doubled over and panting.

"That was the plan?" I gasped, falling to the ground to tremble like jelly until my limbs were working again. I couldn't *remember* the last time I'd run hard uphill… I'd stopped trying in P.E. classes years ago.

"No," she managed to cough out, and sat next to me. She flexed her punching hand, where a vivid red line crossed the tops of her fingers. She was going to have a really interesting bruise tomorrow… Somehow seeing that the goblins could suffer damage when punched made them feel a lot more real. They looked so odd my brain had clearly boxed them in with computer-generated creatures and assumed that, like in films, you could only appear to land a hit on them and someone would edit in the sound effects later by punching bags of flour. "That was unintentional, but pretty satisfying all the same. I don't regret punching that thing right on the beak. I think I read somewhere you could kill a bird by doing that. Hope it works on ugly goblins too."

"Where's Teb?" I raised myself up on my elbows and looked back at the sea of grass. There was a clear line that we'd beaten through it, but in the windless air the meadow had fallen still. Nothing was following us, friend or possible foe.

"She's buying us time," Alana said. "She must have heard and agreed with me when I said she should stay."

"She must have," I agreed, not because I thought it was true, but because I didn't like to think about Teb having defected because she was hormonal. I knew that there was a strong possibility she would up and give herself to a fearsome monster like the Green Man just because she was seventeen and like me had never had a boyfriend before and for her that meant she was a total idiot about anything that might possibly be attracted to her. Yes, even Teb had that problem. I'd seen her almost fall down a flight of stairs when Chris King said hello to her outside her Physics class. Tanya had been adamant we should set them up together, but trying to introduce Chris to our group had been met with a stronger rebuff than we'd ever seen from Teb, possibly because she was scared she'd eventually choke or trip to death if she stayed in his presence for long. When I'd dared to ask her months later how she felt about Chris, she had told me it didn't matter, he probably wasn't interested in her anyway, and froze me out for the rest of the conversation. With something like the Green Man it wasn't so much a possibility that he'd be attracted to her as a certainty. I thought about the maypole they dragged out for him each year at the summer festival and didn't have to wonder hard to guess what his role might be there. "I think we might all be pregnant just from looking at him," I ventured.

"Don't be an idiot," Alana said, although she sounded insecure as she said it. "He's just your harmless local god of spring."

"I wonder what that says about January daffodils," I said, and was ignored.

"We need to get moving," Alana said, peering around the landscape with narrowed eyes. "The green will spread faster near him, but the fact remains this whole land will be in spring by the end of the day. Just because we're still in winter on this patch of land doesn't mean it'll stay that way long. We need to find the Lady, and Tanya along with her."

"Well, if the Lady is winter, and he's summer... Should we go where it's snowing?"

"Snowing?" Alana asked, surprised.

I pointed up at the hills.

In the dim light it was hard to be sure of anything more than a few hundred yards away, but the hills definitely had a white-capped look to them and their trees. Think of how light it gets at nighttime in thick snow, when the light bounces between low clouds and the shining ground cover, to make a weird yellow pre-dawn light even at midnight. That was sort of how the fairy world was lit all the time, except blue, and the glow was strongest at the hills.

Sensing a moment of safety while Alana was still too puffed out herself to tell *me* to go anywhere, I took a moment to look around the rest of the area.

We were sitting in a stretch of shorter grey-blue grass which should have been the town green. Not only was it lacking the colour, it was missing the town to go with it. Just a short way away from us was a line of trees, the edge of the woods. It should have been the high street: it even followed the same route. But everywhere that should have been a house or a shop was another tree. The trees carried on behind that, rolling up the hills, covering everything that should have been my little patch of houses or the cleared fields.

There was one exception to the missing buildings: the church was still around… sort of.

It looked as if all the jumble sales it had hosted had been in vain: one side of the little steeple was gone. The walls had been assaulted too, but a pale glow persisted somewhere in the heart of the ruin, showing through the lead lattice left behind from the broken stained glass.

The huge mound of earth that it was built on top of was still around, though, and a much greater presence than the church. Local lore (and Tanya) insisted it was a burial mound. Right here and now anything seemed possible. I decided that it was time to stop being curious about everything before I met some actual zombies, and that was the only thought that stopped me getting up to go try and peer through one of the high windows to see what was glowing inside.

Perhaps sensing that I was getting restless, Alana struggled to her feet. "We should get moving." She cast a nervous glance back at the Green Man's grove. "You ready?"

I hauled myself back up, using her arm as leverage. "As long as I still have both my flip-flops, I can do anything."

"How have your feet not just, like, fallen off in protest?" she asked, with a curled lip.

It wasn't until we were into the woods that I began to feel a little worried. My meeting with the Piper meant that I had taken being captured by hideous goblins and witnessing the birth of a god with a rather calm head. I mean, he had said that he'd make sure I was safe, that he would help me. And he did not seem like the sort to make empty gestures. I trusted him. I *hoped* he wouldn't have sent me off here on my own if he thought I was going to get eaten by monsters or handed over for a "non-fatal" sacrifice within minutes of setting foot here.

But we had already lost Teb, quite probably for that sacrifice…

Things weren't exactly looking brighter for Alana and me either. We had walked into a forest of a density that I had never known. The obsessive amount of footpaths that the local conservationists cleared religiously was absent. Without a dozen volunteers regularly taking on the undergrowth with rake, shears and machete, we were walking through nettles that sometimes grew higher than I was tall. Even Alana struggled with some of the arches of brambles we came across, and she and the goblins had a lot more in common, height-wise, than I did. They'd left nothing but little rabbit trails where the nettles still touched one side to the other often as not. My ankles were soon covered in red bumps and itching furiously. Alana was exposing rather more skin than I was, and kept whimpering when we came across a new patch of stinging nettles.

While the air was still windless and empty, it was no longer completely temperate. There was a chill that closed around us and got more and more pronounced as we climbed. It was like going up a huge mountain in fast forward. Soon the day before yesterday felt like a warmer time to be reminisced cheerfully about. As frost appeared on the weirdly colourless leaves of the tangled undergrowth, the ground crunched beneath our feet, and the bare branches of the trees creaked under the weight of icicles. Our breath appeared in front of us and hung in little puffs where we had walked, no wind to carry it away.

When we saw snow we knew that we were close. As the snow grew deeper I wondered if the supports of the skate park had been built of re-purposed wardrobe, because there was something disturbingly Narnia-esque about this, except as far as I could recall no one had called "the Lady" a witch yet, and I wasn't sure if it was in the public domain yet anyway (that's when something becomes a bit of folklore, right?).

Teeth chattering, blue of toe, we stopped. Alana seemed to be listening intently, so I turned an ear the same way, hand cupped behind it, and affected an expression of aural concentration. Apparently this wasn't just a thing cartoon characters did, because I quickly became aware of noises coming from not far up the hill. Mostly it was light, rustling footsteps which I might have mistaken for wind in the trees if there had been any movement in the air, or leaves to throw around. Nothing seemed to be talking much.

The undergrowth was thinner here, and I realised that many paths crossed it. I started paying attention to more than watching snow pile up on the toes of my flip-flops as I scuffed over the ground, and thought I recognised the layout of the trees. I'd been here with Alana only yesterday… Whatever was going on here had been happening in exactly the same spot we'd been sitting.

"This is weird," I mumbled.

"*Now* you say that?"

A high sneeze suddenly echoed down from the stone circle, a very familiar cute "Tchoo! Tchoo!" that I'd been hearing pretty much all my life.

"Tanya's up there!" I hissed, and took a stumbling step forwards. Alana grabbed my arm and dragged me back, then led me a few paces behind a tree for good measure.

"Wait," she said in a low voice.

"What for?" I demanded.

"That place is crawling with pixies, and the Lady is there… She may not be the Green Man but she's just as bad in other ways. The Piper said she was cruel and possessive, and we don't know if Tanya is her prisoner or her guest. We have to decide which one we are too!"

"What, so we stroll up and say 'Hi, scary elf queen, mind if we drop by for lunch? I like what you did with the snowstorm this December?' or something?"

"Um… I suppose so. Look, I'll be honest, this is my first real foray into this place, and I've barely met any fairy things before. I told you I've only been working for the Piper for a few months. He gave me some basic guidelines on what to expect, and that was it. I don't think I'm even an apprentice… His job isn't one that requires a second fiddle and I'm definitely not getting much training. I think I'm just a chess piece he moves places, and since I know who he is that just makes it easier for him to make me go where he wants. I don't know what he wants me to do most of the time, or why he's telling me to do it…"

"So you have no idea how to deal with this situation either?" I began gnawing my lip in the silence that followed. Alana scuffed some snow about with her toe. I had a feeling she could have blundered across the Piper as stupidly as I had, and decided I really ought to stop treating her word as truth if that was the case. She suddenly seemed as useless and normal as me, and that was really reassuring on a friendship level, but I'd been rather relying on an Alana who seemed to know everything when I agreed to go on this mission.

"Well, we're doomed," I sighed.

Alana threw her hands up in despair. "Shall we assume you're always right when you're sarcastic and go say hi then?"

"Well, worst comes to worst, we can just be prisoners with Tanya, right? And if she's a prisoner she'll have a plan to get out because this is Tanya we're talking about. And knowing Tanya it relies on us being there, because she always knows what's going to happen somehow."

Alana nodded. "Okay, but don't just blunder in. Let's go."

We stood in the snow for a moment. A large drop of meltwater landed on Alana's hair and she clamped a hand over her mouth to hold back a swear.

"I think spring's coming this way," I said, looking nervously around. The snow already seemed diminished compared to a few minutes ago. The creaking, cracking noises of ice in the woods had changed to a rather drippier, wetter background ambience.

"What are you waiting for, then?" Alana hissed.

"You!"

We glared at each other for a moment.

"Together, then," she said, and held out a hand to me. I took it, and, perhaps just bolstered by how silly it would be to stand there holding hands and not doing anything else, we stepped out from behind the tree and helped pull each other up the remaining few steep feet of the hill.

The stone circle was the same as ever: I had been expecting something a lot more complete, like time had never happened to it, perhaps sucking the good repair from the church or something. But only a few stones remained, and if there was any difference it was that the ones that had fallen over still lay on their side on the site, rather than having rolled away down the hill or out of memory.

Floaties, the same as the weird lights that had mobbed me back in that field, hung in the air like, I guess, strings of fairy lights. Christmas lights, let's call them, so as not to be more confusing than this already is. The small space had been hung with purple and blue banners. Streamers and tinsel decorated the bare tree branches that hung over us.

The local population was a lot less freakish than the Green Man's entourage; they were what I'd assumed were pixies. They wore long white dresses and, though they hadn't quite grasped human proportions and tended towards being small and with extra long limbs and tiny bodies, more than a handful were passingly beautiful, looking like old watercolours of fairies. Some pixies at the side had a roaring fire that they were roasting a hog on, and beside which they were warming big clay mugs of cider, filling the air with the smells of a winter market: spices and charred meat. It was too cold to smell like the fair we'd just come from: the air was too crisp and clean, without hundreds of stinky humans to pollute it. This was very definitely the last holdout of the season. All it lacked was a bizarre cameo appearance from St. Nick, and to be honest it felt like it would be less out of place here than halfway across Planet Narnia. I'd always wondered what Father Christmas was doing there.

And of course, the whole point of this scene was the tall woman lying on the table slab like a reclining ancient queen on a sofa, except it was way too chilly to be fanned with palm leaves by slaves. She was bundled up in furs from some white fuzzy creature I really hoped didn't live in these woods, judging by the size of the skins it left behind. The pixies were swarming around the Lady, as well as doing chores such as the cooking, or just dancing for her entertainment. Her pale face was impassive: I wouldn't have fancied the job of keeping her amused when it was such a harsh face, all arched eyebrows, long sharp nose, and pointed chin. Most of the attention the pixies lavished on the Lady involved grooming and dressing her, rather less viscerally than the way the goblins had apparently assembled the Green Man from twigs and leaves.

Two pixies worked on putting the most elaborate braids into her jet-black hair, weaving spells that put little gold stars in as they went. Some were lacing her boots, tall and pointed with ribbons of spider silk (they had a webby sort of pattern, and since this wasn't a Spiderman cosplay I assumed that was the reason). To the side one pixie brushed out a long fur coat of brilliant gold and green, summer colours that looked stark and washed out here, never mind the fact that fairies apparently bred giant moss-green bears or something for their fur. Again, really would not like to meet them. The Lady wore a thin black dress, a neutral colour of neither season but every night, under the white fur wrap she huddled in at the moment. A couple of fairies were putting gold jewellery on her, and among them, looking perfectly cheerful and at peace with the world, completely native to the scene, was Tanya, sliding shiny silver bangles over wiry wrists as another fairy sat beside her to put heavy grey rings on the Lady's bony fingers.

As Mrs Potts had said, she was dressed up: far more than someone in the woods should be. Her terracotta-and-orange dress she'd bought for the debate society's one disastrous event had mud from the mid-calf hem right up the back, like she had slept on the ground in it, and there was a rip in the lining. Her hair had small bits of leaves and twigs in, and I guessed the messy bun she had it in was not how it had started her adventure. She had abandoned shoes entirely, and walked such big holes in her tights they'd basically just become leggings. Her nose was pink, her fingers bright red.

Alana stopped a respectful distance away, but I kept walking in my distracted state of gazing at my crazy, irresponsible friend and I released my grip on Alana's hand… I'd somehow blundered unthinkingly into the middle of the scene just like I'd been told not to; I wasn't scared enough of the fairies. I stood there with goldfish mouth going, taking in all the details. The Lady didn't even look up at me, but carried on quietly watching her dancers with her disinterested, sleepy look.

In the time I gawped a large blob of snow slid from a branch somewhere behind us. Tiny dark blue buds had pushed out of many of the twigs in the vibrating trees.

"Er, hello," I said.

The queen gave me a look which was almost impassive, save for a slight down turn at the side of her mouth. I think she was confused to see me. I would have been.

"Well met," the Lady eventually said, although phrased almost as a question.

As if she had been waiting for that cue, Tanya burst out with, "Hello Ally! How'd you find me?"

"Alana helped," I said, automatically gesturing over my shoulder. Alana, who had backed almost away behind one of the stones by that point, cringed and gave a little wave as all eyes turned to her. The fairies had all stopped what they were doing. Even the dancers had. One of them in particular seemed familiar, one with long red hair.

"Why have you come here, travellers?" the Lady asked. "My time is almost up. I am holding no court until November."

"Oh, um, we needed to talk to our friend," I said. "Just for a second, if you don't mind."

"I am getting ready to meet with my husband," she said coolly. (Just imagine everything she said was 'icily' or 'in a chilly tone').

"Er… Well, why don't you help the Lady, Alana, while I have a quick chat with Tanya?"

Alana's expression told me what she thought of that. But the Lady subsided back onto her stone recliner and stretched out her arm again. Perhaps only because angering the queen scared her more than serving enraged her, Alana scurried over to take Tanya's place. The bustling work of the fairies stirred up again.

I led my wayward friend aside.

"So, you and Alana teamed up, then? It's nice to see you making more friends!" Tanya chirruped as soon as we were standing beside one of the big stones, away from curious eyes.

"Do you have *any* idea how worried we were about you? What was this meant to prove?" I demanded.

"Then again, two friends might be all you can cope with before you start pulling all your hair out…"

"Normal friends don't run off to live with fairies without even leaving a note!"

"Normal friends are boring. I assume that's why Alana's here instead of Teb?"

"Um… Teb is here…" I instantly went down several gears, awkwardness reasserting itself over my attempt at motherly concern. "We kind of got a bit separated."

"Oh dear," Tanya sighed, like I'd told her we had run out of custard creams. "What did she go chasing after?"

"The Green Man."

"What?" Tanya grabbed both my arms and shook me. It took me a while to realise that she wasn't still joking around. "What happened?" she demanded, voice as hard as ice. (*Her* new friend had rubbed off on her as well, apparently.)

"We got captured because Teb ran off to watch when he woke up, and she opted to stay behind to give us a chance to find you…"

"Is that what she said?" Tanya demanded, but didn't wait for an answer, thankfully. "How could you let her do that? Why didn't you make sure that she came with you? You left me to fend for myself for two nights here: you clearly weren't worried that I was in immediate danger."

"Well, I didn't know how to find you…"

I was ignored, since Tanya was mid-rant. "But you didn't even notice when Teb blatantly was? I thought you were the sensible one!"

A badly timed laugh burst out of me. "The sensible one? Now I know you've cracked!"

"Okay, say the three of us are walking along and we see a wall with a sign that says, 'No Entry'. What happens?"

"You climb over the wall?"

"Come on, Ally. Don't disappoint me again. Overthink this! It's your superpower!"

"Well, okay, so Teb would be all like, 'climb over it! I bet you wouldn't!' and I'd freak out and say we'd all die and get arrested, and then you'd do it anyway… I don't see how that makes me sensible. I could still be bullied over the wall but Teb would never go. She's the sensible one."

"She's the one standing there saying how fun it would be to do something reckless! You don't give me enough credit. I always listen to how much you're freaking out… I only do it anyway if we both know you're just being stupid. You *normally* have really good self-preservation instincts and concern for others that Teb and I both lack. I still don't see how you failed to freak out about Teb and the Green Man."

"I… I blame the Piper."

"The Piper?"

"Uh, you met him, I'm sure of that." I felt my cheeks growing hot, which would have been welcome in the cold air except that I so did not want Tanya to correctly interpret why I had gone so pink.

"I mean, how are you blaming him? Is he here? Did he give Teb to the Green Man?" If anything her grip on me and steely look in her pale eyes got *more* intense.

"Um. I'm not sure… Uh…"

"Are you… blushing?"

"No!" I cried, instantly elevating the mild pinkness in my cheeks to a full-faced beetroot.

"Oh Ally… A first time for everything. I suppose we need to go save Teb from herself now. I'll make my excuses here." She let go of me and glanced over at the Lady, reclining quietly and probably listening to every word we were saying, no matter how sleepy she pretended to be.

I grimaced. "We might not have much time for that. I came to warn you the Green Man is on his way and he wants you."

"What would he want with me? I'm just a visitor here. I haven't interfered in anything."

"Well he might not know about you yet, but when he does he will want you. I guess he's all these rubbish male stereotypes like he thinks anything belonging to his wife is his? So when she goes to sleep for the summer you're going to be his property instead."

"I'll just be his guest… I can leave. The fairies didn't capture me. We haven't made any trades and I haven't eaten anything…" Tanya rubbed her stomach, letting on a little of her discomfort for the first time. "And that cider smells *fantastic.*"

"It doesn't matter. The Piper made it pretty clear this is not a good host…"

"Again, *why* did you leave Teb alone with him?"

"We came here to rescue *you!*" I complained. I was getting almost tearful with frustration. This wasn't how it was meant to go. I hadn't expected to find Tanya ready to pack up and walk off with us… Or for her to be *angry* with me for coming to get her. "I thought it was all costs to get *you* back."

Our argument was cut short when Tanya saw the leaves behind me. There hadn't *been* any leaves behind me when we had started talking.

"He's coming," she said, pointing to a nearby twig which had white blossoms rapidly appearing all down it. "Come on, we have to get out of the way."

"With me," said an unexpected voice. We turned to see the red-haired pixie standing by us. While I was busy jumping violently and miming a heart attack, Tanya said, "Oh, hey Cathy!"

'Cathy' led us around the edge of the circle and gestured for us to sit beside the fire. Alana came scurrying over and sat with us.

"So?"

"We've got to go save Teb, but first the Green Man's coming here," Tanya explained in a low voice. Of course she was in charge. "I suppose we see if she's with him or not and then plan based on that."

"He will come alone," Cathy assured us.

"Well why are we still here?" Alana asked.

"I cannot leave my Lady until she goes off with him," Cathy said. "I wish to help you."

"*Why?*" Alana said.

"I recognise this girl," she said, pointing to me.

"*Me?*" I said.

"You know Ian."

"Do I?" I turned blankly to Tanya, who shrugged.

"Ally, don't make any deals with her," Alana groaned. "Fairies always want to make deals for some reason and it never works out."

"You are from the college, are you not?" the pixie pressed, ignoring Alana.

"I'd hardly say it's our primary identity, but… yes." I suddenly thought of where she might know me from aside from when we'd seen her dance in the town centre. I decided not to mention it. Was something actually about to make sense here? I could hardly believe it.

"Is this… something to do with Mr Brooke, our history teacher?"

"Ian! Yes!" Cathy said, clapping her hands together with delight. Apparently teachers had first names and other people used them. That was disturbing all by itself.

"Didn't you get him attacked by evil spirits or something?" I asked.

The effect on Cathy was to instantly crush her bubbling excitement into a tearful shaking wreck. "He was *what?*" she asked in a quavering voice.

"You know," I said uncomfortably. "That morning when you came to the school… After that he was… was…"

"I didn't know!" she cried. "Oh! I would have gone back at once, but the Piper had been chasing me for three days! I knew he'd take me away soon. I'd seen him the night before! He played outside Ian's house… I knew my time was almost over… Oh, Ian…" And she broke off into more sobbing. Outside *Ian's* house? How many places could the Piper go in a night? Or was it…

As the pixie began to get loud and embarrassing with her weeping I awkwardly patted her on the shoulder, looking to the others for help. Alana and Tanya both shrugged at the same time. Tanya made a complicated series of gestures which I think meant something like "She likes you! What does she want?"

"Um…" I ventured. "What… What could I do for you? To make it better?"

"Oh!" Cathy sobbed wretchedly. "I wanted you to tell him from me that I'd be back as soon as I could, but… but… Will he even want me any more after this?"

I thought about how leggy and pretty she'd been when she wasn't a slightly alien little creature with dark eyes, pointed ears and sharp teeth. Also a bright red nose from the sniffling at the moment. "He'd take you back," I said. "Why can't you go back now?"

"The Green Man always demands a full court," Alana said. "He's only got two months in his humanish form, so he makes the most of them to rule this place and set summer in motion. It takes a lot of work to unravel the Lady's winter.

That's why we needed to get Tanya out of here before he claimed her: even if he intended to let her go, it wouldn't be until May and there would be no arguing with that."

"Well, I'll go to 'Ian' and tell him you've had to go home for, er, a family emergency," I said. "We'll just say I'm a friend of yours and that you're going back to… rural Ireland? That makes sense with the red hair, right?"

"Not with the accent," Alana said. "She sounds local."

"So does Teb, but her parents are from India or somewhere," I pointed out. "Anyway, clearly your family farm doesn't have internet or a phone line, right, Cathy?"

She looked blankly at me. "What farm?"

"I mean, you can't communicate with him while you're here and that will explain why, and he'll be so shaken up from being possessed he might not remember what you even said to him when you said goodbye, so I can make up anything, really, and tell him that he's wrong if he remembers anything to the contrary."

"I… fairies can't lie."

"Humans can," I said. "It's what we're for!"

"How would I… When I come back…"

"Well how did he not find out you were a fairy when you were seeing him before?"

"I just didn't say."

"Come on, pixies are good at dodging questions then. You don't have to say anything untrue to go along with my story. Maybe just say you don't want to talk about it, and hug him or something? He'll forget or forgive you… And I'll do all the talking next time I see him, so he won't need to ask you any questions."

"Thank you," she said softly. "Offering to lie for me… Breaking your honour for a pixie you barely even know…"

"It's no big deal," I said uncomfortably.

"Don't undersell it!" Tanya said. "It's a *huge*, *important* thing you are doing for this pixie. You, a totally good human, are laying down the whole *core of your being* to ensure her happiness! Why, it's the most selfless thing anyone has ever done, I'm sure."

Apparently fairies were immune to hyperbole. Cathy's eyes brimmed up again and she flung herself at me, squeezing me hard. "I will do everything I can to ensure you and your friends can return to your world, so you may lie for me!" she promised.

And that was how I made a deal with a fairy not minutes after Alana warned me not to make any deals with fairies.

Summer Queen

We didn't have long to sit around feeling slightly uncomfortable about the over-emotional pixie that we had befriended hugging all of us in turn over and over. A hush fell over the already muted proceedings at the stone circle, and then we heard his approach.

The trees around us had bloomed first, but turned green last: the blue suddenly leached out of them, and in moments the weird dreamlike darkness of the scene was replaced with the heady scent of warm air and summer flowers. The ground steamed as the last of the snow vanished, and the tall standing stones glistened with meltwater. The very grass around us seemed to stand up taller, almost like the hairs that were raising on our arms. The world glowed liked the sun shone from behind each leaf and blade of grass, though a glance upwards through the now thick canopy of leaves was all the reminder I needed we were under the black, cave-like sky.

Then we heard the crunching of heavy footsteps coming our way. I'll never know how the Green Man navigated the woods which had flummoxed two girls of reasonable proportions, but he came out from between the trees, antlers still wider than most doorways, a hulking eight foot figure. Having barky legs, the nettles presumably did not bother him so much.

The Lady leapt to her feet, the brightly coloured furs sliding from one shoulder. So far she'd been completely lethargic, barely bothering to move her own limbs when a pixie could feed her sips of fairy cider instead. But with the arrival of the Green Man, each movement was as sharp as snapping elastic. She practically quivered from the speed with which she righted herself. And then the two of them stood perfectly still, facing each other, shining silver eyes meeting gold.

The Green Man only had eyes for her, and even at a much closer range than before I was rather less scared of him. He seemed far less likely to glance around and decide he wanted me for a side course. His eyes, more magnificent than gold discs heavily studded with emeralds, barely blinked as they watched her.

Slowly, her furry shawl slid from her arms and landed on the ground. In the instant of its soft flump to the wet grass she transformed into an elegant black and silver doe. Her pale underside turned into speckles like stars across her flanks. Her small antlers shone like they were cast in real silver, and bang in the middle of her forehead was a crescent moon in white fur. Her breath poured out in clouds like she was standing in an icy forest, because where's logic even gone here, and then she bolted into the undergrowth.

The Green Man didn't spare a look at the rest of the pixies, but fell to all fours, likewise a huge green and gold stag by the time he needed front hooves to stay upright. His head raised, shaking out a mane of leaves, and he let out a terrible throaty bellow, steam rising from mossy green flanks. Then he charged after her and was gone.

As the hoofbeats faded, Tanya cried, "That was *it*? I spent five hours dressing her like an overgrown Barbie doll for him to look at her for three seconds, and then they were *deer*? Oh, come on, let's go get Teb and go home."

Utterly fed up with fairies, she pulled herself to her feet and marched off out of the circle without a look back at us.

Still dumbfounded by the utter magnificence we'd beheld, it took me a little longer to shake my head clear and follow. The pixies around us were quietly packing up, taking down decorations and boxing up the discarded garments of their queen. One came over and politely doused the fire in front of us.

"Let's go," Alana said, shaken out of her musings by this action. She and Cathy led the way out of the circle, with me tripping after them. We hurried to catch up with Tanya.

She had stopped a short way down the path to give us a chance. She grinned at us as we trudged down the damp path, the same huge toothy grin Tanya always used when she thought she had got away with something, and she offered me her arm when I was at her side. Despite it being so hard to pick through the woods walking two by two, I did my best. I wanted to talk to her some more anyway.

"So... Did you really decide to run off just to drag me in after you? Or was it that you were compelled to go? You would have gone whatever conversation we'd had? Like when the Piper pulled you through by mistake, did he miss some magic that made you come back?" I'd been hoping it was something like that.

"Of course not: I'd just seen the fairy world for the first time in my life. You think I'd just go home and eat biscuits and maybe update my blog about it? I had to see more. Who *wouldn't* investigate if they just found out that it existed? I was going to offer to bring you along, but you sounded so snooty about it on the phone…" She shrugged. "I thought it would be too much trouble to try and talk you into it when I was burning to go back."

"So *all* this was because you were curious?"

She shrugged again. "I've had adventures with the supernatural before, but always in our world. Boring."

"You were using the real name of this place in your games." Now I just sounded sulky.

She grinned at me.

"Did you *know* the Green Man was going to stake a claim on you?"

"I honestly had it under control. *Really*. If you hadn't come, I was fully planning to make my way back right now anyway. I knew the powers that be would be rather distracted for at *least* an hour when they met. If anything, you being here and bringing Teb just puts me, and all of you, in more danger because it'll take longer to escape."

"She's not lying," Cathy said. "I was to walk her to the grove portal after this. I was going to use that as my opportunity to get a message to Ian, but when his neighbour appeared…" She beamed at me.

"N-neighbour?" I asked, to the accompaniment of an embarrassed flip in my stomach… I'd been sort of hoping she wouldn't get around to explaining her earlier comments.

"Did you not know? Ian lives next to you! I have seen you come and go from your house several times."

"But… if you were staying with Mr Brooke, next to me… And the Piper was following you…" Oh my gods. He really hadn't been thinking about me at all when I saw him that first night. I'd somehow assumed it was special, like a destined meeting. Like he'd gone and sat there just to annoy me, to relay that message to me. But there may well have been no need for it at all if I hadn't been so bad at sleeping.

I'd stumbled onto him while he was working and he'd spent the next two days trying to keep me out of the way because I kept on making his simple job with Mr Brooke and Cathy so much more difficult, with the poking and the dragging my susceptible friend over to watch the banishment, accidentally getting her banished at the same time and then asking too many questions when she got back… I didn't feel like an exciting adventurer any more. I felt like someone who was always clumsily underfoot, who the Piper was dealing with on top of everything else. I must have annoyed him so much… How he had managed to keep a good humour about the whole thing… And that explained why he'd almost sacrificed me to the Green Man, like he said. It would get me out of his hair. He hadn't realised there was anything special about our meeting. Maybe he still didn't. Maybe he took the opportunity to randomly kiss as many girls as he bumped into… He had *said* it was just a spell, however much he'd seemed to enjoy it…

"Uuurgh, I'm such an idiot," I complained out loud.

"Come on, it's not like you were *trying* to stalk Mr Brooke," Tanya said. "I've never seen half my neighbours coming in and out of their houses. For all I know Leonardo DiCaprio lives across the road from me. A history teacher is easy to overlook."

"What?" Alana asked

"What what?" Tanya mirrored.

"Never mind," I grumbled.

"Aw, come on. This isn't about how you are still bitter about the ending of *Titanic* ten years after you first stole Teb's mum's DVD and we watched it under the covers at my house?"

"There was room for them both on that door and you know it!"

"What on *earth* are you two talking about?" Alana asked.

"Life-altering experience, the 1997 movie *Titanic*?"

"Yes I know that, but *why*? We're walking through the middle of fairy land with an actual pixie in our company and all you two can do is bicker about a film? Really?"

"Sorry, Alana," Tanya said cheerfully. "Ally, what do you suppose the symbolism even is that the Lady chose the stone circle to live in? It's traditionally a solar calendar, but she's not even the sun god here; that's the Green Man's job."

"Can we go back to complaining about blockbuster films?" I begged.

*

I have to say I enjoyed the warmth that wasn't even yet showing a hint of itself back in the town we knew (I should know—I'd spent too long wandering around in a T-shirt in that winter air). It made it tempting to saunter and enjoy the summer, because no matter how many gods we crammed under the town, nothing could stop a March day from being miserable. In fact, I had now met the goddess responsible for making it more miserable.

When we broke the tree line, we were in about the same place we'd entered the woods, heading back towards the town green. Back out in the open I was struck by how the sky was still dark. With all the brightly glowing trees, and the very summery feeling in the air, I had forgotten just how creepy and underground-feeling this world was. The sky was a little greener, but only in the way the night sky normally has a faint shade of blue to it.

As we grew closer, the hazy green air revealed a sight I'd rather not have seen or have to describe again either: both twenty foot tall, the Green Man and Lady were stretched out across half the green, *writhing* together. Yes, I'm not dumb, but I'm not writing porn either. Ew.

"Well, isn't that nice," Alana snorted.

"Now what?" I asked. "Can we just go around?"

"Best to," Alana agreed, and we started edging around the field.

I was determined not to watch the ridiculous display of public affection, but Tanya seemed fascinated: ahead of me there was a stream of comments like, "Woah, girl!" "I did not *know* you could do that… Huh." and "I'll remember that one for my wedding night…"

I poked her in the back to keep her moving when she stopped to gawp.

When we were safely down the road and they were out of sight, she turned and gave me a huffy look. "Why are you looking so red and uncomfortable? You weren't even watching!"

"I didn't *need* to with you commentating!"

"Life doesn't have a PG-thirteen rating," Tanya complained.

"Well it should." I grumbled.

We carried on walking, scowling at each other. But Tanya poked her tongue out at me and I laughed and then I had to put Alana between us so I could sulk in peace without her ruining it by making me like her again. Unfortunately, as my best friend since forever, that was extremely easy for her to do.

That way we got back to the Green Man's grove without much more incident or even pointless conversations about off-topic movies.

The grove was still pretty busy, but there were definitely fewer goblins in the area. They were hurriedly dismantling the scene from before, replacing all the natural greens that the new summer trees had swallowed up with something flashier. I saw Piggy and Beaky (still alive, unfortunately) struggling by with a heavy roll of golden cloth between them, not sparing a glance our way. Royal colours with gilt edges shone from banners strung around the branches. With an application of cushions and an elegantly spun frame of yet more gold, a jutting root of the tree had become a throne.

Teb was sitting in the middle of this scene on a heap of green and gold cushions, reclining in a way disturbingly reminiscent of the Lady. I felt almost as scared about approaching her.

She had been dressed royally, fantastic golden cloth draped around her more like a toga than a modest dress. A fair amount of bling had been piled onto her as well, shining on her wrists and neck, huge earrings that were strings of coins. Her hair had gold braids running through it. Suddenly the Lady's decision to only wear silver looked rather classy instead of a second best to the riches of the Green Man. Teb looked like a child who'd raided a princess's jewellery box, and the huge smug grin wasn't helping. She didn't look like a child. She looked like a dragon sitting on its hoard.

She saw us and waved us over with a reasonably friendly expression. When we were standing in front of her, she gestured elegantly at the bare earth in front of her. "You may sit."

We glanced at each other, then crouched or kneeled on the uncomfortable ground. Tanya merrily sat cross-legged despite the dress she was wearing, since it was ruined anyway. I almost toppled over from my non-committal crouching, and hastily copied Tanya's pose. Alana folded her arms but remained standing.

"We found Tanya." I gestured said friend. "Come on, we'd better get going before the Green Man comes back. Thanks for distracting him, by the way."

"Why?" Teb said. "I want to stay a bit longer. Tanya had her fun here. Why can't I?"

I blinked at Teb stupidly, wondering what she was playing at. What the end game was here.

"Just take those stupid bangles off and let's go," Alana grumbled, not in the mood for sugar-coating. "We don't have much time."

"No," Teb said. "I like it here. The goblins have been lovely!"

"They're little perverts," Tanya said, cheerfully, so I hoped nothing had happened to her. "You don't want to overstay your welcome, trust me. They help you because you're lying about in a translucent dress which wouldn't leave much to the imagination if it *wasn't* made of cheap fairy-gold tissue paper."

"Well I'm waiting for the Green Man to come back. He said I could be his summer queen."

"Do you even know what that means?" Tanya asked, now also tipping her head and giving Teb a longer and more thoughtful look. "You're not going to be royalty..."

"You're jealous I got the attention off the Green Man, aren't you? You just got some boring winter queen in your time here. You wouldn't want to kiss her even if she wasn't frigid as an icicle."

I decided not to weigh in on what we'd witnessed just up the hill from here. Apparently Tanya was too busy taking Teb's comment personally to remember or analyse.

"I wouldn't be bothered if she *did* want to kiss me. I've kissed a dozen guys already... I didn't turn my first kiss into some sort of religious event like you are. *Literally*."

"Oh my god, you slut!" Teb laughed, meaning it in that joking friend way, but naturally it was hard to feel it while she was dazed with power. "When did you even find time?"

"Um, we go to a college full of male specimens? Not all of them are the dweebs you think they are. I mean, I didn't fancy dating any of them in the end, but it was worth a go..."

"Well at least *Ally* has the sense not to let morons steal her first kiss."

"Heh," I said. I still wasn't decided on that moron thing anyway. It was me or the Piper who was the moron, and for once I wasn't completely sure it had to end up going my way.

Teb's eyes narrowed at me. "Not you too! I thought we agreed boys were stupid!" She really did sound like she'd been dazed back to a playground mentality, but Teb was sharp, always, even when she seemed to be completely unable to see the bigger picture here.

"We were *eleven* when we said that... That was seven years ago. And, um... We should... go. Don't you think that's more important?"

"Oh my god, it was the Piper, wasn't it?" Tanya butted in, distracted into the playground gossip of who was pulling whose pigtails.

I went pink and hunkered down, looking intensely at the dirt in front of me. Tanya was far braver than I was to even risk Teb's wrath on this matter. Had I avoided boys this long just because I didn't want this reaction from her? I agreed with her that I'd never want to marry any of the boys from college, at least in their current larval state, but maybe I would be weirdly more balanced, like Tanya, if I had been braver and dared to live a little. I think it said a lot about what had been done to Teb and her filters and walls that I had suddenly realised for the first time that Tanya was the normal one here.

On the other hand, perhaps my moment with the Piper would not have felt so special... Perhaps I would not have had it at all if I had been an average teen, who texted and giggled about boys and lived or died by the attention they gave me.

"Oh my *god*," Teb complained, echoing Tanya's words with much more displeasure and more than a little despair. "Even *Ally* beat me to having a first kiss? Urgh!"

"Now we've established you're the biggest loser, and nothing, not even making out with the god of summer, will fix that, how about we stop being so stupid and go?" Alana suggested.

I looked up to see Teb's furious expression. She was clearly of the belief that *only* making out with the Green Man would solve her problem of me beating her to the finish line for not being a total loser who failed the basic premise of going to school with fellow teenagers. Which I had still technically failed as well, since the Piper was not enrolled at the college... *As far as I knew* (Wait for the sequel, when we segue into a high school anime and somehow we all have to wear Japanese school uniforms all of a sudden, never mind we were leaving in a couple of months).

"It was hardly a real kiss," I lied, because I wanted her to drop this and then drop the Green Man. "I mean, he basically just grabbed me to un-magic me and it was the fastest way to do it. It's not like we're going out or anything now. You could still be the first of us to get a real boyfriend. I mean, you always complain about all the boys in your science classes trying to get your attention... But some of them are reasonably cute and any of them would be your boyfriend in a second if you asked. Chris King is nice! He keeps holding doors for you and getting stuck with, like, the entire of the year nine group coming through under his arm!"

"All of them? They're so... *boring*."

"Cross my heart, boring guys are fine," Tanya said, thankfully getting back on task with wheedling Teb. "Interesting ones always have loads of issues anyway. It's what makes them interesting. Like that guy in my philosophy class with the pale make-up? He asked me out and I thought, 'well okay then, people will talk!' But by the time we got off the bus in Bilsworth I decided he wasn't worth the movie he was going to take me to. So *angsty*. And I don't own enough black clothes to keep up.”

“But you still kissed him, right?” Teb pointed out.

“Well yeah, just in case he did have some redeeming factors.”

Teb scowled. She may have been annoyed Tanya never told her all this, but considering the amount of fun Teb would have made in normal circumstances, I could understand it.

“Come on, Teb,” I said. “You’re never normally the one who climbs over the wall. You make me and Tanya do all the dangerous stuff so you can make fun of us. Why are you being this way now?”

“Because maybe I’m fed up of you two always running around having all the adventures!” she snapped, some of the clarity coming back to her eyes in a way that wasn’t exactly helpful. “Maybe I want to do something everyone will talk about for a change! I’ve done nothing but study since we started the GCSEs and now the A Levels are almost over and I’m still as boring and rubbish as I was four years ago… And you and Tanya always have some ridiculous story to tell! The actual Pied fucking Piper outside your bedroom window! Accidental day trips to the fairy world! I want to be a part of it! And then Alana comes along and she’s suddenly doing all this stuff with you as well and I’m even more left out!”

“Er, thinking of leaving out, why don’t you just leave me out of this?” Alana said, shuffling back a little.

“No! What makes you so special? Why do you get to start telling us what to do? What did you do to make this weird Piper thing take you on to work for him? What are you even?”

“She’s helping us!” I butted in, my loyalty to Teb quickly evaporating as I saw how much of a brat she’d become. Maybe the fairy gold was enchanted and she had a spell on her to make her want to stay… Maybe she really had been sitting with us day after day thinking how unfair we were when all she should have done was stop passive-aggressively trying to get us in trouble so she could have something to laugh at, and just joined in. Knowing Teb, it was actually suddenly very hard to tell myself it was the first thing, no matter how obvious it had been a moment ago. “That’s all you need to know, and if you ever gave her the time of day instead of trying to bully her away because you’re jealous that we can make friends who aren’t you, maybe you’ll find out more one day. I’m not even asking about how she knows about fairies and portals to other worlds and demons and things… I trust her to tell us in her own time. Maybe some things you don’t have to tell friends you’ve only known three days, but they can still be friends.”

Alana rubbed her eyes, and I think she needed a few seconds to do that before she could speak. She sounded choked up. “It’s okay, Ally. Calm down.” She turned to Teb. “What I did wasn’t special… I was as stupid as you are now when I found out about the supernatural living on our doorstep. But I work for the Piper now: he saved me from myself, and now I’m here to help others do the same, because he gave me back my life and I feel I should pass on the favour. *That* is all you need to know. Well, that and the witchcraft. Did I mention the witchcraft?"

"No," I said.

"Well it works a hell of a lot better in this world, so I am about ready to curse Teb stupid and carry her out of here. The Green Man may not be much longer, and I'd rather not get caught just sitting around here like a willing sacrifice." Just like that tearful Alana was gone, and the fiery girl I knew a lot better was back. It was almost a relief. Except for the part where she was terrifying.

"You wouldn't dare," Teb said.

"Watch me," Alana said. She stood up and raised her hands.

"Wait!" I complained. "You can't just curse Teb! I mean, she's our friend!"

"I've known her two days. I don't really care," Alana said.

"But she's still *my* friend," I said.

Alana hesitated. "How about we just give Teb to the Green Man, on the condition he takes his 'sacrifice' from her, and then we scram?"

"Alana!" I complained.

"What? Just because no one's said it yet doesn't mean she isn't practically begging for him to fuck her on the grass same as he's doing to the Lady right now... They can't *actually* hold her against her will with their magic. If she wanted to go, she'd go."

I quickly turned to our so-far silent companion, feeling my cheeks heating up again and tears prickling my eyes to hear the way Alana talked. Mostly because I was scared it was true. We were seventeen or eighteen. We were adults. And we had taken too long for that fact to catch up with us, comfortable in our little bubble, and now that it had... It hurt to think of my friend putting a random god she'd just met in front of me and Tanya. "Cathy... What can you do?"

"Teb wants to be here," she confirmed. "I can't do anything about that... Maybe we *should* wait for the Green Man to come back. We could find something to trade with him so we can take her back with us."

"But what do we have?" I complained.

We looked hopelessly at each other. We hadn't come to this world with anything more than the flip-flops on our feet. Well, I hadn't anyway. Equivalent for the others, except with more sensible fashion choices.

Tanya reached up and thoughtfully pulled on the hair tie holding up her bun. The fine blonde hair quickly unravelled itself. "We have Ally," she said, fluffing up her hair in a way I'd only seen her do once before: the time she smacked Jess Standerwick in the face the time she tried to convince Tanya she could do with a better set of bimbo friends. She was about two seconds away from smearing mud on her face like warpaint. "That would do."

"Do what?" Alana demanded.

"Yes, what?" Teb asked, struggling to sit up to scowl at me properly, like I had a hidden weapon in my jeans pockets.

"Please tell," I added in a tiny voice.

Tanya grinned, and beckoned me aside.

Awesome Coat

I instantly lost all hope in Tanya's barely explained plan the moment I was standing in front of the Green Man.

The god of summer was seated in the throne, having shown up right about the time the goblins finished buzzing around making everything perfect. The woods had filled up too: hundreds of fairies of various descriptions were packed into the grove now. The most magnificent were standing or seated close at hand. Higher in the trees, or bustling around at the back, dozens more of the lesser sort of goblins still pulled strings behind the scenes. Cathy had taken a place with a group of other handmaidens to the Lady. Of the winter goddess there was no sign: Alana had explained that she'd gone back to the stone circle to sleep off the summer until the first frost. Maybe she needed all that time to recover from her liaison with the Green Man, a thought that made me none the more confident about talking to him.

Teb had been moved next to the throne, and the Green Man had paid her plenty of the attention she craved already, kissing her and holding her between meetings with the various goblin high command who came to petition him. It made me feel ill to see her perched on his knee, the blissful smile on her face... It was most sickening that she was too bedazzled to even look back to smirk at us. I had to hope there was still at least a little mood-altering magic at work here, making her chill, whereas the Piper had made her grumpy and headachey: it was maybe the only way I could have my friend back when this was over, and the only thought that was keeping me fighting.

The hedgehog-spined goblin in half-moon glasses had been rushing around sorting out the court, and had determined the order of our petition. Since there were a lot of fairy politics to sort out first, well before our human problems, we had been standing at the edge of the crowd, watching proceedings for some time. I had actually forgotten the script that Tanya had suggested completely by the time Spike came scuttling up to us and told me to step out to stand before the king when the last petitioners left.

So I stumbled on out, feeling all the curious dark eyes on me. The crowd rustled with wings and stomped hooves, chattered like monkeys and squirrels and birds, but fell silent when I attempted my traditional greeting, giving a wobbly curtsey before the Green Man.

"Um… Hi?"

His gold eyes watched me steadily. I crossed and uncrossed my arms, feeling flustered. I was far from traditionally attractive, with neither figure *nor* looks nor personality to help. Somehow his gaze broke through that shell. I was female and therefore attractive and he would find a way to make my awkward elbows and knees and snorty laugh the most sexy thing that could ever be beheld. He would dress me in gold and sit me on his knee like he had with Teb…

I snorted with laughter.

No, that was just stupid.

"Mr Green Man," I said, starting again. "I would like to propose a trade with you."

He nodded.

"Um, okay, so, right. There's Teb here, and, um, Tanya there, right?" I gestured Tanya, standing with all her blonde hair finger-combed out and loose, her dress pulled down off one shoulder a little to throw some befuddlement into the mix for him (and bewilderment to me that she wasn't talking to him herself). "Following me so far? Okay, so Tanya was here with the Lady, right, and she was her guest, except she's still here so you own her now except you don't because she's your guest. And as I understand it you can't own guests because they didn't eat anything or something like that. I think that's fairies, someone said something about it earlier. Maybe it's also the underworld too? Or is this actually the underworld? We're underground, aren't we? I'm not entirely clear on the cosmology. Although I suppose there would be more dead people around and I'm not even sure there are zombies in the church…

"*Anyway*, either way, guests are somehow important here, I gather, and, like, you don't own me or anything because all I've done is wander around and look at things. Teb here, you seem to have already met. I think she wants to trade herself for Tanya. Or Tanya wants to trade herself for Teb or something. I'm not entirely sure any more. We went over this but Tanya was being all 'FAIRY LOGIC! FAIRY LOGIC!' and so I think she wants to say she wants to trade with Teb and she was here first so maybe Teb's staying? I can't remember if I'm supposed to be speaking backwards or not. But basically we want to just offer you Teb, right? And Teb wants to stay here, so that's all fair, right, but we don't want Teb to stay, which is why we're offering to trade Tanya for her, since you don't actually own Tanya yet, but then I think the point was Teb hasn't actually made a formal sort of 'I want to stay here' gesture either so she's also just your guest so you don't own either of them yet? Or us."

I glanced over my shoulder at Tanya. She gave me a thumbs up. I think Alana was crying. Jury out on laughter or horror.

"Um. Hang on, I think I lied about the wrong thing there. Can I start over? Basically what I am trying to say is that we want to take Teb back with us so we're offering a trade and maybe it's actually up to you which one you trade for which but it doesn't matter because you don't actually have either of them? And I'm just supposed to make you see that? Maybe? Anyway—"

"*Stop. Please stop*," Spike complained, scurrying forward, carrying a long scroll of paper and a broken quill that was, to my surprise, literally smoking from the speed he'd written my words down at. "Can you repeat that a little more slowly?"

I took a deep breath.

I almost choked when the sound carried on, turning into a high-pitched note from a wind instrument: I hadn't realised I'd stopped breathing in and I had to start coughing to make sure I was using my lungs correctly.

Meanwhile the playing continued.

"Aw crap, you destroyed logic forever," Tanya complained as the music grew louder. I *think* what had actually happened was Alana summoned the Piper, but it could well have been me. Come to think of it, there hadn't been a script: Tanya had just said, "Babble about who owns who until something happens"… It was a plan we all knew I could remember.

"So now the world itself has no idea which one of you and Teb is meant to be here?" I asked hopefully. "You were all trying to work out what I was saying? Because if you want to be more confused I could attempt to explain that Tanya was basically an illegal immigrant here, working even though she was only a visitor, and since she still hasn't eaten anything and isn't a part of this world, her visa is technically invalid. She didn't get a work visa so technically she should be deported for working for the Lady. I mean, not like a literal visa, but there are rules for visiting, aren't there? None of us were tricked into this world except for Tanya technically once, but the Piper brought her back and that was all squared off except then she came for her holiday and…"

"That's enough, you've confused even me." The Piper stopped behind me, and cut off my desperate speech by putting a hand on my shoulder. Shakespeare I was *not*. "Well met," he said to the court at large.

I didn't dare turn, though I was addressing him sort of when I tried to clear things up a bit more. "Okay, but when you're sorting this out, is there anything about the gifts that Teb took from the fairies which affect this in any way? I mean, the Green Man gave her a lot of presents, but does that give her an obligation to stay or does it mean she has to leave because…"

The Green Man suddenly decided to weigh in on this matter. Having watched and maybe followed all of it, he gave a bright, sunny laugh that came from deep inside, cutting off my latest ramble. I found my eyes fixed to him again, as my memory filled up with all those beautiful summer days I'd lived through. For the first time he spoke, and I understood him underneath all the rumbling. Perhaps because the words were about me: "I will keep them all."

"*No*," said the Piper behind me. He took another dramatic stride forwards to stand directly next to me. I glanced out of the corner of my eye and saw The Coat. It was everything I could ever have dreamed of: floor-length, black and white leather, sewn together with big thick stitches and lots of safety pins. The side facing me, the main length of the coat, was black, with a long white sleeve and heavy collar, spotted with mismatched black buttons. The other side was white with a black sleeve, black collar, and white decorative buttons beside white-threaded buttonholes. All the pockets were edged in opposing colours to their backgrounds, and there were a lot of pockets. *Now* I knew he was definitely, without question, everything I had hoped.

In his hand was a long white recorder, with a black mouthpiece and end cap thingy and that lump in the middle. He spun it between his fingers. Though I doubted many recorder players in orchestras had one with an inner glow; one that seemed to fill the same role as Gandalf's staff, a presence I'd always take for granted until the moment he whips it out and does something awful to the Nazgûl and then you remember why he is written out of every moment when he'd just be *too* helpful for there to be a challenge for the other characters. Well I was more than happy to have a deus ex machina summoned for us.

I remembered what Mum said. I wasn't sure this wasn't what drove her crazy, more than the fairies and the fairy world. I'd been doing okay so far.

I looked up at his face anyway.

He was *beautiful*. And still had an awkward, heavy face with a thick nose and dark eyebrows. He looked like a guy off the street. He *glowed* with otherworldly power. The facial piercings were still there, the confident smile was still there. But he had the blank, glowing white eyes to back it up. He turned to me and smiled wider, the snakebite piercings stretching apart on his lower lip. Now I could see why I'd rejected the Green Man's smouldering look. The Piper didn't smoulder because he didn't need to. He knew he wasn't attractive and he didn't care. He thought I was funny and he certainly didn't mind that he was tripping over me everywhere he went that week because it made him laugh, and that was not a bad thing. He had a nice laugh.

"No?" the Green Man demanded, surging upright. I could see Teb cringing away from him. She was giving the Piper the most fearful look I'd ever seen. I'd have been just as terrified if his level of cheeky confidence was turned against me. Even though the debate had barely started, he already stood like he'd won it.

"As my friend here so eloquently put it, none of these girls belong to you right now."

"Eloquently?" Spike spluttered beside me.

"They are here," the Green Man said. He reached down without looking, grabbed Teb by the arm and pulled her upright, squeezing her to his side. She was stubbornly trying not to look terrified by this turn of events, but I knew her too well for her stern façade to work. He'd grown in his anger: she came pretty much to his waist. "They danced for me. They are mine."

"And when was the last time you accepted a summer sacrifice?" the Piper said. "Seems to me my job is to enforce the Ritual happenings of this universe. If, say, you had a virgin sacrifice *every* year, I'd be compelled to hand over one of these lovely ladies immediately, no questions asked. Tell me… Do I have a reason to do that?"

"They are *here*."

"Every year I make sure Troutespond dances that little dance for you, and bring all your court home to you, play sweet lullabies to put the Lady to sleep so you can rule without unexpected sleet storms in July… Do you want to see what happens when you break the Ritual? It means I lose interest in helping you. Maybe I have to tidy *you* away."

"But I *want* to stay," Teb blurted out at the Green Man's side. "Why can't I be his summer queen?"

The Piper sighed, quietly enough that only I heard it (I was rather more used to huge melodramatic sighing, what with being surrounded by flouncing teenagers and engaging in a little of that behaviour myself). "Teb, I said before… This did not have to be your story. Even if you forgot those words, the meaning of them should still have stayed deep in your mind these last two days. Your determination to ignore my advice is staggering. Think carefully before you throw away two months of your life. They are important months." They only happened to contain all the remaining months of revision and work we had to do before our life-deciding exams in mid-May. I doubted we'd be able to bring Chemistry textbooks into the fairy world for her if she chose to stay.

"I've made my decision," Teb said.

"Please don't do this!" I begged. "If you say you want to go home, the Piper will get us all out of here and we can leave. *Think* about it!"

Teb shook her head. "I'm staying."

The Piper turned to me, head lowered. "I'm sorry, Ally," he said for my ears only. "I am unable to affect a decision someone has made. It is my job only to ask them to change their mind." Then he turned to the Green Man. "If I give you Teb, will you allow the other three visitors to return home?"

The Green Man's eyes ran over us all: me standing at the Piper's side, quivering and quickly turning tearful. Tanya, with her messy hair and inexplicable smile, more trouble than a pixie. Alana with her arms folded and furious scowl directed at Teb. Then he turned to Teb and weighed up his golden little mistress, still doing her best to pout and not be rubbish like the rest of us. If only I'd realised

Teb was so repressed, I thought. I had been given plenty of opportunities to agree with Tanya's self-called 'zany schemes' to set her up with a boyfriend, but I'd been all about respecting her privacy and decision to be aloof and scary. How was I to know that wasn't the whole extent of her personality?

It took forever for the Green Man to admit it, especially in front of his whole court, but he was scared of the Piper. I could tell he was not the sort to give in normally. "They may leave," he rumbled at long last. "I will replace Teb to the letter of the law."

"There's no need to—" the Piper started, but the Green Man bellowed something over the mild-mannered voice the Piper used, and a creature stepped out of the crowd. It was sort of greenish, a completely ambiguous, plain pixie. It was more like a blank doll than anything, waiting for someone to paint features onto it and dress it up.

"Oh dear," the Piper said.

"What is this?" I asked him quietly.

"I think I may have frightened the Green Man a little too effectively. In times past, well…"

"Summer Queen," the Green Man ordered, "tell my changeling your true name so it may take your place."

"Oh sweet Jesus no," Alana said somewhere behind me. "Piper, stop him!"

Teb fixed pleading eyes on me. "Should I do it?" she called to me. "I can't vanish for two months! This way you don't have to lie to my family for me… You can pretend I never left."

"Don't tell it your name!" Alana shouted, furious. "That thing is not going to be like you, whatever you think!"

"It can go home for me," Teb said.

"Don't do it," Tanya said. "Don't give your name away!"

"Tebster Magee!" I blurted.

"What?" Alana asked, bemused.

"Ally!" Tanya cried, sounding horrified.

"Her name's Tebster Magee," I said again, more confidently, meeting the Green Man's eye.

"No!" Tanya wailed.

The changeling looked hard at Teb. And then it *changed*. One second it was green and plain… The next it was Teb, dressed in the same purple T-shirt and shorts as she had been at the fair. It tossed a ponytail just like Teb's. And it turned to grin at me with wicked, sparkling green eyes. I felt sick.

"How did you do that?" the Piper asked in a low voice. Genuinely bowing to my expertise. *Genuinely shocked.*

"The news van," I said. "Teb's 'name' went out to anyone who tuned into the lunchtime news. Stories about missing teenagers always make national news… Especially when they have a cute blonde mug shot like Tanya's to stick up on the screen. And Teb recorded a segment with that as her name."

"That should *not* work."

"I don't think it did. Look at the changeling."

Only on the surface was it Teb. Everything about the way it moved, the strange eyes, the sharp teeth in its mouth looked wrong. It was very, very clearly an alien creature in a skin stretched over the surface to resemble our friend.

"Now leave, before I reconsider," the Green Man said, not noticing his creature's failure to copy Teb. He wouldn't have the first idea what 'human' was meant to look like.

The changeling skipped up to Tanya and Alana, who both recoiled in horror from it.

"Let's go. We can deal with it away from the court," the Piper said. And just like that, he vanished.

I suddenly felt all the eyes of the fairies on me, and fled to my friends. And the horrific creature portraying one.

"The Piper says deal with the changeling after this," I said. "Let's get out of here."

"No need to tell me twice," Alana said. She grabbed the changeling roughly by the arm and dragged it away. We broke through the curious crowd and fled through the trees. We only stopped when we were right down among the stacks of loose stones that made up this world's version of the skate park. Apparently fairies hadn't invented concrete yet, which was why they had to keep coming through to ours to play.

"Okay, now explain how that worked," Alana demanded, hands on her knees to catch her breath. "Fairy magic doesn't work unless you have the real name of a person you're casting the spell on."

I shrugged. "I don't think it's so black and white as that. Wouldn't you say a changeling should be a bit more effective than that?"

"Don't mind me," the changeling said, still grinning its awful sharp toothed grin. We all shuddered away from it.

"That will never pass for Teb," Tanya agreed.

"I can fix this!"

We turned to see Cathy panting as she hurried our way. Even her run had something akin to dancing in it. Maybe that was why she was so puffed out and far behind us.

"Fix it how?" Alana demanded.

"Give me Teb's true name, and I will cast a spell to bring her back to you. We have a body here, linked to hers… Somewhat. Why not steal her from under the Green Man's nose? He can't do anything to snatch her back without her true name, and once you step back into your own world you will be out of his reach."

"Sounds good," I said with a shrug.

"Ally, no more snap decisions, deals with fairies or even talking to them," Tanya said. "You helped us dodge a bullet with the Magee thing, but now you've bought us some time we need to use it to think about this properly. Let the grownups handle this."

"If we do what Cathy suggests, we'd be breaking the agreement the Piper made with the Green Man," Alana weighed in. "Where did he go anyway?"

I looked around in case the Piper stepped out from behind the nearest stack of stones. We *really* needed his advice. Every time someone looked at me I felt closer to screaming than reeling out a confident plan. Maybe Tanya was right. "He said that he'd meet us here. I think."

"He's not here because he can't let us do this," Tanya said. "Oh my gods, he knew Cathy would make this offer. He left us to decide for ourselves because he can't tell us to do it."

I bit my lip... It was mind-boggling the sort of issue on the table, but we could flap our arms and run around in headless chicken circles or try to understand it. "Well, why can't we do it? The Green Man *hardly* took Teb for her personality, do you think he would notice the difference?"

"We *can't* do it," Alana said. "It's gross and unnatural and we don't even have Teb's permission."

"What we have is a monster who doesn't even belong in our world. If we bring it back with us, we're messing up everything," I said, gesturing at the leering changeling that Alana still had a strong grip on. "If we swap it for Teb then we leave a fairy in the fairy world and take a human girl to the human world."

"*In the body of a changeling that's only pretending to look like her.* What if the spell doesn't even last? What if she still looks like *this* when we put her inside?"

"Changeling magic is strong," Cathy said. "The spell will not break; in fact, the body should adjust to the soul within it, and she will be fine."

"Dammit Piper, get over here!" Alana yelled up at the dark sky, perhaps frightened by all the logic and reassurance we were presenting.

Nothing happened.

"I think he wants us to do it," Tanya said quietly.

I pulled on Cathy's arm until her pointed ear was level with my mouth. "Teb Nandi."

"Wow," she said. If not for fairy name-grabbing magic I probably would have had to guide her through it syllable by syllable.

"Oh Ally," Alana sighed, although she'd had plenty of opportunity to tackle me to the ground while I'd been telling Cathy the name. Oh, except that the changeling was trying to get free of Alana's grip on it, ready to flee now it realised we were so serious about this.

Cathy skipped up to the changeling. It desperately tugged on Alana's arm, but she held it in place. It hissed furiously.

Still wrestling it, Alana tried to avoid this neat and tidy solution the best way she could: "Cathy, I'll stop Ally talking to Ian if you do this."

"No you won't. She made a promise," Cathy put a hand on the changeling's disturbing face, covering it completely. She whispered something that I didn't catch, and pulled her hand back.

The look on the face had changed completely: it wasn't malicious and twisted anymore. It seemed pretty much authentically Teb, though very, very confused. She fell over, like her whole body was too heavy. Alana tugged on her arm and then, looking around, chose to just disappear through to the normal world, before Teb could throw up a fuss here.

"Well, time to go back for us too," Tanya said. "Are you okay, Ally?"

"Yeah, I'm fine," I said. "I mean, I'm emotionally scarred, for sure, but… I mean… We're all going to make it back?"

"If we go now. It'll be pretty obvious what we've done back at the grove: the changeling is not going to keep quiet about the switch."

"Right." I turned to Cathy. "I'll speak to Ian right away," I promised.

She nodded and fled back up the path, not even bothering to dance.

Tanya held out a hand to me. "Come on, useless."

"I'm not useless!"

"It's your superpower," she said with a grin. And then she tugged me back to Normalsville, Normalshire, Normal Land.

Well, okay, it was back to Troutespond, but that sentiment is still somewhat true.

Still Friends

I looked around, breathing in the cold evening air. The sky was going through every shade it was allowed to throw at us, light and dark. Away from the blotchy pink clouds around the pale horizon, I stared upwards, still a bit dazed, at the zillions of faint stars I was used to seeing in the indigo sky—and all of them staying in place and doing as they were told. *Physics.* I sat up to see the lights of the town right where they were meant to be as well, the sleepy glow of a good long day settling in on our home, the noise of the pub audible even out here, practically outside town limits. The motorway, low and out of the way again, gusted with the sound of rush hour traffic. A plane was roaring high overhead, lights flashing regularly. *Normally.*

A skateboarder came rattling down the road and almost hit us, a pile of confused girls sitting in the middle of the road.

"Don't you have fucking brakes on that thing?" Teb yelled at the hapless skateboarder as he swerved around us with a yelled swear. My heart swelled, and I threw myself at her, knocking us down again.

"TEB!" I cried. "You're you again!"

"What the hell am I doing back here?" she demanded. "How did you do that?"

"Magic," Alana shrugged.

"You… You did this! I'll kill you! I'll…" Teb stopped, startled by the movement of her own arm as she made a fist. Slowly she unclenched her hand and rotated it, wiggling her fingers.

"This isn't me. This is the changeling. Am I the changeling?"

"Um… Maybe," I said. She looked just like Teb again, but I suppose you do know your own body better than anyone else. Maybe it was something as simple as a nail that wasn't broken all of a sudden or feeling hungry despite being full of fair food not too long ago. If you had just witnessed a copy of yourself being made, and were as quick on the uptake as Teb…

"Urgh! That's… That's… Horrible!"

"The way you were fawning over the Green Man was horrible," Alana said. "We had to bring you home. I don't like the method, but if Ally and Tanya were in agreement, well, they know you best…"

"I wasn't *fawning*." It was a relief to see that Teb had brought some regret back with her: she wouldn't blatantly lie to us if she didn't feel she'd gone wrong somewhere.

"You were acting so unlike Teb I almost didn't care if we brought back something strange," Tanya butted in resentfully.

"*You* would have thought it was fun anyway," Teb shot back.

"Please… don't argue," Alana groaned. "At least not irrelevantly. We need to go find the Piper. He'll help us sort all of this out…"

"Sort what out? We're home!" I said. I was still sitting around feeling relieved while everyone else had moved onto their own issues. I wouldn't say that I ever lost faith, but it was wonderful to be back on ground I was certain wouldn't change colour depending on the season.

"Like to tell us what the hell we're supposed to do now we have a Changeling-friend!" Alana snapped back. "Never mind explaining if we're going to have any further trouble from the fairies now they know that they've been swindled of their human girl."

"You make me sound like currency," Teb complained.

"Hey, you're the one who sold yourself. You always hear about people making deals with demons, but you'd think at least *some* common sense would tell you not to do the same with fairies and the like!"

"You said that he was a god!" Teb suddenly sounded wounded, and more than a little anxious. "How could it have been bad? It felt… really right. Like I was meant to do it." In just the few seconds we'd been sitting on the road she seemed more and more unsure as she tried to defend her decisions. The sheer normality of the surroundings was working on her as well, whether a spell was disappearing from her brain or not. Being home made our adventure in the fairy world seem that much sillier, more unbelievable. The things that we'd done there were sorted into different folders from our normal programming files, a sort of secondary fairy world personality, reading from a completely different script. I'd felt like some sort of action hero for a bit while we were there, but I knew exactly how loud I'd scream if I saw a spider in my room. I wasn't taking any character development home if I could manage it.

Alana groaned with frustration, still trying to get Teb to understand some sort of moral lesson. "Well then he found your head easier to crack open than anyone else's to put those ideas in it! The fey are not to be taken lightly… If you feel compelled to do something out of character you can still *not do it*. Fairies give you a choice. They don't force you to do anything, not like demons. I mean, Tanya spent days there and still strolled out without trouble. Our rescue could have gone along without any trouble but then we started giving and taking from the fairies… I thought after what I told you about fairies literally ten minutes before you wandered off to live with them, you would have had at least some common sense about it. Apparently you were just really easy for them to buy over, and there's a group of goblins who'll carry on thinking humans are stupid and small-minded…"

"Would you *stop*?" I complained. "Look, we made it back, we shouldn't be fighting. We should be thinking about how lucky we are!"

"Ally's right," Teb said abruptly. She now actually looked genuinely embarrassed: maybe she'd happily gone along with the idea of being the Green Man's mistress because she'd been telling herself she had no choice. Perhaps that look was her remembering that she'd been coherent enough to hold a full conversation with us. Maybe she just didn't like Alana standing up to her and sounding like she might be right. "Come on, let's go home."

Alana shrugged. "We still have to face the music."

I looked sharply over at her.

"*Not* an intentional pun," she groaned.

I felt a little giddy at the thought of seeing him again.

*

The Piper cornered us as we arrived back in the centre of the town.

Tanya flung herself at the statue of the war hero as soon as it was in sight and was snuggling up to him as if nothing else so far had reassured her she was home. The rest of us were mooching along in silence, all sulking for one reason or another. Alana clearly felt it was extremely unfair that Teb was blaming her for everything, and Teb clearly felt it was extremely unfair that *Alana* was blaming *her* for everything. I was stunned and going into shock as I trudged along, thinking about the things that had happened and the stuff I'd seen. My relief to be home was so overwhelming I just couldn't be angry with Tanya *or* Teb, as much as I wanted to be. I'd still chosen not to talk to them. Fortunately, someone was there to be angry for us.

"Well met," a cool voice said behind us as we flopped on one of the benches in the town centre. He didn't sound like he meant it.

The Piper was standing on the edge of the glorified traffic island that was the centre of the town. He looked different to me. His eyes wouldn't go back to how they were meant to now that I knew what he was meant to look like. My weirdness filters were broken and didn't think there was anything too strange about the Piper hanging out in Troutespond high street, so didn't censor him into something human to make me feel better. I couldn't really see the aura of terrifying power he'd had in the fairy world, though. I wondered if the others could still see him like that. I couldn't remember if Alana had ever mentioned how attractive or not she found him.

At the moment the Piper looked, as Alana had predicted, *highly* unamused.

"Are you going to send me back?" Teb asked, stepping forwards. She sounded only cautiously optimistic, and a little bit fearful: I wasn't sure if it was of him now, or of the fairies. I *hoped* she had been steadily building up regret. I think she'd already guessed what he said next:

"No, I have more than enough damage to repair without balancing a changeling in the town for two months."

"So in the end the only reason Teb stays here after she said she wanted to stay there is because the paperwork is too much hassle?" I asked, putting an arm around Teb, protective mother bear style.

He smiled at me. "I think teenagers find new ways to be stupid every year. I've been around a long time, but episodes like this prove I should never let my guard down or say that I've seen it all."

"What are you going to do then?" I asked, hoping that because I'd made him smile he was going a little easier on us.

"After so much exposure I need to cleanse all of you. And you must make a decision. Who is going back to living a normal life?"

"Normal?" Tanya laughed, sliding down from the statue. She skipped up to the Piper, grinning defiantly. "No thanks. I'm happy with this life."

"What would you actually do to us?" I asked a little more cautiously. Like Tanya, I wasn't sure what was really *normal* anyway. Would he end up stripping away half my personality just to keep us all in line?

"I can offer a return to the lives you had before. I can erase your memories of these events, and you will continue your lives as if nothing happened."

"Will Alana still be our friend?" I asked.

"Am I your friend?" Alana asked incredulously.

"You are mine," I said. Beside me Tanya gave a sort of shrugging nod. Like, *sure, why not?* Teb didn't look too encouraging though. My brief hope from earlier in the day that this might turn into a bonding experience for Teb and Alana had completely fizzled out a while back.

"Um… I probably shouldn't affect your decision," she said, glancing nervously at the Piper. "I don't get a chance to go back to normal. Even if all three of you did… And we stayed friends… Then I would still be working off my sins with the Piper. Maybe you'd find out all over again. I can't say you'll never be dragged into things if you hang around with me." Maybe she was turning her head away so we couldn't see how shiny her eyes had gone. I glimpsed a tear before she looked fully away, though.

"Well you are definitely my friend." I planted my hands on the part of my torso where other girls had hips. "Never mind anything else, I don't want you to be a stranger after this. I'd keep twice the horror of what I've seen today to make sure you don't go so soon."

"Well, I suppose I was about ready to stab my mother after a month of distance learning and home schooling... I suppose staying on at the sixth form can't hurt."

Tanya followed me over to Alana's side. "What?" she asked. "I treasure the contents of my head. And I get the feeling Alana's got plenty of interesting things to tell me in her own head."

We looked at Teb. Peer pressure either was the biggest deciding factor of her life... Or completely useless. I hadn't quite worked that out yet.

She shook her head. "I don't know... I don't know." She sat down on one of the benches and put her head in her hands. For a moment there was an uncomfortable silence. I wanted to go over and hug her, but I was worried that the Piper would choose that moment to wipe our memories or something. I didn't want my thoughts to be caught in the crossfire.

"I don't like this," Teb said at last. "I don't like knowing. Today has been the worst day of my life. I... I was so scared in the fairy world. I don't know why I did and said those things. It all seems so stupid now. And now I'm apparently a changeling? I can't live normally after this. Piper... When you do your magic thing, will I be safe?"

"With Alana as a friend, you will never be far from help," he said.

"But, I mean... I'm *changed* now. Changed into a changeling! How does that affect me?"

"It doesn't have to."

"So if I didn't remember it happening..."

"It would be like nothing had ever happened to you."

She nodded.

"I'm sorry, guys. This is just... Just... I'm not the same person I was, in every single imaginable way, and I don't *like* that. The more I look at these alien hands, the more I want to use them to reach back in time and smack myself this morning, tell myself to stay home. If the Piper can't fix what I am, but he can make it so I don't know... I know it doesn't fix my mistakes, but I don't know what else I can do. Are they even my mistakes? If I was under a spell and now I'm in a different body, can I even be blamed for any of it?"

"Yes," Alana grumbled for my ears only. I poked her, probably too hard, to offset the tension of watching one of my closest friends mentally wringing herself out. I'd feared that Tanya would be messed up by this: I could never have imagined Teb being the one who would be destroyed. But she was the least prepared, and it turned out that had made her the most fragile.

She turned her tearful eyes on us, finally looking up from examining her hands. "Can you cope with not telling me what I am? What I've seen? Definitely never ever ever what I did? I feel moments away from screaming and never stopping. I think I need to not know what happened to me."

"Easily," Tanya said, trying to sound jolly instead of choked up. I was far from over blaming her: she was the one who had run off because she thought we all needed a bit more magic in our lives. I secretly hoped she felt dreadful for seeing what that created in practice.

I nodded, tears pretty much gushing down my face. "Of course."

"I'll do my best," Alana said.

Teb scowled. "I hope I still don't trust you afterwards."

"Teb!" I complained. "Alana wasn't the one who did this to you."

"Look, you guys are winning *that* argument. For my own sanity I want to forget… But when I do, I'll forget that Alana is *poison* and if I can't stop you being friends with her, once I have no idea… What if I like her? What if we become friends? If the last thing I can do is tell myself not to be friends with her, then I will do that and hope *something* remains to help me not fall for it."

"Whatever," Alana said. "I hardly think after you say something like *that* I'm going to try to be friends with mind-wiped you."

I poked Alana again, mostly for my own benefit.

"Are you ready for me to perform the ritual now?" the Piper asked. "I still have to cleanse all of you. The clock is ticking on that one."

We all agreed on that point. He herded us into a huddle. A huge magic circle burst into bright white lines around us—the whole town square was rigged, it seemed. The sounds from the pub only a dozen feet from us became utterly muted. The world darkened around us, the weak glow of the sickly streetlights cutting out entirely, the amber glow from house windows fading away to mere points of light. It was just us and the glowing circles that surrounded us. I stuck a foot out, and the white line (like his eyes, I thought) stretched with my foot. He turned and glared at me. I grinned.

"Your natural curiosity is *not* endearing at a time like this," he informed me. "Stand still and don't nod off."

Shamed, I endeavoured to be good.

The cleansing was every bit as bad as he'd threatened back in the tent, and I knew better than my friends how much nicer and faster the alternative was. Even the gentle tones of the song he played weren't distracting enough to stop me thinking of how much my feet hurt. I stared at the patterns in the circle. There were no odd eldritch symbols: it was just a few concentric circles, with smaller circles trapped between those lines, a triangle in the middle. The light pulsed a little with the intensity of the music, but if I stared too long I began to get sleepy. I slid an arm through Teb's and stared up at the dark streetlights instead. Tanya put a hand on my other arm as well, and pulled Alana closer.

Finally the music ended. I shook my head hard. The three of us needed no extra telling to leave the circle when the Piper ordered us to.

With just Teb left inside it shrank a little to accommodate her. Outside the circle the world seemed less dark, although still silent and cut off.

The Piper approached the circle, and pocketed his recorder for a moment. He beckoned Teb to the edge of the circle and reached across the line to give her a proper kind of medical examination, peering in her eyes and mouth, tapping bits of her, feeling her pulse with two fingers pressed against her wrist. I noticed that he never let an inch of her outside the circle, and never stepped fully into it himself.

"You're lucky they had enough power over you to put in your kidneys," the Piper eventually snapped, but he let go of Teb, stepping back from the circle and rather hastily putting some space between him and it. "Fortunately, even without your name, you gave one recognised well enough as your own. But the fact remains that you're still technically a pixie…" He frowned. "I wouldn't be doing my job if I didn't fix this. But there aren't many ways to do it without banishing you like any other fairy, or swapping things back to the… admittedly fair arrangement you had before."

"You wouldn't dare!" I snapped.

He shook his head. "Fair to the fairies, but not to this world. Teb belongs here. The troubles the swap causes in the Green Man's court are nothing compared to having a pixie loose in this world." He turned to us, speaking specifically to Alana. "I can remove any pixie powers she may have. If she doesn't realise there's anything strange, and if nothing strange is attracted to her, then *maybe* nothing will stop this being a permanent, effective body swap, where she never need know she is no longer human. It is up to you, and Ally and Tanya, to keep her safe from any memories, to protect her should something happen."

"Teb was just getting cool!" Tanya grumbled to herself.

"Shut up," I told her, "I like her *human*."

"Thanks," Teb said, rolling her eyes. She looked down at her body again, and shuddered. "Do it." She turned to look directly at Alana and fixed her with a fearsome glare, as if trying to bore some mark of hatred directly onto her face as a reminder for when her memory was gone. It made me feel sad to think that was the only thing she wanted to keep from the whole venture. If I was getting a mind-wipe I'd have asked to keep a mental image of the fairy world as dream… Maybe my glimpse of the Piper's true looks.

He raised his tin whistle to his lips and started playing again. I wondered how much easier he could have fixed it with a kiss or two, then decided I probably didn't want to hate Teb so badly, and he could do it this longer way.

The song he played was haunting—more so in the still and darkness of this place he'd created where the only light came from his magic circles, and the only sound his pipe. But it wasn't directed at us—Teb was the one to whom the recital was aimed, and she didn't look like she was having any fun with it, frowning and wincing in turn, trying to keep her eyes on Alana. The song ran on and on, and I knew it wasn't for any musical interest, as even the Piper's amazing playing began to tire on me. I was sure if he actually wanted me to *enjoy* the song he'd have had me listening raptly for hours, even if he was only playing three notes over and over. Teb's eyes closed more and more often.

Finally the song ended, and Teb was left standing, apparently fast asleep on her feet, in a fading circle.

"You can sit down," the Piper said, and Teb walked over to one of the benches and sat down.

"You made her into Zombie Teb instead!" I protested. "How is that better?!"

"Only until morning," the Piper assured me. "Unless you feel like explaining this scene to her?"

I looked about the strange town square, weirder even than the empty grass and trees of the fairy realm by how *familiar* it was, just with a hefty whack of magic over the top.

"I guess not," I said. 'Power outage' probably wouldn't clear this one with Teb immediately after a detox from magic.

And then pub-noise washed over us again (and I could tell the karaoke was going well, or, as badly as it ever did here), and we were back to true Normalsville. The Piper was still standing by us—I'd expected him to vanish during the transition back.

"I never want to have to do so much for you girls again," he said, but it was in his old good humour, now the balance had been set right and we were all as normal as we'd ever be. It was enough to fit in, anyway.

"I wouldn't be so sure about that," I said, "We're all going to university at the end of the year."

He frowned. "Make it through the summer at least, *please*." And he turned and walked off.

"I guess we should get Teb and Tanya home," Alana said, "Tanya's dad will be so happy to see her again, and Teb's a liability like this."

I nodded. "Wait here with them a minute, though."

She didn't get a chance to question me or tell me to stay—I was off, running after the Piper, my flip-flops slapping on the tarmac pavement.

I caught him by the church, just before the road split.

"Wait!" I called after him. He stopped and looked at me with those strange eyes, a smile on his face. I'd never imagined monochrome eyes could express so much. The way they crinkled up at the corners was more than enough.

"You can't keep chasing after me," he said. "There's nothing else for me to do here for now, for one thing. The rituals are all over, spring has happened, and your friends are back to normal and in their right places. What else am I supposed to do here?"

"I... I wanted to say thanks," I gasped, still out of breath from the run. "You rescued us from the fairies, kinda... Not sure how or what happened..." I shrugged.

"That was all you. I just stood there and looked intimidating."

"Still... Couldn't have done it without you."

He nodded. There was definitely a bit of a smug smile going on there. He knew it was all about him.

I looked away, desperately seeking for something else to say to keep him around. I cast my eyes up at the church, looming over us, though only in the quiet way of an old building, not the intrusive way everything had sat in the landscape in the other world.

"Do you miss it?" I said softly, my thoughts bouncing around crazily. My mind was still working overtime. Images of the changeling becoming Teb, the drugged smile she had when we found her, the look of the fairy world, all hung in my mind. All loads of good nightmare fuel for the next months. If I ever slept, that is.

"Miss what?" he asked.

"I dunno… This town? You come from here, don't you?"

He nodded. "I travel far and wide, but this town is special. I don't *need* to come here in person, normally. Perhaps I would have this year, *after* you swapped Teb back. But before that… I was only here because it was here."

"And now you have to leave again?"

"Unfortunately, yes. I used to live among the people here, but that—" he gestured the church "—was the last time. It was a long, long time ago."

I thought of what Alana said about it, how he'd saved someone. "You stayed because you fell in love?"

He nodded. "It was a uniquely depressing experience."

I understood what he meant. He must have buried her somewhere in the graveyard we stood beside, but no markers would remain… Maybe not even the bones either. The church was terrifyingly old.

"Don't look like that," he said, trying to smile for me as I cast almost tearful eyes across the dark graves. "I've moved on. It was a long time ago."

I cast desperately around for something else to say, and found myself taking in his amazing coat again. "Well, you have a cooler coat than you must have done back then, anyway."

He laughed, "You liked it?"

I nodded. A moment later I almost collapsed under its weight as it landed on my shoulders.

"Ack!" I said, almost ruining the moment as I tried not to topple over backwards. It was really warm. And *really* heavy.

"I haven't seen you in a coat since we met. This warm spell won't last—it'll snow again before the summer, Green Man or not."

"Um, thanks," I said, threading my arms through the sleeves. I hugged the coat close. Tall as I was, he was taller and the bottom crumpled on the ground behind me. The sleeves hung over my hands. There was an awkward moment—a long pause between us, as I ran further topics of conversation through my mind. *Just let him go*, I thought. But here we were, standing on a dark street, having the moment I'd wanted back at my first sight of him.

"I should go," I said, at last. "You must have a lot of work to do."

"No more questions?" he grinned.

I shook my head. Then, "What was so important about when I spoke to you?

I mean, why was everyone so insistent that I had to? What did you do?"

He laughed, "I didn't do anything. The world has a way of reflecting things back to people who've had too much exposure to the strangeness. I thought it would be funny, since you love all that random significance on things which shouldn't really have any meaning, and so everything started playing with you, making it seem more important than it really was. If you hadn't been so curious in the first place, you wouldn't have seen or heard anything."

"And Teb would still be normal," I said rather bitterly.

"She is now."

"Yeah, well… It was a close one. So, Alana… What's the story there?"

His smile sank a little. "She will tell you in her own time. Or lie to you about it first. It is a story that needs more than four days' trust to share. Maybe even four months won't do the trick."

I cast around for another question, and picked the wrong one: "Will I see you again? I mean, if you come when there's trouble, and I'm me…"

"I don't think it would be a good idea to meet again."

"Oh."

He stepped closer, broaching the awkward distance between us, and without stopping to ask me for permission, had me in a hug. It was so unexpected I squeaked in surprise, and stood there with my arms sticking out to the sides. I mean, a *hug*? After all that?

When he let me go I could just about accept that he was going—that for all my jokes about getting into epic trouble as soon as the seasons changed again, I wasn't going to see him again.

"Bye," I said pathetically.

He turned, pulling his tin whistle out of his pocket, and walked off down the street, playing and walking. Soon even the carrying sound of the whistle faded as well. I pulled his warm coat tighter around me, and headed back for the town centre where my friends would be getting very annoyed with me.

"Still, Better Hairy Legs Than Barky Ones, am I Right?"

It proved surprisingly easy to take everyone back to their rightful places. I walked Tanya, who lived pretty much on the town centre, up to her front door to make absolutely sure she went in and was not going to nip right back out again to go poke some pixies. I left Alana on the street to guard Zombie Teb.

When we were sort of out of earshot of Alana, Tanya flashed me a grin. "I don't regret this," she said.

"You should!"

"Ally… I said I wanted to show you stuff, to open your mind. I mean, not like you were close minded, but you weren't going to grow up any time soon because you're so scared of the big wide world. And look at you! You turned your terrified babbling into something productive! I hope if nothing else you'll feel like you learned more about the world. And when we go away to university… We'll be closer because we have such a big secret to share."

"Teb doesn't."

"Teb is the sceptic in the group. She always has been and she always will be. I think she was very unstable when we took her scepticism away. Maybe that's how the fairies got to her: she didn't have anything to stand on, so they offered her a new platform. And she took it, because even with our warnings, she just didn't understand. It's not that she couldn't cope with knowing. It's that she couldn't cope with the hole that left in her when she found her strength undermined. Sometimes the moral lesson is maybe someone didn't need to learn a moral lesson: they were doing fine before the lesson. The Piper gave us the chance to undo a mistake, and Teb herself knew she had to take it."

"Because she is a *changeling*, living in some monster's skin," I hissed, glancing back down the steps to where Alana was uncomfortably propping up the snoozing Teb. "You say babbling nonsense is my super power, but look at what you just said!"

Tanya laughed. "Well, once you've slept this off, you'll forgive me. You always do."

I shook my head. "Go home."

Tanya smiled a little more sadly and put her key in the door. I trudged down the steps, suddenly feeling a lot wearier for the conversation. I wished Tanya didn't always feel like she was right. Talk about moral lessons bouncing off people: was I the only one who had learned something today, that being, it was probably safer to stick forks in electrical sockets than let my friends near the supernatural?

Alana nodded to me, and I felt a little of that emotional weight lifting as we took one of Teb's arms each and set off towards her house. This had been an unorthodox way to make friends, but I didn't even know if I could do things normally. And the results spoke for themselves. Alana had been there for us: a passenger in a story that might have happened all the same without her, yet somehow we'd all made it home and I had a feeling we wouldn't if the story had been all down to me and Teb finding this out on our own. Maybe she would say she was only staying in the group to look after Teb on the Piper's orders, but the fact remained we were now a group of four and I couldn't be happier that my new friend had turned out to be the only dependable one of the lot.

Or, we would be once Teb had recovered from her little incident. She walked into her house on autopilot. Alana and I waved dully to each other as we went our separate ways. After all that she gave me a muted "Laters." I supposed I would see her on Monday at college, so I had no reason to treat this as a formal goodbye.

My street was quiet; no mad cats were wandering up and down it, no lurking weirdoes with recorders.

I walked right on past my front door, mentally replaying that scene from my first meeting with the Piper. When I stopped where I'd stood before, I couldn't bear to look at the patch of pavement where he had sat. Instead I turned and looked behind me, at my neighbour's house... The house that he had been watching before I interrupted him.

I rarely spared a thought for my normal neighbours, and the blandness of the house was probably why. It was one of the neater ones along the road, with a paved driveway without any weeds growing on it and a recent coat of paint on the pebbledash walls. The car wasn't familiar to me from any of those charity car washes we'd done in the school car park, because as far as I knew, Mr Brooke walked to work hours before I was usually out of bed.

I went right up the drive and pressed the doorbell. I only wondered if it was the right house after the incident. What if I didn't recognise the car because it wasn't his? My heart started hammering away, and I realised I probably looked crazy—in a big heavy patchwork coat, with hair gone wild, flip-flops sticking out the bottom…

An older woman opened the door and looked suspiciously at me.

"Is, um, does Ian live here?" I asked. I was careful not to call him Mr Brooke in case he had a thing against students coming to his door: his mother would probably be wise enough to turn anyone away who didn't know the password.

She frowned, but then, having weighed me up, turned and yelled into the house—"IAN! You have a guest!"

"Who is it?" a familiar teacher-ly voice yelled back.

"Some weird-looking girl!" the woman (his mother?) replied. I rolled my eyes while she was looking the other way.

There was a silence, and then from some room off the hall, Mr Brooke shuffled into view, wearing big fuzzy slippers and a dressing gown of epic proportions. He looked tired, but healthy and no longer obviously tormented by evil spirits.

"…Ally?" he asked, after a pause to remember my name. He seemed disappointed. Had he hoped Cathy had come back? I wondered if she had actually been living with him here. I could have had a fairy next door to me!

"Heh, turns out we were neighbours all along," I said, "Funny. Small world, isn't it? I thought most teachers commuted from Bilsworth."

"Is this a prank?" he asked. He glanced around for a sign of Tanya hanging out of a bush with a camera phone pointed his way. Yes that's a specific thing to guess he was looking for, but we had past form with other teachers

I shook my head emphatically. "I have a message for you… from Cathy."

He glanced at his mother, who was glaring at him with mounting annoyance. "Can I have a moment alone?" he asked her.

She glared harder. I began to get the impression she didn't know who Cathy was.

He stepped out of the house and shut the front door on her. Well, there was something we had in common—going outside in our pyjamas. I decided he wasn't so bad after all. The fairy girl could keep him, though. Uck, hairy, hairy legs. And, again, big fuzzy dressing gown. Okay, he was on a break from work while he recovered, but the man needed to have some standards. For all I knew he'd been lazing around in boxers playing video games until I turned up.

"You met Cathy?" he demanded when he had led me a few paces down the drive, out of range of any elderly ears pressed to the door. "Where was she? How is she?"

I shook my head. "I… How much do you remember, of when you were, um, ill?"

He said nothing.

I decided not to push it in case he had a relapse. Also, I'd made a deal… One lie coming up. "She's, um, a friend of my Mum's… Small world, like I said.

Heh. Anyway, someone she knows… A cousin or sister or something is ill… In Ireland. The bit with all the sheep and none of the phones. Somewhere like that. She had to rush out to get a flight… Come to think of it, that might have been what she told you the other day… Before she left? Do you remember? Sorry if that's reminding you of what caused your nervous breakdown. Um. Please don't go weird and shouty again. But she wanted me to tell you… She's sorry. Please wait for her. She will come back. It might be a couple of months but she will be back for you as soon as possible. Okay?"

He nodded sadly. Like the goblins not long before, he was sporting an expression of extreme concentration as he picked apart my hundred-miles-an-hour babble. It seemed to pass without raising any flags. (He was a history teacher, not geography, so he was unlikely to hit me with statistics on sheep to phone proportions in Ireland. Come to think of it, wasn't Wales the one with the sheep? I probably ought to have said potatoes. Did they still have those after the famine? I wasn't going to ask the history teacher in case it blew my story wide open.)

While I chewed my lip, he finally found an answer. "Thank you, Ally."

Then without stopping to chat, maybe ask me if I'd picked a subject for my coursework yet or something, he turned and hurried back up his drive. When he started ringing his doorbell I felt a sudden moment of sympathy for him. It was a familiar situation.

"Um, hope you feel better soon," I ventured, "I'll see you in college." I fled. My day was *not* going to get so surreal I was going to see one of my teachers, in his pyjamas, being yelled at by his mother. No. Just… *no*.

*

I had thought it absolutely impossible for anything else to happen between Mr Brooke's house and my own. It was a space of like two feet of hedge between the properties. But as I set foot on the pavement I caught a glimpse of someone standing across the road. I froze, but relaxed when the person opened their eyes, and two points of white appeared, bright as the moon. He crossed the road in just a few strides and stopped right in my personal space, using the hedge as shelter from the windows of my house.

"Uh… I thought that you said you could never see me again?" It was a surprisingly coherent thing to say, considering in that moment he reached out and brushed my cheek with warm fingertips. I was pretty sure that hit the 'off' switch in my brain. It seemed dumb to keep such a switch in so obvious a place.

"I decided that decision to never see you again couldn't be made with a rational mind. I walked off far too quickly: only a tormented soul would say something as stupid as 'We will never meet again'. If I intended to keep it, for the good of both of us, then I shouldn't have left without saying another word."

"Huh? What? So why are you still here?" I asked, because, see above, off switch.

His hand fetched up with his fingers buried in my tangled hair. His other hand was on my waist again. I *somehow* anticipated what he was after, and even managed to tip my head up and lean forwards to meet his kiss, bumping his lips accidentally too hard. He didn't mind. I didn't wave my arms at my side like a startled penguin as I'd done in the hug, but dared to touch him. He felt awfully real for an imaginary friend. A shared hallucination. Even for an honest-to-whichever-gods powerful supernatural entity.

Then he broke away from me and took a couple of rather hasty steps back.

"Now I can regret my decision properly," he said. "Farewell, Ally Guardian." And… he blinked out of view.

I went to go ring my own doorbell, after a ten-minute search for my key, because *really* who would remember locking themselves out hours before?

"No More Fairies."

Mum ran me a hot bath, had a mug of tea waiting for me when I came out, and braided my hair while we sat on the sofa as I unwound. I told her the whole story. The living room looked empty without all the turtles on every surface. Aside from a couple of half-finished ones she'd ruined along the way, and some unsold turtles who had joined the legions of failed art projects poking out from above the DVDs, under the chairs, amongst the coffee table clutter, atop the mantelpiece, etc. Okay, so the living room didn't exactly feel empty so much as no longer inhabited by a turtle hoarder.

"I feel bad for Tanya and Teb," Mum said, when I was done. "You still sound annoyed with both of them."

"I know… But the way Alana kept explaining it, it was like I shouldn't be angry at the fairies. They were just doing what they always do. It's like complaining that the trees are being green. Tanya's the same as them. They both just do what they like. They all annoy me. But we need them. It's not like Teb… She showed a side of herself I'd never seen before and it frightens me. She got herself into stupid amounts of trouble and I'm still not sure how much she did deliberately and how much the fairies tricked her. And now she's had her mind wiped, I'll never know."

"Thinking of trouble… You should have Alana around for tea again. She's a nice girl, and you need some more friends."

"I am finding the dullest university in England, and going there no matter how lame the course is," I decided. "And I will make new boring friends. We will sit around and eat biscuits and talk about Wuthering Heights. It will be vanilla."

"What if everyone on the course is escaping just like you?" she teased.

"Then we shall *never* mention it. Halloween will mysteriously not happen on campus. We shall all grow up as businessmen with briefcases and neat hair."

Mum tugged on one of my new plaits, "Nice try, but you'd not last a week."

"Maybe you should do sculpture next time you do an art project," I concluded, hoping I'd get a ton of clay to play around with.

"I was thinking cardboard fairies," Mum said, as she finished my hair.

"*No more fairies*," I insisted.

She giggled. "Just messing with you, kiddo. I think it's about time you went to bed, after a day like that."

I stayed up all night watching the street. Nothing moved. The world was exhausted, unlike me. I was still digesting what, on reflection, taken all as one event, might even have been able to claim second, or even top, most strange thing to have ever happened to me. It depended on if we sorted out that last kiss as a separate incident or not.

I pulled the Piper's coat closer around me, and fell asleep with my forehead pressed against the glass as the sun came up, the streetlights shining softly along the length of my street shortly before they winked out, like white eyes closing.